"Marriage isn't an option for me,"

Caleb said. "When I leave Washington Island, I'll leave alone."

Nancy's eyes widened. "Caleb, I wasn't expecting you to propose to me, if that's what you think. We've only known each other a week. I'm no more eager than you are to rush into a long-term commitment."

That wasn't exactly the truth, and she knew it. She knew that Caleb was the man she wanted for her husband, the father of her children. And she had no intention of staying behind when he left the island.

He reached over and covered her hand with his. "Just so long as you understand my position." His tone was cold and tight, and the loud rumble of thunder that nearly drowned out his words added an appropriate chill of foreboding. "There's something else, though, that you need to know about me...."

Dear Reader,

Got the February blues? Need a lift? You've done the right thing—you've picked up a Silhouette **Special Edition**. Among the guaranteed-to-cheer-you-up offerings this month is a particularly inspiring love story by Bay Matthews, *Summer's Promise*. The compelling portrait of a family torn apart by tragedy, then made whole again by the miraculous healing power of love, it's a very special kind of romance, a radical departure from "boy meets girl."

Whether they're traditional or innovative, written by your Silhouette favorites or by brand-new authors, we hope you'll find all six Silhouette **Special Edition** novels each month to be heartwarming, soul-satisfying reading.

Author Bay Matthews says: "I believe we all read romances to recapture the breathless, sometimes bittersweet feelings of falling in love. As well as fulfilling that promise to the reader, Silhouette **Special Edition** features exciting plots grounded in the psychological and emotional makeup of the characters. **Special Edition** allows me to stretch the boundaries of romance, to create realistic people and explore their minds, their souls and the entire spectrum of emotions ruling them. As a writer *and* reader, to me, that's special."

Let us know what's special to *you*—all the authors and editors of Silhouette **Special Edition** aim to please.

Warmest wishes,

Leslie Kazanjian

Senior Editor
Silhouette Books
300 East 42nd Street
New York, N.Y. 10017

PHYLLIS HALLDORSON
Ask Not of Me, Love

Silhouette Special Edition

Published by Silhouette Books New York

America's Publisher of Contemporary Romance

SILHOUETTE BOOKS
300 East 42nd St., New York, N.Y. 10017

ISBN: 0-373-09510-4

First Silhouette Books printing February 1989

Printed in the U.S.A.

PHYLLIS HALLDORSON

met her real-life Prince Charming at sixteen. She married him a year later, and they settled down to raise a family. A compulsive reader, Phyllis dreamed of someday finding the time to write stories of her own. That time came when her two youngest children reached adolescence. When she was introduced to romance novels, she knew she had found her long-delayed vocation. After all, how could she write anything else after living all those years with her very own Silhouette hero?

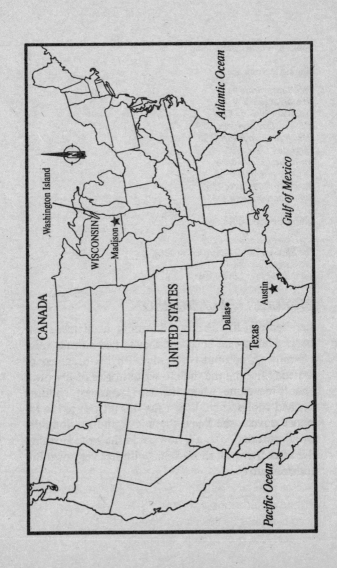

Chapter One

Caleb Winters carefully lowered his gaunt, five-foot-ten-inch frame onto the uncomfortable chair in the empty physician's office. A hiss of pain escaped him involuntarily.

Dammit. Would the nightmare never end?

For eleven months he'd looked forward to this day, but in his imagination he had always strode out of the hospital with head held high, shoulders back, well and whole again, the past miraculously blotted out and the future at least bearable.

He muttered a bitter oath as he subconsciously rubbed the throbbing leg that stuck out at an awkward angle in front of him. It hadn't exactly turned out that way. Instead he would hobble to Barry's waiting car on a three-legged cane and be driven off into a future of uncertainty, loneliness and ever-present torment.

Maybe he was wrong to insist on leaving the hospital now instead of waiting another two months as the doctors had advised, but he knew he would go mad if he didn't get out of here, away from the enforced confinement, the lack of privacy and the long hours with nothing to do but remember.

He shifted restlessly as he heard footsteps approaching. Then the door opened to admit a big gray-haired man in a white coat, and a smaller, younger, dark-haired man with a mustache. "Sorry to keep you waiting, Caleb," said the white-coated physician. "I got sidetracked, then caught up with Barry, here, just as he was coming down the hall."

Caleb nodded in acknowledgement as the doctor sat down behind his desk and the man called Barry took the chair next to Caleb. The doctor frowned and spoke. "You can still change your mind and stay here until we feel you're ready to be released. You've healed nicely in all areas, and the minor elective surgery checks out safe, but you'd benefit from more therapy, both physical and emotional. Are you sure you're ready to start handling this thing alone?"

Caleb shrugged. "I guess I won't know until I try, but I can't stay cooped up here any longer."

"I understand. Well, you have the medication you've been taking and prescriptions for refills. Barry will give you the name and address of the physician you've been referred to. It's imperative that you see him for regular checkups and that you do the exercises we've outlined. Take moderate walks, eat nourishing meals and spend as much time as possible in the fresh air and sunshine for the next three months. It shouldn't take too long to put on some weight and lose that hospital pallor."

The doctor stood and walked around the desk, then put out his hand. "Good luck, Caleb. You're one hell of a determined man, and it's been my pleasure to be your friend as well as your physician for this past year. You're an inspiration to the whole staff, and they've asked me to give you their best wishes. If you ever need me you know where to find me.''

At Dulles airport Barry requested a wheelchair. "I don't need to be pushed around. I can walk," Caleb answered angrily.

"This is a big airport," Barry said, "and you've got to conserve your energy for the two-hundred-mile drive from Chicago to Washington Island. I've made arrangements for you to be met with a wheelchair at O'Hare, too."

Caleb grumbled, but allowed himself to be helped.

At the gate where his plane was being loaded Barry dismissed the attendant and handed Caleb his tickets. "Okay, you remember the plan. The man meeting you at O'Hare is named J. T. Ross. You have his picture, and he's studied pictures of you. He'll turn over to you a two-year-old blue Ford Mustang that has been registered to Caleb Winters. Be sure he gives you the pink slip.

"There's a room reserved for you at the airport hotel. Stay there and get a good night's rest, then leave tomorrow morning and drive to Washington Island, Wisconsin. The route is marked on the map I gave you. Also, you have the directions for getting to the house you've rented for the summer."

He put out his hand and Caleb took it in a strong grip. "Keep in touch," Barry said. "What the doc said back at the hospital goes for me too. You're a great guy, and I'm looking forward to hearing from you at least once a month. More often if you have any problems."

Embarrassed, Caleb murmured thanks, then slowly made his way down the ramp and onto the plane.

It was a curious feeling starting life over again at the age of thirty-six. Until a week ago he'd never heard of Washington Island and he wondered what the future would hold for him there.

Nancy Lloyd drove her silver-gray Nissan Sentra off the ferry and onto the Washington Island dock. She continued toward the old, two-story, yellow frame house that had been remodeled into a first-floor medical clinic and a second-floor apartment. She hummed along with the music on the tape player.

It was a beautiful Saturday in June. The early afternoon sun sparkled on the waters of Lake Michigan and took the chill out of the slight breeze. Already tourists were arriving, and the year-round residents insisted that as many as one hundred thousand people would visit the picturesque island by summer's end. It was easy to understand why. The setting was unusual, the pace was slow and the fishing was great. Numerous summer homes dotted the beaches, and the handful of hotels and motels were preparing for the influx of business.

Nancy turned into the steep driveway and drove up to the closed garage door, then set her emergency brake. The island contained both sandy beaches and rocky bluffs, and most of the terrain in between was either up or down.

She gathered the various packages and bags from the seat beside her and carried them into what had originally been the kitchen but was now converted into a supply room and small laboratory. After putting away the medical supplies she'd had Dr. Gunther order for her she picked up the other bags acquired during her shopping trip in the tiny town of Ellison Bay on the mainland. She was on her way to the staircase when the doorbell rang.

She wondered if it was a personal or a professional visit as she hurried to the front of the house. The clinic wasn't officially open on the weekends, but everyone knew she lived above it so if they cut a finger or had a sniffle they just wandered on over, certain that she would drop everything and take care of them.

The problem was that she always did just that. Nancy wouldn't really mind except that Dagmar Harvey, the middle-aged nurse who assisted her during the week, wasn't available on weekends so she had to work alone.

The bell rang again before she reached the door, and she put down her sacks and opened it to find a thin, black-haired man of medium height wearing faded jeans and a white T-shirt standing on the porch, his face devoid of color and a blood-soaked towel wrapped around his left arm. His right hand gripped a three-legged cane, on which he leaned heavily.

"Oh, my," Nancy exclaimed and without hesitation put her arm around his waist and helped him into the nearest examining room. She led him to the padded table, but when she asked him to lie down he sat on it instead. "I'm all right," he said stubbornly. "I just had a little accident with the hatchet."

Nancy's hazel eyes widened, but she bit back a retort and slipped a clean lab coat on over her navy blue and white print dress. She scrubbed her hands and started to unwind the bloody towel, exposing a long, deep gash that ran diagonally across his arm just below the elbow. It was bleeding heavily, but not spurting as it would if an artery had been cut. Nevertheless she didn't feel qualified to repair it on her own.

She tore open a sterile gauze packet and applied pressure directly to the laceration. He cringed, but made no sound. "I'm sorry," she said, "but I have to stop the bleeding. Can you tell me what happened?"

He took a deep breath, and she was alarmed by the whiteness of his face. "I was chopping kindling, and the hatchet slipped," he answered tonelessly.

"Accidents do occur," she said, "but we're going to have to take you to the mainland and have a doctor suture this."

He looked startled. "Aren't you a doctor?"

She shook her head. "I'm the nearest thing they have to a doctor on the island, but I'm a nurse practitioner. That's a registered nurse with extra training in treating patients under the supervision of a physician. I can diagnose and care for minor medical problems, but a surgical procedure of this sort should be done by an M.D. As soon as this bleeding stops I'll make arrangements to transport you. Do you have a family doctor in the area?"

"Dr. Arnie Gunther at Ellison Bay has my medical records."

"Good," Nancy said, "he's the physician I report to."

The man's pallor was definitely not a good sign. "I'm sorry, but I'm going to have to insist that you lie down. If you lose consciousness and pitch forward I won't be able to hold you."

He didn't argue this time, and, still applying pressure to his wound, she helped him to stretch out on the table. "I'll need more information later, but right now I'll settle for your name and address. I'm Nancy Lloyd, by the way."

He shifted until he was comfortable. "I'm Caleb Winters and I'm renting a cottage down on the waterfront for the summer."

He told her the address and she nodded. "I know the area. It's very pretty with all the trees and flowering shrubs. Where are you from?"

He looked at her oddly. "From?"

"I mean your permanent address. Where do you live the rest of the year?"

He scowled and looked away. "That is my permanent address for the time being. I've spent the past year in hospitals. I was blown halfway to hell in an industrial accident in Baltimore."

Nancy was too good a nurse to let her emotions show, but the picture his few terse words produced was unnerving. She was aware of the shattering damage an explosion could do to the human body, and it was evident that Caleb Winters was still enduring the aftermath, even before this latest assault.

The bleeding had slowed to a trickle, and while she cleaned and tightly wrapped the gash she kept up a conversation in an effort to distract him from the pain she was causing. "Have you been on the island long?"

"Only a week. It felt so good to be out of the hospital that I guess I overestimated my strength with the wood chopping." There was self-derision in his tone. "I sometimes wonder if I'll ever be a whole man again."

For the first time Nancy really looked at him as a person rather than a patient, and what she saw left no doubt about his manhood. He was too thin, but his bone structure was impressive. His shoulders were wide, and his chest was broad. His muscle tone was good considering he'd had a year of inactivity, and with a little time and some body-building exercises he would not only be normal but impressive.

She looked at him and grinned mischievously. "Take it from me, there's nothing wrong with you that a few pounds and a little exercise won't put right. Are you getting physical therapy?"

The muscles around his mouth relaxed a little in response to her lighthearted teasing. "I have an exercise routine that I do every day, but it takes so damn long to get results."

"Tell me," Nancy said as she finished dressing his arm, "was there any machinery damaged in that explosion?"

He hesitated. "Yes."

"What happened to it afterward?"

"It was junked."

She nodded. "Exactly. But your body has been repaired and it's still whole and functioning. Don't you think it's a little unreasonable to expect it to be good as new?"

He sighed. "You're right, of course, but this past year has seemed like an eternity."

He had clear, dark brown eyes that betrayed the depth of his frustration, and her heart lurched as his gaze connected with hers. It was all she could do to keep her hands on his arm instead of moving them up to stroke his pale cheeks and brush the lock of ebony hair back from his forehead.

Down, girl. You know better than to get emotionally involved with a male patient.

She got a tight grip on her errant thoughts and turned away for the examining table. "The next ferry leaves for the mainland in twenty minutes. You lie there while I call Doctor Gunther and arrange for him to meet us at the hospital."

"No hospital!" The words thundered through the room.

She turned around to find him struggling to sit up, and hurried to ease him back down before the bleeding started again. "Caleb, be reasonable," she said as he continued to struggle. "The emergency room at the hospital is the only place that's set up to take care of this type of injury."

"No hospital," he repeated, but relaxed and lay back down. "You can sew it up right here."

She helped him to get comfortable again. "No, I can't. I'm not a surgeon. I'm not even a physician, and this wound is deep. You don't want an ugly scar, which I can guarantee you'd have if I sutured it."

"One more scar won't make any difference," he muttered.

She put her hand over his where it lay across his waist, and he captured her fingers in his. His grip was strong despite the latest injury to his arm. "Yes, it will," she said gently. "You don't have any that show, and I'm not going to add one."

"Pull up my shirt," he said tersely.

Nancy stared at him.

"Oh, come on, you're a nurse, and I'm in no shape to make passes. Just pull up my shirt."

With her free hand she did as he asked, then understood why he'd demanded it. His chest was crisscrossed with scars, and one at the side ran under the waistband of his jeans.

"Now tell me about the importance of not adding another one," he grated. "If you're really interested I'll show you the ones on my back and legs, too."

Nancy struggled against the lump of tears that had formed in her throat and managed to subdue them before they reached her eyes. He really had been through hell!

"All right," she said when she was sure her voice wouldn't quaver, "I'll tell the doctor to come here. You said he has your medical records, but has he examined you yet?"

"No, I've never met him, but I do have an appointment scheduled for later this month."

Nancy carefully withdrew her hand from his and regretted the necessity. His touch made her feel feminine and needed, and from the way he'd clasped her fingers she knew that he drew comfort from the contact.

When Doctor Gunther's exchange connected her with him she explained what had happened. He recognized the patient as a referral from Walter Reed Hospital in Washington, D.C., and agreed to catch the next ferry for the island.

When she hung up the phone in the reception room she returned to Caleb and smiled. "The doctor will be here within the hour," she said. "Meanwhile he's ordered a shot to make you more comfortable."

As she reached for the syringe Caleb's gruff voice stopped her. "No, I don't want it. Believe me, I've hurt a hell of a lot worse than this. Besides, I've had so much pain medication that I've developed a tolerance for it. It won't do me much good except in massive doses, and I've had all of those I intend to take."

He smiled at her skeptical expression. "I'm fine, really, except that this table is killing my back. Don't you have a chair I can sit in while we wait?"

"There's a sofa in the reception room you can lie on."

She helped him to sit up, then handed him his cane and walked along beside him into the front room.

She made him comfortable, propped up on the couch with two large bed pillows, then fastened a medical record form to a clipboard and pulled up a chair beside him. "Do you feel able to answer some questions now?"

He closed his eyes. "I told you I'm fine. What do you want to know?"

"How old are you?"

"Thirty-six."

"Your place of employment?"

"I'm unemployed."

Nancy looked up. "You mean you were fired because you were injured?" There was outrage in her tone.

"Not exactly. I've obviously been unable to work, and I got a big settlement from the company so we parted by mutual consent."

She wanted to ask him what his occupation was, but since it wasn't called for on the form she didn't feel she could.

"Who do you want listed as next of kin?" she asked instead.

"I don't have a next of kin. My parents are dead, and I have no brothers or sisters."

"Wife or children?"

His mouth tightened in a grim line. "No."

"Aunts, uncles or cousins?" she persisted.

"No, no one." He opened his eyes, and his tone was impatient. "Not everybody has a family, you know."

Nancy sighed. "I know that very well. I'm alone, too."

He looked surprised. "You?"

She nodded. "I was abandoned on the playground of a child-care center in Chicago when I was two. My parents never returned and no one knows who they were."

"But surely you were adopted."

Her smile was pensive. "No. By the time all the obstacles were cleared away and I was available for adoption I was too old and too ordinary-looking to appeal to prospective parents."

This time it was he who took her hand. "Too old, maybe, but too ordinary?" His voice was gruff. "Good Lord, woman, don't you ever look in a mirror? I've been trying to be a gentleman and not stare ever since you opened the door and let me in, but your combination of rich, dark brown hair—" he reached up with his uninjured arm and stroked the soft curls that had been tangled by the breeze earlier "—creamy skin—" he moved his fingers to outline her high cheekbone and rounded chin, "and slightly almond-shaped eyes that change color from brown to green to tawny, add up to classic, undisputed beauty."

Nancy felt a hot flush of pleasure color her face. "Thank you," she murmured breathlessly. "I—I guess I improved as I got older."

The tips of his fingers lightly brushed across her full, generous mouth, then dropped away leaving her lips tingling. "You're a very lovely lady, Nancy. You must have to fight the men off. Tell me, who raised you?"

She shrugged, but her voice wasn't altogether steady as she answered. "Oh, I was in a series of foster homes, and in between those I stayed at the orphanage, but we're getting off the subject. We're supposed to be talking about you. I really need someone listed on your record to notify in case of emergency."

He released her hand and scowled. "You can notify Barry Young." He gave her a post office box number in Washington, D.C., and added, "He's a business acquaintance. Anything else you want to know you can get from Dr. Gunther. It's all in the records he has."

He was telling her, politely but firmly, that he wasn't going to answer any more questions. She capped her pen and stood up, anxious to put some distance between them and calm her fluttering heart. "Can I get you anything to drink? Juice would be best, but I have sodas and coffee if you prefer."

"Juice will be fine, thanks. Whatever you have."

She went into the lab, where she took a can of apple juice out of the refrigerator, poured the contents into a glass, then added a flexible straw.

"I'm sorry it's taking so long to get your injury taken care of," she said as she handed him the drink. "Some of these rural communities are really strapped for medical care. Before this clinic was established two years ago, the citizens of Washington Island had to go all the way to the mainland to see a doctor. It got pretty hazardous in wintertime when the lake froze and the ferry had trouble getting through."

He took a long swallow of his juice. "Have you always been in charge?"

"Oh, no. I've only been here a month. After I got my master's degree as a nurse practitioner with a concentration in family care I spent a year working with a group of doctors in Chicago before going out on my own. This is just a temporary position until the regular nurse practitioner returns from spending the summer in Europe with her husband. They're celebrating their twenty-fifth wedding anniversary with a second honeymoon."

The phone rang, and Nancy excused herself to answer it, then spent the next fifteen minutes placating an anxious teenage mother whose baby slept all day and cried all night. By the time she'd explained the intricacies of an infant's timing device, Caleb was sleeping.

She walked carefully across the maroon carpet and stood looking down at him. Even in sleep he was tense and restless, and she knew that the injury was more painful than he had admitted. His face wasn't quite as pale as it had been earlier, though, and there was a little color in his cheeks.

He had an interesting facial structure but not enough flesh over it. She wondered if he'd been eating properly since he left the hospital. It had been her experience that men alone didn't, but surely he knew how important it was to his general health to gain weight. He needed to relax and regain his strength, so why on earth had he been chopping kindling?

Not wanting to disturb him, she picked up her packages and headed for the stairway and her apartment upstairs. Originally the second story had consisted of five bedrooms, but now the larger one was a living room, the small one at the back was a bathroom, and the one in between a kitchen. One of the rooms on the other side of the hall was still a bedroom, but the smaller was used as a walk-in closet. The whole apartment was newly painted, roomy and clean, and there was a spectacular view of Lake Michigan from the recently installed picture window in the living room.

Nancy quickly changed into jeans, loafers and a lightweight pink pullover sweater. Then she repaired her lipstick, ran a brush through her thick, shoulder-length hair and scooped up her lab coat as she hurried down the stairs. The staircase was in the front hall, and from the last few steps she could look through the open door and see the couch in the reception room.

Caleb was sitting up with his feet on the floor. He raised his head when he heard her coming down, looking upset and sounding a little dazed. "I must have dozed off. When I woke there was no one around and I thought you'd deserted me."

She tossed the lab coat on the back of a chair and walked over to him. "I just went upstairs to change into my working clothes. Are you all right? Was there something you wanted?"

He hesitated for a moment, then spoke in a husky murmur. "Yes, I wanted you."

It was a perfectly innocent answer, but for a moment as their glances met and clung the sensual tension between them was thick and shimmering. "I—I mean I've wakened in so many strange rooms lately that for a minute I wondered if I'd dreamed you." He rubbed one big palm over his face. "Oh, hell, isn't it about time for that doctor to get here?"

She sat down beside him and put the back of her wrist against his temple to see if his temperature was elevated. His forehead was cool, but when she moved her hand away he captured it and clutched it in both of his with a hint of panic that instantly alerted her.

She forced herself to remain calm as she looked at him. "Caleb, I can still give you that shot if the pain..."

He shook his head. "It's okay, I'm not going to freak out. It's just that my dreams aren't usually very pretty."

"But you weren't asleep long enough to dream," she protested.

"At times I only have to close my eyes to start. Also, I was a little disoriented when I woke up." He gave her a grin, but she knew it was forced. "I never had a nurse that looks like you before," he teased. "I guess I didn't want to believe that I'd just imagined you."

She was casting around for something to say that would match his attempt at lightness when the front door opened and Dr. Arnie Gunther, all six-foot-two, two hundred and fifty pounds of him, walked in.

Chapter Two

Repairing Caleb's wound was a lengthy procedure. When it was finished the doctor removed his lab coat while Nancy applied a clean bandage. "I hope you're not planning to cut more wood anytime soon," Dr. Gunther said. "Hell, man, didn't they tell you at Walter Reed to take it easy for a few weeks?"

Caleb, who was still lying on the examination table, looked up. "Yes, but I'm tired of being an invalid."

A look of compassion flitted across the physician's face, then vanished. "I can understand that—" his tone had lost some of its gruffness "—but you've got to work up to these things. You're mighty lucky that gash wasn't any deeper. I see by your records that you're living at the Jenssen place."

Caleb eyed him speculatively. "Oh? Are you a native of the island?"

Arnie grinned, and his blue eyes sparkled. "Sure am. Born and raised here. Would have come back to set up a practice after I got out of school and finished my army time, but by then there were so few permanent residents left that I couldn't have supported my family. Instead I took over for the only doctor in Ellison Bay when he retired, and now I serve all of the northern end of the Door County Peninsula. We have a small hospital, and that's where I'm going to insist you spend the night."

"No." Caleb's tone left no room for argument.

Dr. Gunther argued anyway. "Believe me, I can sympathize with your aversion to hospitals, and I wouldn't be so insistent if it weren't for your general physical condition, and the fact that your blood pressure and pulse rate are high. It's probably just a reaction to the shock of the accident, but they should both be monitored."

Caleb opened his mouth, but the doctor hurried on. "Also you gouged yourself with a dirty ax. Nancy and I have cleaned the gash, but your resistance is low and it not only could, but probably will become infected."

Caleb snorted. "That's a crock. I've been pumped so full of antibiotics that no self-respecting bacterium would come near me."

"Not lately you haven't, and your records indicate that you may be developing a resistance to some of the medication. Come on now, dammit, be reasonable. You won't have to stay more than a couple of nights—"

"No!" Caleb interrupted. "No way. Now look, doctor..."

"Call me Arnie."

"All right, Arnie, I'm not going to the hospital. I can always get in touch with Nancy if I think there's a problem."

"Oh? Have you had a telephone installed at the Jenssen house?"

Caleb looked momentarily nonplussed. "Well, no, but—"

"Then just how do you intend to contact her in the middle of the night if you should start running a high temperature? Or if your arm starts bleeding again? Or if your blood pressure shoots up and you have a stroke?"

Nancy had been listening to the heated exchange between the two men while she bandaged Caleb's arm, and she was torn between sympathy for him and the certainty that Dr. Gunther was right. Caleb shouldn't be alone, at least not tonight, but she could understand his aversion to hospitals.

This time it was she who interrupted the conversation. "That couch in the reception room folds into a bed." She looked at Caleb. "Why don't you stay here? I live upstairs and I can keep an eye on you."

For just a moment she thought he was going to accept, but then stubborn determination hardened his expression again. "Thank you, but I'm going home. Even here I feel like a prisoner. I'd never be able to sleep, and there's no reason to keep you awake. If you'll just help me get off this table I'll be fine."

He started to sit up, and after a quick glance at the doctor Nancy helped him.

Arnie, who was every bit as stubborn as his patient, growled angrily, "So be it, but if you insist on going off by yourself I won't be responsible for you."

"I don't expect you to be," Caleb snapped. "Now, if you'll hand me my cane..."

Nancy gave it to him, and he slid off the table and stood while Arnie washed his hands and put on his tweed sport coat.

"You can't leave just yet," Nancy said to Caleb as she directed him to the sofa. "I still have to get some information about your insurance and then you need to sign some forms."

Caleb sank down on the couch and leaned back. Nancy knew his limited strength was rapidly diminishing, and a plan began to form in her mind as Dr. Gunther handed a small bottle of pills to Caleb.

"Here," he said, "and don't give me any more of your lip. When the local anesthetic wears off that arm is going to hurt. When that happens take two of these and go to bed. After four hours take another one, and repeat every four hours as needed."

"Thank you," Caleb answered, without making any promises to take the advice. "And thanks for coming over to sew me up. I realize I'm being a pain in the rear, but I can't seem to help it. It comes down to the fact that I'd rather suffer at home than be comfortable in the hospital. Stupid, but..."

Arnie smiled, his expression warm and forgiving. "Not so stupid, considering. Come in to see Nancy on Monday, and that's an order. I'm not kidding about infection."

He turned to look at her. "Walk to the car with me."

She nodded and followed him outside. "Can you keep an eye on him?" he asked, and there was concern in his tone.

"I'll stick like glue," she answered, laughing.

"Honey, the guy's injured, but he's not dead," Arnie drawled. "Don't stick too close."

Nancy knew she was blushing and that made her all the redder, even though she was used to his teasing. Arnie Gunther was sixty years old. He had been married to the same woman for over thirty years and had six grown children, but he loved to tease Nancy about the parade of male patients, with everything from headaches to hangnails, who had sauntered into the clinic since she had arrived.

Suddenly his playfulness disappeared, and his next words were spoken seriously. "I wish he'd come to the mainland with me and go into the hospital. If you get a chance you might stop by his place tomorrow and make sure he's all right. If he doesn't come in on Monday, give me a call."

Nancy patted his arm. "I promise I'll take good care of him even if he does growl and bare his teeth."

Back in the reception room she picked up the papers she needed and sat down on the couch beside Caleb. After getting the necessary insurance information she had him sign the forms, then she put them aside and looked at him. "Have you had anything to eat today?"

The corners of his mouth quirked. "Is that going to be noted on my medical record?"

She grinned. "Absolutely. We don't want you to die of starvation after all the work we've done to patch you up."

"Oh, well, in that case the answer is yes. I had bacon, eggs and toast at about six-thirty this morning."

Nancy glanced at her watch. "It's almost six now, and long past time for you to eat again. Do you like spaghetti?"

"Next to hot dogs it's my favorite food."

She rolled her eyes in exasperation. "Men! Fortunately you're in luck. One of my grandmotherly patients keeps bringing me food, and last night she showed up with a pot of spaghetti. I'd ask you to share it with me here, but you'd have difficulty climbing my steep staircase. How about if I drive you to your place and warm it for us there?"

She held her breath, afraid he would reject her offer. She knew it wouldn't be safe if he stamped off by himself.

He looked at her speculatively. "You're tempting me, but suppose you tell me the real reason you're willing to go to all this trouble?"

Nancy held his gaze. "I told you the *real* reason. I want to be sure you eat. You won't get your strength back on only one meal a day. Also I don't like to eat alone, and I have to take you home, regardless, because it's too dangerous for you to drive your car."

He opened his mouth, but she put her fingers to his lips and continued, "You've been seriously injured, and your left arm has been anesthetized. You have no reflexes in it, and if you had to stop suddenly, or swerve, you'd wreck the car. Now don't argue. After all, you should be honored. You're the first man I've invited to dinner since I left Chicago, and you'll also be the first man I've gone home with."

While she was talking he put his hand over hers and placed a lingering kiss in the palm, then closed her fingers as though to hold the kiss in. The gesture tugged at erogenous zones she hadn't even known she had and interfered with her breathing, to say nothing of her ability to speak.

He clasped her small fist in his big hand and rested them both against his chest. "In that case I can't very well refuse, can I?" She could feel his heart beating under their joined hands. "I have French bread, a treeful of cherries and a bottle of wine to contribute to the meal."

She would have breathed a sigh of relief if her own pounding heart hadn't short-circuited her whole respiratory system. "Sounds delicious, but we'd better forego the wine. You can't drink alcohol while you're taking those pills the doctor gave you."

Fifteen minutes later they pulled up in front of the cottage Caleb was renting. It was small and white, and stood only a few yards from the water's edge. In front of it was a trim green lawn surrounded by bushes and a huge weeping willow tree with slender, leafy branches that touched the ground.

Nancy waited as Caleb laboriously got out of the car and walked slowly to the front door. She wanted to help him, to put her arm around him and encourage him to lean on her, but she knew she couldn't. That Caleb was a fighter had become evident even in the few hours she'd been around him, and he needed to be encouraged in his independence, not made to feel weak and helpless. Her job was to support him without making him aware that she was doing so.

Inside the cottage was a room with a huge stone fireplace, which served as both living room and kitchen. Off that was a hall with a door on each side, which Nancy assumed led to a bedroom and a bathroom. The furnishings in the front room were rustic, but clean and neat.

She put the pot of spaghetti down on the stove as Caleb closed the door. The evening breeze off the lake was still chilly in June. While she lit the burner and turned it down low, Caleb made coffee. She'd intended for him to rest while she fixed dinner, but didn't suggest it as he moved about the kitchen. Obviously he didn't want to be coddled.

"If you'll point me in the direction of that tree you told me about I'll go pick some cherries," she said as she stirred the spaghetti.

"No need," he answered and limped to the refrigerator. "I have a container of them right here. As soon as I build a fire in the fireplace I'll wash and stem them if you'll fix the French bread." He grinned. "I suddenly have an aversion to knives and other things with sharp edges."

They worked together companionably, and when the meal was ready they ate sitting beside the wall of windows that provided a magnificent view of the small cove, the vast lake beyond and the tree-studded shoreline.

"This is a wonderful place to convalesce," Nancy observed as she dished up a second helping of spaghetti for Caleb. "How did you happen to come here? Are you from Wisconsin?"

He reached for another piece of bread. "No. Uh...a friend suggested it, and the hospital made all the arrangements."

She was surprised that a hospital would be involved in that way, but a big government facility such as Walter Reed probably did a lot of things that smaller, private hospitals wouldn't attempt. "Did they also refer you to Dr. Gunther?"

"Yeah. Hey, do you suppose your grandmotherly patient would cook a meal for me three or four times a week? I'd pay her, of course, and I wouldn't want anything fancy."

Nancy was aware that he had changed the subject rather abruptly, but she shrugged mentally and answered his question. "Her name's Emma, and she loves to cook. I'll ask her."

By the time they finished eating Nancy noticed that Caleb was furtively rubbing at his injured arm. She knew that the local anesthetic was wearing off, and it probably throbbed all the way from his shoulder to his hand.

She stood and began gathering up dirty dishes, then asked casually, "Where did you put those pills the doctor gave you?"

"In the medicine cabinet in the bathroom." His answer was equally casual.

She put the dishes in the sink and went looking for the bathroom. It was on the left side of the hall, and she returned with the small container of strong analgesic. She shook two of them into her hand and brought them to Caleb, who was still seated at the table. "Here, take these," she said, and held them out to him.

He hesitated. "I don't think—"

"Caleb, don't be so stoic," Nancy said impatiently. "It'll get you nothing but a lot of pain and a sleepless night. Arnie Gunther is an excellent physician. He would never have given you medication you didn't really need."

He looked at her, then took the pills, put them in his mouth and washed them down with his coffee.

Nancy was standing beside him and she was so relieved not to have to insist that she patted his shoulder, though it turned out to be more of a caress than a pat. He put his arm around her and pulled her close, then laid his head between her breasts. With no will to resist she clasped him to her and stroked his thick black hair.

He was so slender, all bone and muscle, but even so his hold on her was strong and firm—the embrace of a man and a woman, not of a patient seeking comfort. What was there about Caleb Winters that attracted her so strongly? That circumvented her conscience and her common sense and left her operating on pure emotion?

She'd had her share of infatuations, including the intern during her hospital training days who had been her first and only lover, but she had never felt this magnetism before. The pull was sensual but not necessarily sexual, and it had radiated between Caleb and her almost since she opened the clinic door and saw him standing on the step.

She lowered her head to snuggle her cheek in his hair. The only logical explanation for her feelings was a natural compassion for a wounded and still suffering man, but she knew she was too good a nurse to let her emotions become involved with a patient merely because of his medical problem.

Caleb rubbed his face against the fuzzy pink sweater covering Nancy's soft breasts. They were warm and full and he could hear the heart that beat beneath them, and smell the fresh sweet scent that was a natural part of the woman.

He cursed himself for a fool even as his arm around her tightened. The doctors at Walter Reed had been right, he shouldn't have left the hospital yet. His judgment was impaired, and his emotions were unstable. He had only been out a week and already he'd injured himself by his carelessness and been caught under the spell of the first woman who offered sympathy.

God, but it felt good to be held like this again. He hadn't realized how much he'd missed the soothing, sensual touch of hands that caressed, of breasts that pillowed, of a flat, firm belly fitted against his chest. He'd had scores of women handling him during the past months, but they'd been nurses, doctors, lab technicians. Skilled professionals who had been friendly but impersonal, sexless to the point that he had seldom differentiated between the men and the women who had ministered to him.

So why was Nancy Lloyd an exception? She was part of the medical profession, sort of halfway between a nurse and a doctor, and he was her patient. She was no different than those faceless, sexless caregivers who had poked and probed and put him back together again, inch by inch. His gratitude toward them was boundless, but he'd never had to fight the urge to touch them, or sleep in their arms, as he had almost from the moment this beautiful creature put her hand on him and tenderly but firmly took charge of his well-being.

Nancy's fingers stroked the back of Caleb's head, his nape and the tense muscles in his shoulders, and he forgot the burning pain in his arm and relaxed. He would have purred if he had known how. The odd part was that he wasn't sexually aroused, although his body was giving warning signals that if this went on much longer he would be. He somehow knew that his need for her was more than sexual, not less, and that idea was terrifying.

There was no room in his life for anyone, but certainly not for an emotional relationship with a woman. He'd been celibate for a long time and a physical encounter would be a welcome relief, but not with this lady of the tempting curves and the sweet and loving disposition. She would tie him in knots, and he already had more emotional baggage than he could handle.

As the stirrings in his groin increased, he took a deep breath and forced himself to speak. "I think you'd better leave before I do or say something out of line."

He didn't loosen his hold on Nancy, but his tone was strained and she knew he was right. It was past time to put some distance between them. "I will," she said, but it took all her willpower to disengage herself from him. "First I'm going to make sure you get to bed all right, then I'll clean up the dishes and go home."

He started to protest, but she handed him his cane. "If you need help, call me," she said and stood back as he got awkwardly to his feet.

He glowered. "If I let you undress me, it wouldn't be to sleep."

Nancy smiled as she watched him make his way across the room, his annoyance apparent in the way he held his shoulders back and his head high. Annoyance was safer than the feelings that had been growing between them just now. It was better for both their sakes that he had rebuffed her offer of assistance.

When she'd finished washing the dishes she heard Caleb come out of the bathroom and cross the hall to the bedroom. A few minutes later he appeared, wearing light blue pajamas and a dark blue robe. "Now are you satisfied?" he asked, as he stood in the middle of the room and let her inspect him.

"Very nice," she answered, and meant it. He was an extremely appealing man, not too tall or too short, and his gauntness touched her maternal instinct, although *maternal* was definitely not the word she would use to describe her feelings for him. He was thoroughly masculine, but he had a vulnerability that she was quite sure was an integral part of his makeup and not just a result of his bad experience. "Did you get your bandage wet in the shower?"

He lifted the sleeve of his robe to display a dry covering on the wound. "I learned long ago to shower or bathe without getting bandages wet," he said testily. "I also brushed my teeth and washed behind my ears, so now you can stop fussing over me and go home."

"Not until you get into bed," she said and bit back a grin at his look of disgust.

"Are you always this bossy?" he demanded.

"Only with mule-headed patients," she answered cheerfully. "Come on, I'll tuck you in."

She expected him to protest, but instead a slow, seductive smile lit his face. "Oh well, in that case..." His voice was husky, and he put his arm around her waist. "Come along. I like to be tucked in."

His tone left no doubt that his idea of being "tucked in" differed drastically from hers. Her eyes widened. "You wouldn't?"

"Maybe not," he said in that husky drawl as his hand settled on her hipbone, "but you don't know for sure, do you? It's been a long time since I've been with a woman, and I've got all the normal male drives. I'd advise you not to trust me too far."

He had outmaneuvered her, and she hadn't even seen it coming. She was certain that he wouldn't try to force her, but if he actually set out to seduce her she'd be in big trouble. She wasn't sure she could refuse him, not when her pulse pounded and her knees turned to jelly just thinking about his hands seeking and memorizing her curves, his lips teasing and tasting, and his body joining with hers in the ultimate intimacy of love.

Love! Good grief, she really was coming apart at the seams. They'd known each other all of six hours or so, and love didn't even enter into this far-out fantasy of hers. It was lust, pure and simple, and she'd better pull herself together and put a stop to it.

She backed away from him, and he let her go. "Okay, you win," she said, wishing her voice was steadier. "But I'd appreciate it if you would get into bed while I dry the dishes. Shut your door so I don't disturb you, and I'll leave as soon as I finish."

Their gazes met and melded, and again Nancy was lost. Caleb put out his hand and wound a strand of her dark hair around his finger. "You know I'd never harm you, don't you?" he asked softly.

"Yes." It was little more than a whisper as his hand curled around her nape and drew her toward him.

Without breaking eye contact they moved closer together. "Thank you for being here when I needed you," he murmured just before his lips touched hers tenderly, clung for a moment, then moved to the tip of her nose and finally to each closed eyelid, breaching the spell of their heated gaze.

Before she could open her eyes his hand dropped away and she heard the thump, thump of his cane as he walked toward the bedroom.

Nancy lingered over the dishes in hopes that Caleb would doze off before she left. The pills Dr. Gunther had given him were strong, and two of them should not only dull the pain but put him to sleep. If they didn't, if he had built up a tolerance to medication, then he was in for a thoroughly miserable night, and she didn't want to leave before she knew which it was going to be.

It was nine o'clock when she turned off the light and sat down on the sofa. The scene outside the window was breathtaking. A full moon silhouetted the maple, beech and birch trees on either side of the cove, illuminated the peaceful water and penetrated the inside of the cabin as well. The fire in the fireplace gave off enough heat and glow to create a restful, shadowed effect.

She leaned back and listened to the lullaby of the crickets with an occasional bass obbligato from a bullfrog. It was a storybook setting, a tiny corner of paradise where a battered body could be restored and a bruised soul renewed. If only Caleb would cooperate and give nature a chance.

After a while her eyes began to droop, and she knew she'd better move around or she would fall asleep. She got up and went to the bathroom, then moved across the hall to knock softly on the bedroom door. There was no response so she opened it and looked in. This room also had a large window, and Caleb hadn't pulled the drapes. The combination of moonlight from one side and the hall light from the other made the area bright enough for her to see him.

He was thrashing around restlessly, and his breathing was labored, but he was obviously asleep. She walked quietly across the room and stood by the bed, wondering if she should wake him. He'd mentioned having bad dreams earlier.

Suddenly one arm flailed out, and she caught his hand just before it hit her. He jerked, and she thought he was going to wake up, but then he clasped his hand around hers and tugged. She sat on the side of the bed, and he tucked their joined hands under his cheek and sighed peacefully as he settled down.

Nancy put her other hand to his forehead. It was warm, but not alarmingly so. She didn't feel it was necessary to wake him to check his temperature, but neither could she leave him alone until she was sure he was all right.

Her touch seemed to quiet him, and she sat there until his grasp on her hand loosened and she knew he was sleeping deeply.

Back in the front room she turned on the light beside the couch and pulled the drapes. It was growing chilly, and she put more wood on the fire, then found a paperback spy thriller in the bookcase and settled down on the couch again. She'd stay for another hour, then check on him one last time.

An hour later he was sleeping peacefully, but he still felt warm. She hated to wake him so decided to give it another hour.

The fire had burned low and she didn't want to build it up since she'd be leaving soon, so she got a blanket from the linen closet at the end of the hall and wrapped it around her as she settled down to her book again.

Minutes later the print on the page blurred and her eyes closed. A short nap wouldn't hurt, she thought dreamily. Just long enough to take the edge off her drowsiness . . .

* * *

Nancy smelled the coffee before her mind focused on anything else. Then she became aware of the cramped position in which she was lying. She shifted, trying to get more comfortable, and realized that she wasn't in bed.

Her eyes blinked open, and for a moment she was disoriented. Where on earth was she?

Then she remembered. Caleb! Good heavens, it was daylight, and she'd slept all night on the couch in Caleb Winters's cabin. Her gaze moved to the other end of the room, where he sat at the table sipping from a thick mug and reading a paper.

With a low groan she defied her aching muscles and sat up. "Good morning," Caleb said, and she was relieved to see that he was smiling. "If you'd told me you were going to spend the night I would have given you the bed."

She knew she must look a mess with her hair mussed, her makeup stale and shiny and her clothes rumpled. She ran her hands through her hair and felt the tangles. "Oh, my. I'm sorry. I only intended to wait a little while to make sure you were all right."

She fought her way out of the twisted cover. "It must have been the blanket that did it. The fire was going out so I wrapped up in it and fell asleep. I'm so embarrassed."

He stood and limped slowly across the room to stand in front of her. She noticed that he wasn't using his cane. "Don't ever be embarrassed with me," he said, and there was a catch in his voice. "I can't tell you how much it means to me that you cared enough to stay, even after I'd practically ordered you to leave." He took her hand and pulled her up to stand beside him. "Now, what can I fix you for breakfast?"

A good night's sleep hadn't done a thing to lessen the attraction that seemed to radiate between them. "If . . . if you'll just give me a few minutes to freshen up, I'll make breakfast."

He shook his head. "You cooked dinner last night, so this morning it's my turn. Do you like ham and eggs?"

She'd already learned not to argue with him. "Love them. I won't be long." She turned and started toward the bathroom.

"There are new toothbrushes in the medicine cabinet," he called. "They gave me several when I left the hospital, as well as the most complete first-aid kit I ever saw."

Nancy had a comb, brush and lipstick in her purse, and after a quick shower she dressed again and managed to look presentable when she joined Caleb at breakfast.

He insisted on waiting on her, and since she knew it was important to him to assert his independence she let him. She was surprised that he wasn't using the cane and asked him about it.

"I don't usually use it in the house," he said as he poured her a second cup of strong, hot coffee. "I don't want to depend on it any more than is necessary. Yesterday, with the shock of the accident and all, I needed it, but I feel fine this morning. I slept soundly last night. Must have been the pills you gave me."

"Have you taken any more of them?"

"No, the pain's not bad any longer, and I like to have all my wits about me."

Nancy noticed that he looked much better this morning. There was more color in his face, and he looked rested. "They are strong," she agreed. "That's why I didn't go home right away after you went to bed. Also you had a period of restlessness, and you seemed quite warm."

He looked thoughtful. "I sometimes have bad dreams, although if I had one last night I don't remember it. I've always been warm-blooded, too." He cocked one eyebrow. "In fact, I've been told that at times I positively radiate heat." He said it with a straight face, but she caught the teasing note in his voice.

She grinned and looked him over boldly. "I'll just bet you do," she answered, her tone a husky exaggeration.

He reached across the table and covered her hand with his. "I'd be happy to demonstrate," he said hopefully, his deep brown eyes filled with amusement.

She felt the heat they were talking about kindling in her body, and took a deep breath to keep her voice under control. "That's very generous of you, but we'd better make it some other time. I have to leave in a few minutes."

Immediately his expression changed, and he squeezed her hand. "I'm sorry, I was only teasing. Please don't run away."

"Oh no," she hurried to assure him. "I have to go home and check my answering machine. Since I'm the only qualified medical person on the island I'm never really off duty unless I make arrangements in advance. You don't have a telephone here, and I haven't been able to check my messages since last evening."

"Yes, of course, I didn't think." He sounded disappointed. "I'm afraid I'm being selfish, but I'd hoped we could spend the day together."

She smiled. "If that's an invitation, I accept. Why don't you come to the clinic with me while I look things over there? That way you can bring your car home when we come back."

He brightened. "Sounds great. Just promise me one thing."

She almost said anything, but checked herself in time and nodded instead. "Promise you'll forget that you're my nurse and be my friend for today."

When he looked at her with those compelling brown eyes she was afraid she would agree to anything he asked. Fortunately, this request was easy since the line between their professional and personal relationships was already hopelessly blurred.

"I'll always be your friend," she said simply, and wondered how long friendship would be enough for both of them.

Nancy suspected that she was caught in an emotional web that could change the course of her life, but whether for better or worse she wasn't sure.

Chapter Three

Nancy and Caleb saw each other every day during the following week. Each afternoon after she closed the clinic Nancy drove to Caleb's place where they had an early dinner, then went for a walk. The first day it was a very short stroll down the road in front of the cabin, but each time they lengthened it a bit, took it slowly and enjoyed the scenery along the lake. Everything was so green, and the red, yellow, lavender and blue of the tulips, daffodils and hyacinths, as well as the flowering bushes, added a riot of color to the quaint little island.

Caleb had a telephone installed so Nancy could stay in touch with her message machine. He spent the daytime hours while she was working soaking up the sun and faithfully continued his exercise routine. As he replaced the hospital pallor with the beginnings of a golden tan he also strengthened his muscles. His appetite improved as did the nutritional quality of his meals with Nancy's supervision, and he gained two pounds in six days.

On Thursday she removed the sutures from his arm and noted that it was healing better than she'd anticipated. The infection she had feared had never materialized, and she could tell that the scar, though raw and angry-looking now, would fade with time and be less noticeable.

As if by mutual consent they ignored the electricity that continued to crackle between them and made a determined effort to keep their relationship friendly and, if not impersonal, at least neutral. They never discussed the sensual pull that became more difficult to ignore each day, and they kept touching and intimate eye contact at a minimum.

Nancy knew that if either of them reached out to the other there would be no holding back, but neither was ready for a deeper commitment yet. It was happening too fast. They were little more than strangers, and Caleb was her patient.

That bothered Nancy most of all. Not only the ethics of it, but the fact that it was a misleading and dangerous situation. She'd always been strongly empathetic and felt a compulsion to ease the pain and unhappiness of others. As a small child she'd pretended that her dolls were sick so she could take care of them. As she got older she was the one the other kids came to for sympathy and bandaging when they were hurt.

Nancy was a natural caregiver and she'd always known she would be a nurse when she grew up. It was this aspect of her personality that made her distrust her feelings for Caleb. He was the most emotionally needy patient she had ever had. He'd been severely injured, had spent long months in hospitals and apparently had no family or close friends to turn to.

He desperately needed someone to care about him enough to make sure he ate properly, got enough exercise and didn't overtax his limited strength, and Nancy had a matching need for someone to care for. They gravitated toward one another because it was their nature to do so.

As the professional, Nancy was charged with the responsibility of keeping her emotions separate from her professional caring when dealing with a patient—no matter how appealing that patient might be to her. She wasn't doing that. Something about Caleb had tugged at her heartstrings from the beginning, and she hadn't had a prayer of staying impersonal with him.

She knew he was fighting the same battle, although they never talked about it. He told her with his burning glances, his restrained touch that nevertheless warmed her, and the huskiness of his voice when he inadvertently said something deeply personal to her. The sensual tension between them was too strong to be one-sided, but were they confusing their individual needs to care and to be cared for with a deeper, more binding emotion?

Would they still feel the heightened awareness when he was well and strong and no longer needed or wanted her protective compassion? Or would they find that they had nothing else in common but a mutual need that was no longer applicable?

At five o'clock on Friday Caleb, who was lying on the lounger in a sunny spot on the lawn, closed his book and went into the house to shower and put on some clothes. When he was alone during the day he only wore abbreviated bathing trunks in order to take advantage of the sun's tanning rays. The homes along the waterfront were far apart and secluded by the heavy growth of trees and bushes, and there was little danger of being observed.

He hadn't always been reluctant to appear nearly nude in a public place. He'd done so regularly at beaches and swimming parties, and once he'd even modeled swim trunks in a charity-sponsored fashion show. But that had been when he'd had a body to be proud of, when he'd weighed thirty pounds more and had rippling muscles and firm, unblemished flesh.

Now he wouldn't expose anybody, not even Nancy, to the full effect of the scars and burns that marred his pale, thin frame. He always wore long pants and a shirt if there was any chance of being observed.

He'd just finished dressing in clean jeans and a sweat-shirt when he heard Nancy's car. His pulse speeded up and he quickly ran the comb through his still damp hair, then walked carefully, without the aid of his cane, to the front room just as she came through the open door.

She always changed out of the white uniforms she worked in before she came to him, and this time she was wearing red slacks cinched at the waist with a white woven belt, and a red and white striped long sleeve shirt. His hard-to-discipline gaze noticed the fullness of her breasts and hips accentuated by her narrow waist. It took all his wavering control to stand where he was and greet her instead of going to her and taking her in his arms.

"Hey, you're early," he said pleasantly. "You almost caught me in the shower."

She gave him that perky little grin that always alerted him to the fact that she was going to say something outrageous. "Sorry I missed it, I could have washed your back. I'm very good at backs."

Just the thought of her nude under the shower with him and rubbing a washcloth over his back made him ache with longing, but he laughed and followed her to the kitchen end of the room. "I'm sorry, too. Maybe next time," he said as lightly as he could manage.

She was carrying a sack of groceries, which she set down on the counter. "You said you were going to barbecue steaks, so I brought salad makings." She began taking lettuce and fresh vegetables out of the bag.

"Thanks," he said. "If you want to fix it, I'll heat up the grill."

An hour later they'd finished dinner and were starting out on their nightly walk. Caleb still relied on the cane while navigating the uneven terrain outdoors, and Nancy took care to stay close beside him. Although she never took his arm or offered to help he knew she was coiled and ready to spring if he should stumble.

It was the same when they ate together. She never scolded him for not eating enough, but she would teasingly coax him to have another piece of meat, or a second roll, or more ice cream. He was quite sure that he would gnaw on the table leg if she looked at him with those luminous eyes and smiled her sweet, tender smile while she told him it would make her happy if he did.

He shivered and said the first thing that came to mind in an effort to shift his attention to something else. "I met an old man at the grocery store yesterday who told me that this island has the largest colony of Icelanders in the United States."

"I'm sure that was true in the past," she said, "and maybe it still is, but according to the last census, people of Danish and Norwegian extraction outnumber the Icelanders."

Caleb glanced at her. "How come you're such an expert on Washington Island history? You haven't been here much longer than I have."

She laughed. "True, but when I found out I was coming here I did some research. Did you know that the narrow strait that separates Door County Peninsula from Washington Island is called Death's Door because between the sixteen- and the nineteen-hundreds countless ships were caught in the treacherous crosscurrents and sank?"

She had piqued his interest. "In that case I'm surprised the island was ever settled."

Nancy shrugged. "The Scandinavians were always a hardy people, but those early pioneers endured extreme hardships. The temperature has been known to drop to forty degrees below zero here in the winter."

"Brrrr..." Caleb shivered. "Remind me not to stay past the first of September. My ancestors weren't Eskimos."

"Who were your ancestors, Caleb? What's your ethnic origin?"

He was once more on guard. "Who knows? A little of this and a little of that. What's yours? Isn't Lloyd an English name?"

"Welsh, but the name was given to me in the orphanage. I have no idea what my real one was, so I know nothing about my background either."

The idea of her being alone with no one to care about her was intolerable, and he reached for her hand and clasped it. "My precious little orphan," he murmured. "We're a good pair. Maybe I should adopt you as my niece. Then I'd be your uncle and we would both have a relative."

Nancy squeezed his hand, but shook her head. "No niece should ever feel about an uncle the way I feel about you." There was shyness in her tone, and she wouldn't look at him.

All his good intentions vanished in a rush of gladness and a need too strong to resist. He turned and took her in his arms, and she made no protest but snuggled against him.

For a moment they just stood there holding each other. He had played this scene often in his mind, but the reality so far exceeded the fantasy that he wondered if he would ever be able to release her. Her body was firm and round with no sharp angles, only soft curves that melded against him, and her fragrance made him think of springtime rain and fields of wildflowers.

He kissed the shining darkness of her hair. "And no uncle would feel about a niece the way I feel about you." His voice shook in spite of his efforts at control.

Without saying more they turned and with their arms around each other's waists, started back in the direction of the cabin.

The two of them were becoming a familiar sight walking on the road at this time of the day, and several people in cars waved or called greetings.

Caleb and Nancy responded with happy abandon to the friendly strangers, continuing on until at last they turned into Caleb's driveway. Once inside the house he shut the door and took her in his arms. She lifted her head as he lowered his, and their mouths met and clung.

Her lips were soft and warm and responsive, just as he'd known they would be, and he pulled her even closer as he felt her small fingers stroke his hair and his nape. She was trembling in his arms like a frightened doe, but he knew she wasn't afraid.

It was only then that he realized he was trembling, too, and that did scare him. He knew he was perilously close to losing both his objectivity and his self-control, and if he did it could have a devastating effect not only on his future, but on hers as well.

Nancy felt as if she were floating as Caleb's mouth held hers, and his hands roamed slowly over her back and shoulders. She breathed a sigh of relief. All week they'd been edging toward this until the tension between them had become almost alive.

At first she had been grateful for his restraint because she wasn't sure she could trust her own, but the last few days had been torment. In spite of the many reasons why a relationship between them was both inadvisable and unprofessional she was glad he'd finally given in before she had been reduced to begging him to hold her and kiss her.

She pressed closer against him in an effort to assure him that he needn't hold back any longer. That she would give whatever he wanted, take whatever he offered and worry about the consequences later. Right now they needed each other, and that was all that mattered.

They broke off the kiss slowly, reluctantly, and when he spoke his voice was unsteady. "I've wanted to do that ever since you first touched me. It's taken all the control I possessed to keep my distance and not come on too strong too soon." His lips touched hers briefly. "It's still too soon, but I can't play the waiting game any longer. I need you in my arms."

She rubbed her cheek against his. "I'm glad," she whispered against his ear, "because I need to be in your arms. I was afraid you didn't want to kiss me. That I was just imagining the tension I felt in you."

"You must have known better than that," he said as he nuzzled the hollow at the side of her neck, making her shiver. "The vibes I was giving out couldn't have been misunderstood. I've wanted you so much."

They stood there silently for a moment, then turned and walked over to the couch where he gathered her in his arms once more. He was very strong. The muscles in his upper arms and shoulders flexed when he moved, and his touch was gentle but sure. Even so, she was careful not to lean too heavily against him, a maneuver he recognized almost immediately.

"Relax, sweetheart," he said and settled her closer. "I'm not an invalid."

His tone was brittle, and she knew he was upset by her caution. "I know." She rubbed her hand over his chest. "I just don't want to hurt you."

His expression softened. "The wounds are all healed, and the bones have knit. You aren't going to do any damage by snuggling up to me."

He tipped her chin up and their mouths met again. She put her arms around his neck, and he cupped one of her breasts. It seemed to her as if it swelled beneath his palm, and she felt the pull deep in her womanhood.

He moved his hand to unbutton her blouse and release her bra, then bent and kissed her nipple before taking it in his mouth. She gasped as a wave of pleasure rippled through her, and her hand plunged under the loose neck of his sweatshirt and caressed his bare back.

His skin was rough with small ridges that would be the aftermath of skin grafts. He'd mentioned that his back had been burned, and her sympathy for his sufferings overwhelmed her good sense as she murmured, "Oh, Caleb, I'm so sorry."

He released her breast and lifted his head, then put his hands on her shoulders and held her away from him. "I don't want your sympathy, Nancy," he growled and turned away from her.

She was sick with the knowledge that she'd blundered badly. "I—please, darling, I didn't mean it that way..."

"I should have known." There was more sadness than anger in his tone, as he got stiffly to his feet. "I hoped that since you're a nurse you'd be more objective."

"I am," she said desperately. "I never let my emotions get in the way of my judgment."

The words were hardly out before she realized how untrue they were in this case. She had let her strong attraction to Caleb interfere with her professional demeanor. It was only natural that he'd mistaken it for pity.

Caleb ran his hand through his hair and walked over to stare into the empty fireplace. "I think you have this time." His voice was hollow. "You feel sorry for me, and you've confused that with a deeper, more basic emotion. For someone as caring as you are that's to be expected. You've sensed my desire for you and you feel sorry for me, but that's not fair to either of us."

She was appalled that he could actually believe what he was saying. "That's not true! I'm twenty-five years old, Caleb. Certainly old enough to sort out my own feelings." She rearranged her bra and started buttoning her shirt.

He continued to stand with his back to her. "Are you still a virgin, Nancy?"

Her fingers fumbled with the button as her hand jerked. "No. I had a lover when I was in training."

"Was he a patient?"

The slash of pain couldn't have been more severe if he'd slapped her. So that's what he thought. How could she have degraded herself so! While she was falling in love with him he was assuming that she gave herself to all her male patients who were in need of a little extra attention.

Her trembling fingers could no longer manage the buttons, and she rubbed her palms on the leg of her slacks in a gesture of despair. "No, Caleb," she said, surprised at how icy calm she sounded. "He wasn't a patient. I'm sorry if I've given you the impression that I take care of my patients' sexual needs as well as their medical ones. I can see that I've been behaving unprofessionally with you."

He whirled around and almost lost his balance as he reached out and clutched the fireplace mantel. He looked shocked. "My God, Nancy, I didn't mean..."

She was no longer listening as she picked up her purse and stood. "I'll let myself out," she said, holding her head high as she crossed the room.

"Nancy!" he shouted as she opened the door, then closed it behind her. Even with it closed she could hear him shout her name again, and she ran to her car. She knew he couldn't catch her if he tried, but she had to put distance between them as quickly as possible before she made a fool of herself by breaking down and crying.

The phone was ringing as she unlocked the front door of the clinic and stepped inside. She ignored it and went upstairs to her apartment where she heard Caleb's voice as it was being recorded on her answering machine. "Nancy, dammit, answer the phone. I want—"

She disconnected the phone and shut off the recorder.

Obviously he wanted to apologize, but she was in no mood to listen. Oddly, it wasn't him she blamed as much as herself. It was her own fault. By acting like a lovesick simpleton she'd set herself up for just what she'd gotten.

She burned with shame. How could she ever face him again? She knew she'd have to. She was the only medical person on the island, and there was no reason for him to have to go to the mainland every time he needed to be checked over.

She sank down on the sofa and put her head in her hands. She'd only been in charge of the clinic for six weeks

and already she'd botched things. Caleb was right in a way.
She did have trouble separating her various feelings for
him. She responded to him on all levels, and had from the
beginning. She couldn't help it, it just wasn't possible to
compartmentalize her emotions for him. They all blended
together—compassion, friendship, love.

That last one frightened her. Love wasn't an emotion to
be bandied around lightly. Was it possible to fall in love
with a man you knew almost nothing about? It might be,
but it definitely wasn't wise. To her, love meant marriage
and babies and fiftieth wedding anniversaries. Love was
forever, and only a foolish, immature woman would reck-
lessly allow her heart to be stolen by a stranger.

How could she have allowed that to happen? And what
was she going to do about it now that it had?

Nancy spent the weekend avoiding the phone. She was
afraid Caleb would call, and in the next moment she was
afraid he wouldn't. He didn't. Or if he did it was when she
wasn't there to receive it.

By Monday morning she was existing on raw nerves. It
didn't help any that Dr. Gunther was coming that day for
his monthly schedule of office surgeries and appointments, and Caleb was due at eleven o'clock to have the
doctor check on the progress of his arm injury.

She couldn't assist. She just couldn't. She would make
up a reason for leaving the office at that time and ask
Dagmar Harvey, her assistant, to take her place.

Unfortunately when the doctor was there they were always fully booked so that it was eleven before Nancy realized it. She had stepped into the lab for a moment and
when she came out she heard Caleb talking to the doctor
in one of the examining rooms.

Her first thought was to escape, but Dagmar was tied up on the phone so there was no one to cover for her. Well, her ethics where Caleb was concerned may have been marginal, but she was a good nurse and she wasn't going to let her personal problems interfere with her work performance. She'd done some acting in college and maybe her training would come to her rescue now.

She squared her shoulders, tilted her head up and walked into the room.

Caleb was sitting fully clothed on the table, and Dr. Gunther was looking at his medical chart. Nancy took a deep breath and even managed a passable smile. "Good morning, Caleb," she said and was relieved that her voice sounded bright and impersonal.

"Nancy..." He stood and reached out, but she stepped back before he could touch her.

"The doctor would like to check your heart and lungs, so if you'd just remove your shirt—"

"Nancy, I've got to talk to you."

"Certainly," she said and picked up a thermometer. Before he could say anything she stuck it into his mouth, even though taking his temperature wasn't necessary. "Put this under your tongue and hold it there."

He glowered as she waited the few seconds for the electrical instrument to register, and she caught a glimpse of the doctor looking from one of them to the other with a perplexed expression.

She took the thermometer from Caleb's mouth, noticed that it registered normal as she'd expected, then took the chart Dr. Gunther held out to her.

"Okay, Caleb," the doctor said, "take off your shirt and we'll make sure everything's functioning. You're looking good. Gotten a little tan, I see. Hope you've given up playing around with hatchets."

He laughed, but Caleb's expression remained serious. "I'd rather not take off my shirt. You can lift it up if you need to."

Nancy understood that he didn't want her to see his bare chest and back. Maybe he's afraid I'll throw myself at him in unrestrained pity if I get a full view of his scars and burns, she thought bitterly, then hated herself for her pettiness. He had a right to whatever privacy he wanted.

"I'll get the next patient settled in the other examining room," she said and put down the chart. "Call me if you need me."

She started to walk away, but Caleb's voice stopped her. "I'm not leaving until I've talked to you, Nancy, and I can be a real pest when I'm frustrated."

She closed her eyes for a second, but didn't turn. "I'm sure you can," she said lightly, "but we're awfully busy today. Perhaps if you have a problem you should take it up with the doctor."

"Do you really want me to discuss this with Arnie?"

He was beating her at her own game again. Why did she even try to outsmart him? She was discovering that Caleb Winters had a very good mind, indeed.

She sighed. "All right, Caleb, we'll talk. I'll be free from noon till one-thirty." She walked out and closed the door behind her.

The doctor was with Caleb for quite a while, longer than they'd budgeted time for, and there were still two patients to see before the lunch break. Was something wrong? Had Caleb developed a health problem that she hadn't been aware of?

She shook her head to push the unwanted thought away. No wonder he thought she couldn't control her emotions. Apparently she really couldn't where he was concerned.

Now she understood why doctors never treated those close to them. It was impossible to be dispassionate.

When Arnie finally called her Caleb was fully dressed and standing beside him in the small room. "The next two patients are just routine checkups," the doctor said brusquely. "Dagmar can assist me. You stay here and get things settled with Caleb." He hurried away before she could protest.

Caleb didn't try to touch her or keep her from moving farther away from him. Instead he put his hands in his pockets and spoke softly. "I took your advice and talked to Arnie."

Nancy gasped. "But I didn't mean you should talk to him about our personal problems."

Caleb shrugged. "I know, but I need help in dealing with you, and the good doctor has been married to the same woman for thirty years and four of his children are daughters. He's obviously learned after all this time how to handle his women."

"I'm not—"

"My woman," he finished the sentence for her. "I know, but you're very dear to me, and I can't let you think that I was criticizing or accusing you the other night."

He leaned back against the edge of the examining table, taking some of the weight off his shattered leg. "Nancy, when a man is injured the way I was and spends months in hospitals it does things to his self-image. For weeks I was taken care of like a baby, and for months I had to be helped with everything I tried to do. There were times when it would have been all too easy to give up, and I had to fight against that. I've finally reached the point where I can live alone and take care of myself. The day I left the hospital was a personal triumph, but I still see only pity in people's eyes when they watch me limping along. They don't see it as a victory that I walk at all, but as a defeat because I limp.''

She knew how difficult this was for him, and she couldn't let him put himself through any more of it. "Oh, Caleb, I don't pity you." Her voice broke and she tried again. "Believe me, I know how far you've come and how difficult it's been, but I can't help feeling compassion for you. I feel it for anyone who's hurting or disabled. Any person with an ounce of sensitivity would, but I never would confuse it with love, or even friendship. Sometimes I don't like the people that my heart goes out to, but that doesn't keep me from wanting to ease their pain.''

The outrage that had deserted her was coming back. "However, I do that in socially and medically approved ways, not by going to bed with them." Her tone was strident.

Caleb winced. "I know, and I'm sorry I overreacted, but I swear I wasn't accusing you of anything like that. You misunderstood what I was trying to say. I want so much more from you than compassion, and I asked if your lover was a patient because the affair apparently didn't last. I can't believe that any man would walk away from you, so I wondered if he was a patient and you lost interest once he was well and strong and no longer needed to lean on you.''

Nancy wasn't altogether flattered by that analysis of her character, either, but she finally understood what he was getting at. He wanted to be sure that she could separate the man he was from the patient he had become.

For the first time she managed a real smile, albeit a small one. "Theo was an intern at the hospital where I was training. We truly thought we were in love, but we were both so busy, and our schedules never meshed for more than a few hours together now and then. I guess you could say our relationship died of neglect. Of course that would never have happened if our feelings had been as deep as we first believed."

Caleb looked thoughtful. "Don't be too sure. Sometimes love just isn't enough. It takes a combination of so many things to make a marriage work."

Nancy felt a stab of uneasiness. Why was he talking about marriage when they'd been discussing affairs? He had answered no when she'd asked if he had a wife or children, but... "Are you married, Caleb?"

His eyes widened in surprise. "No. I told you I wasn't. Do you honestly think that I'd come on to you if I had a wife?"

Oh damn, now he thought *she* was accusing *him* unjustly. She wouldn't let that merry-go-round get started up again. She hurried over to him and put her hand on his arm. "No, I don't. I'm sorry. I know you're an honorable man, but it's a question I had to ask."

He put his arms around her and widened his stance so he could hold her between his legs as he leaned against the table. She tingled all the way to her toes as she hugged him around the waist and cuddled closer. "Oh, darling, don't let's have any more misunderstandings." She choked back a sob.

"I don't want to quarrel with you," he murmured as he rained tiny kisses down her cheek and throat. "It's been a hellish weekend. I finally gave up trying to contact you because I knew I'd be seeing you today, but I missed you so much. I didn't fully realize until then how vitally important you are to me."

She tilted her head to give easier access to his tantalizing mouth. "I missed you, too. Several times I actually started out the door to go to you, but then I would remember what you thought of me—"

"No," he muttered huskily and stopped her words with his lips.

Everything fled from her mind but the feel and the taste of him. Oh, it was so good to be back in his arms. He smelled clean, like bath soap and shampoo, and his face was smoothly shaven. He held her so tightly, but still with a tenderness she'd never experienced. As though telling her without words that she was very special to him.

He moved his mouth to the side of hers. "Do you want to know what I told Dr. Gunther?"

"Yes." She flicked her tongue against his cheek, then planted a moist kiss there and felt the stirring in his loins.

"I told him I thought I was falling in love with you."

A shock of exultation lurched through her and left a corresponding pull in her femininity. "Were you telling him the truth?" They were both speaking just slightly above a whisper.

"Only partially," he said, and her newfound elation was shaken until he continued. "To be absolutely truthful I should have told him that I *am* in love with you. It wasn't what I planned, or even wanted, and until I met you I would have said it wasn't possible to fall in love so quickly, but it happened and there didn't seem to be anything I could do to prevent it. Now I can only hope that you feel something more than just friendship for me."

Nancy wondered how it was possible to be so happy and so frightened all at the same time. Their feelings for each other had gotten totally out of control, even though each had fought against it. How was it that such a thing could happen to two adult, intelligent, well-educated people?

Well, it was too late to worry about it now. She ran her hand carressingly over his shirt-clad back. "Oh, my feelings for you are a great deal more than friendship," she assured him. "I had faced the fact that I love you by the time I got back to my apartment on Friday night."

He raised his head, startled. "Then why did you put me through two days and three interminable nights of torment?"

She pulled back slightly to look at him. "Don't forget," she said sharply, "that you had just told me you thought I 'comforted' my male patients in the same way I was 'comforting' you."

His expression hardened. "Do you still believe that's what I was saying?"

She relaxed and shook her head. "No, of course not, but I did all weekend—and that's what we were talking about."

She leaned against him once more and felt his arms tighten around her as he breathed a sigh of relief. "Will you come to the house and have dinner with me this evening?"

She teased his earlobe with her tongue. "Yes, but I'll be later than usual. We have appointments almost till six."

When he spoke again his voice was tight with tension. "Will you spend the night?"

She hesitated for only a moment, then smiled. "Darling, I was afraid you weren't going to invite me."

He pulled her closer and tightened his thighs around hers, leaving no doubt about his need for her. "Oh, Nancy," he said, and there was desperation in his tone, "I love you so much."

Chapter Four

Even though they were busy at the clinic the afternoon hours seemed to drag by until finally the last patient was gone, followed a few minutes later by Dr. Gunther.

Nancy left Dagmar to straighten up and hurried upstairs to shower and change. The hot, pulsing spray unknotted her tired muscles and left her feeling relaxed and clean, then a quick, invigorating dash of cold water revitalized her and sent her flagging energy skyrocketing.

She took her most expensive underwear—beige satin trimmed with delicate lace—out of the drawer, and it was then that the enormity of what she was planning to do hit her. Caleb Winters was a stranger! She wouldn't invest money with a man she knew so little about, but she was not only willing but eager to give her body to Caleb, and in the process gamble with her future.

Some of her happiness dimmed, and she pulled her robe more tightly around her as she looked at herself in the large mirror above the dresser. Never in her life had she behaved so irresponsibly. Not even with Theo. She had known him six months, learned his family history and met his parents before they made love. Since that affair broke up she'd gone no farther than a good-night kiss with her dates.

She fingered the soft, sexy material of the garments she held. Was she being a fool? Would she wake up some morning alone and hurting? Feeling used and bitterly regretting her impulsiveness?

The last thought made her smile. "Oh, come on Nancy," she said aloud to her image in the mirror. "You're not Little Red Riding Hood being lured to some unspeakable fate by the Big Bad Wolf. So what if he hasn't given you a signed and notarized pedigree? He's sweet and thoughtful and kind, and you're in love with him. This is the 1980s, for heaven's sake. Nobody gets ironclad guarantees these days."

She shook off her doubts and turned away from the mirror to begin dressing. All her life she'd been practical, careful not to make mistakes, not to anger her various foster parents, not to care too much because no one wanted her permanently. This time she was going to take what she desired so fervently. Surely a night in Caleb's arms wouldn't exact too great a price, even if it never went any further.

She loved the feel of the silky underwear against her body and considered not wearing the bra, but a glance at her high, bare breasts in the mirror convinced her that their fullness really needed the light support the abbreviated garment would provide. Besides, she shouldn't appear to make it too easy for Caleb. The thought left her tingling, as she slipped into a yellow cotton dress with a full skirt and a plunging neckline.

Nancy didn't need much makeup. The renewed excitement of anticipation brought a peach glow to her cheeks, and her happiness shimmered in her eyes. A lustrous coral lipstick and a touch of mascara added the little accent required. She grabbed her purse and a shawl and raced downstairs and outside to her car.

Caleb looked at his watch. It was 6:35, exactly five minutes later than the last time he'd checked. It seemed like an hour.

Running his hand through his thick, dark hair he resumed pacing. He knew he was being overanxious. Nancy had said she would be later than usual so why was he so concerned? She had promised to come, and he'd never known her to go back on her word.

Could it be that he was in such a state because he was afraid she *would* come?

He stopped his pacing and stood still as the unbidden thought shook him. No, that wasn't possible. He wanted her. More than that—he *needed* her. The weekend without her had been pure hell.

He shook his head and walked over to stand in front of the window. The sky was cloudy, and small waves lapped at the low breakwater that separated his front yard from the lake. It was going to rain. In his short time in Wisconsin he'd found that to be a common occurence—cool, gentle showers that started and stopped almost without warning, but kept the grass, leaves and flowers looking dewy, clean and bright.

His thoughts returned to Nancy, and he ached with longing for her. Wasn't that really what had him so upset? He was rapidly approaching the point of no return. If he gave in to his longing, made love to her and got used to having her beside him when he went to sleep and when he woke up, would he ever be able to walk away from her when the summer was over? Even more important, could she give herself temporarily to him, or any man, without incurring lasting scars?

He shuddered. Marriage was out of the question. The very fact that he loved her made a future for them impossible. He had nothing to offer her, nothing at all. He wasn't even sure how he was going to support himself once he was able to do so.

But overriding everything else was the possible danger. He was already cut off from the two people who were most dear to him and he couldn't survive losing Nancy, too. Not if she were ever truly his.

Caleb heard the car turn into the driveway from the road. It had become a familiar sound in the nine days that he'd known Nancy, one that his whole being was now attuned to, and all thoughts fled from his mind but the fact that she had finally arrived. That she hadn't changed her mind. That tonight they would be one in body and in spirit.

Nancy spotted Caleb standing in the open doorway when she walked around the front of the house after parking the car. He'd dressed up, too, and was wearing brown slacks and a green plaid shirt open at the neck. Funny how just looking at him could make her feel so alive and happy.

His face lit with a big smile when he saw her, and he held out his arms. She almost flew as she ran across the lawn, onto the porch and threw herself into his embrace.

His arms closed around her and he held her close, rocking them both back and forth. For a long time they just stood there, not speaking, cherishing the physical contact between them.

Caleb was the first to break the silence. "The past six hours have seemed like a week." His voice was husky as his hands roamed over her back.

"I know. They have for me, too," she said breathlessly. "I thought we'd never get the clinic closed up." She planted kisses on his jaw and chin. "I told Dagmar I'd be unavailable tonight and asked her to check the answering machine at intervals."

He nuzzled her neck. "That's good, because I've already unplugged the telephone."

He kissed her, and her body fit itself to his, a fusion that blended them and made them one whole being. Nancy wasn't aware of anything but Caleb's caressing hands, his gently insistent mouth and the electricity that flowed so strongly between them.

When he finally moved his head it was to reposition his lips against her cheek. "If we keep this up I'm going to carry you off to bed and forget about dinner," he said in little more than a whisper.

She turned her head slightly so she could kiss the corner of his mouth. "I don't mind if you do," she whispered back.

"But I do." He nipped at her lower lip. "I don't want to lose control. I want to make this last. To seduce you slowly and let the excitement build until neither of us can stand it any longer. I want it to be memorable for you, too, my darling."

A lump formed in Nancy's throat, and she blinked back tears of...gratitude...joy...love? His thoughtfulness was almost unbearably sweet.

"How could it be anything but memorable with you?" Her voice broke, and she swallowed before attempting to say more. "Have I told you lately that I love you?"

"You can never tell me too often." He kissed her lightly. "I need to hear you say it."

She stroked her fingers through his hair. "I love you, Caleb." She kissed him. "I love you." She kissed him again. "I love you."

This time he kissed her, and for a while they were both lost in wonder.

A rumble of thunder finally broke the spell that bound them, and Caleb pushed her away from him. "We'd better get inside before the clouds open up," he said in a voice that was unsteady, then ushered her through the door and closed it behind them. "Besides, I've arranged a surprise for dinner. Can you smell it?"

Now that all of her senses weren't concentrated on him, she was aware of the delicious aroma that penetrated the small house. She took a deep breath. "Emma's stew," she guessed.

He put his arm around her waist and led her to the kitchen area. "Right. I called her and told her someone very dear to me was coming for dinner and asked if she would fix the meal for me. She seemed really pleased to be asked."

They had reached the stove, and Nancy took the lid off the simmering pot. "Mmm," she sighed blissfully. "Now I understand why you wanted to eat before we got caught up in...other things."

He looked at her, and a small smile twitched the corners of his mouth. "No, I don't think you do, but it might make the time pass a little faster."

He ladled the tender beef and vegetables covered with thick mushroom gravy into bowls while she shredded lettuce onto small plates and put squares of molded fruit salad on top. French rolls and a rich red wine completed the meal, and in a gallant gesture Caleb seated Nancy, then leaned down and kissed her before taking his own chair. She felt loved and cared for, and she'd never been so happy.

They ate slowly to the ever-increasing accompaniment of thunder and lightning while Nancy told him about her busy day at work. Then Caleb recounted the conversation he had had with Emma when she'd brought the food to him. "It didn't take her long to find out who my guest was going to be," he said with a grin. "I'm sure it will be all over the island by morning that the man with the limp is sweet on the pretty lady who runs the clinic."

Nancy laughed. "It's hard to keep secrets in a community of three hundred residents."

Caleb was suddenly serious. "Keeping secrets can be very difficult anywhere." His tone was almost grim, and for a moment his eyes held an empty, haunted look.

A cold breath of apprehension blew across the back of her neck, and she reached out and put her hand on his. "Caleb?"

He picked up her hand and kissed the palm. "Sorry," he said, and the look that had disturbed her disappeared. "It's nothing, just a passing thought." He pushed back his chair and stood. "Time for dessert." He began gathering up their dishes. "I hope you left room for a piece of Emma's coconut pie. It's topped with whipped cream."

They lingered over the pie and coffee, but Caleb seemed thoughtful, almost preoccupied, and again Nancy felt uneasy, though she told herself it was just her imagination.

Finally she stood, intending to clear the table and start cleaning up, but he clasped her around the wrist. "Leave it, Nancy," he said, and his tone was almost curt. "Please sit down. There's something I have to discuss with you before we go any further."

She sank back down on the chair, and her unease changed to full-blown fear. Whatever it was he had to say she didn't want to hear. Now that she'd faced her own uncertainties and come to terms with them she didn't want anything to keep them apart.

"I—I'd rather you didn't. Whatever it is that's bothering you won't make any difference to me. I want you."

"And I want you," he said tenderly. "I can't even begin to tell you how much, but all I can offer you is a summer romance. When I leave Washington Island, I'll leave alone. Marriage isn't an option for me."

Nancy's eyes widened and she felt the blow that his words carried, but it was more the pain of hearing them spoken than of surprise. "Caleb, I wasn't expecting you to propose to me in the morning if that's what you think. We've only known each other a little more than a week. Don't you think it's too early to talk about marriage? I'm no more anxious to rush into that type of long-term commitment than you are."

That wasn't entirely the truth and she knew it. She recognized that it was imperative that they get to know each other better before they decided to spend their lives together, but she also knew that Caleb was the man she wanted for her husband and the father of her children. He claimed that he loved her, and she knew she loved him. If that love flourished and grew during the next few weeks she had no intention of staying behind when he left the island.

She breathed a little easier. Once they'd spent the summer together he would never be able to leave her, any more than she would be able to leave him.

He reached over and covered her hand with his, but there was no lessening of the tension in him. "Just so long as you understand my position," he said. "There's something else, though, that you have a right to know. Nancy, have you read my medical records?''

She blinked. ''Well, yes. That is, I've gone over all the things I need to know. Your file is huge, and I skipped the parts that don't apply to the care you're getting now.''

He nodded. ''In that case you probably missed the notation that I had a vasectomy three months ago.'' His tone was cold and tight. ''You won't have to worry about an unplanned pregnancy. I've been tested. I can't father children.''

The loud rumble of thunder that nearly drowned out his words gave her a chill, and Nancy's stomach felt as though she'd been dropped one full story in an elevator—a shocking swoosh that left her gasping. Caleb couldn't give her children! Was that why he was so reluctant to marry again? It was an obstacle and a big one. She had never been the type who couldn't resist cuddling every baby and small child she saw, but having children who were flesh of her flesh, blood of her blood, had always been important to her.

As an orphan she'd grown up lonely, unloved and unwanted. Her heritage was a total blank—no name, no nationality, no medical history. And because of that she'd dreamed of being the founder of her own line, generations to come that would assure her immortality. It sounded rather egotistical, but because she had no past she'd always felt the pressing need of a future.

Damn him! Why did he have to break the lovely, romantic mood they'd woven by bringing up his aversion to marriage and his inability to get her pregnant? She certainly hadn't expected him to ask her to spend the rest of her life with him on the strength of one night of lovemaking, and since she was a nurse, she knew all about birth control and had come prepared. He must have known that she would. He'd even given her advance notice of his expectations, so why did he find it necessary to deliberately shatter the sensitive awareness that had held them enthralled?

Was he having second thoughts, too? The idea was unnerving. Was he trying to back out as gracefully as possible before it was too late? Had she battled her own doubts only to be humiliated and defeated by his?

She was grateful for the anger that surged within her. She would never have been able to stand the pain without it as she pushed back her chair and stood looking down at him. "If you're trying to tell me that you've changed your mind and don't want me to spend the night after all, then just say it," she said hotly. "Rejection is nothing new in my life, I can handle it. What I can't tolerate is your insistence that it's for my own good. For God's sake, Caleb, admit that you can't make a firm decision and stop blaming your waffling on me."

She whirled around and headed for the door, but Caleb beat her to it. "Oh no," he snapped, "you're not going to run out on me again." He stood barring her only exit. "Is that the way you handle all your anxieties? By running away and refusing to face them?"

"Me!" she yelped. "You're the one who keeps beckoning me with honeyed words and caresses, then, at the last moment, throwing obstacles in our path. I don't play games, Caleb, and I don't like men who do."

"Games!" Now he was the one who was shouting. "I'm trying my best to protect you, to make sure you know what you're doing and where we're headed, and you call it playing games? Do you think this is easy for me? Have you any idea what I'm putting myself through by waiting and strewing obstacles in our path as you so picturesquely call it, instead of rushing you off to bed and to hell with any regrets you might have later?''

Nancy blinked. She hadn't thought of it like that. If he really did want to make love to her it would be difficult for him to go slowly and make sure she understood his terms. But the operative word was *if*. Did he truly want her, Nancy, or was he having attacks of guilt because it was just a woman, any woman, that he needed and she was the only one available?

"I can't answer that," she said, her anger still clouding her judgment. "My intimate experience with men is severely limited, but I think if you really loved me and wanted me, you'd quit stalling and get on with it."

His expression changed. "So, it's the macho approach you like, is it?" His tone was harsh as he reached out abruptly and pulled her to him. "Well, never let it be said I left you wanting."

A sheet of lightning flashed through the room, and the loud crack of thunder shook the floor beneath them as he crushed her against him. Nerves, muscles and flesh meshed along the full length of their bodies and an exhilaration as electrifying as the pyrotechnics in the heavens fused them together. His mouth took hers in a kiss that branded her his woman. When she gasped, his tongue darted through her parted lips and engaged hers in a duel of such startling sensations that she eagerly opened to his erotic invasion.

With one hand he pushed her into the cradle of his groin and let her experience vividly the urgent state of his arousal. With the other hand he cupped one breast and rubbed her hard, erect nipple through the barrier of her clothes.

Nancy was caught in a whirlwind of passion that swirled through her and whipped her unwary emotions into a frenzy of desire. Her arms tightened around his neck, and the throbbing ache deep in her womanhood drove out every thought but her need to be possessed by this man who had so quickly captured her heart and soul.

"Come," he said harshly as he clutched her around the waist and led her quickly across the living room and into the bedroom. He pulled his shirt over his head and dropped it on the floor, then pulled off his shoes and socks while she wiggled out of her dress and stepped out of her pumps.

"Here, let me," he said, his tone still raspy with impatience as he speedily stripped her of her lacy underwear without even noticing it except as an unwanted impediment.

Nancy was aware that it was all happening too fast. The tender romantic interlude Caleb had planned had been overpowered by the urgent need that had been unleashed by her idiotic accusation. But her disappointment was fleeting as he pulled back the covers and lowered her to the bed, then unzipped his trousers and stepped out of them before joining her. His body covered hers, and her mouth opened to his. She wrapped her legs around his hips and welcomed him with unconditional acceptance just as another flash of lightning and an almost simultaneous bolt of thunder ripped apart the black, swollen clouds and released a torrent of rain.

While the two on the bed moved together in the urgent, thrusting furor of passion Nancy was unable to distinguish between the storm outside and the one that raged inside her. The sound of water beating on the roof and their mingled cries of soaring release exploded in a symphony of nature unfettered.

It took them both a long time to relax after the hurricane that had been their loving. They lay quietly, arms and legs entwined, chests heaving and hearts hammering as they each struggled to calm down and figure out just what had happened to them.

Nancy had never experienced anything like the earth-shattering explosion that had annihilated her control and left her quivering, spent and overwhelmed. She'd thought she was in love with Theo, but nothing like this had ever happened with him. What kind of spell had Caleb conjured up to enchant her so?

It was all over so quickly. They'd argued, kissed, undressed and fallen into bed, and after that there were only the violent waves of ecstacy that tossed her higher and higher until, with a cry of wonder, she'd burst into a million tiny pieces.

Her cheek was resting against his chest, and she could feel his heart pounding and his breath coming in short, uneven pants. She lifted her head and kissed his throat. "Are you all right, darling?" she asked, knowing that if this had affected him the way it had her it was definitely not what the doctor would have recommended.

"I'm not sure," he answered, but she could hear the amusement in his tone. "I didn't know I was tangling with a beautifully wrapped package of explosives. What in hell did you do to me?"

She chuckled. "I was just wondering what you did to me. It felt like I'd shot into orbit without a space suit and then disintegrated."

He kissed the top of her head. "I know what you mean, but that's still no excuse for the way I behaved. I wanted to lead you gently, not ravage you."

There was no more amusement in his tone, it was heavy with self-disgust.

She lifted herself up on one elbow and looked down at him. It was nearly dark, but she could see the condemnation in his eyes. "Oh, Caleb, you didn't ravish me. Or if you did I was ravishing you too. Besides, it was my fault you lost control and caused me to do the same. You were trying to be a gentleman until I taunted you."

She lowered her head and kissed him. "I'm sorry for being such a wi—"

He put his fingers across her mouth, shutting off the word. "Watch your language, young lady, nobody calls my girl nasty names. However, I hope you believe me now when I say that I really do want you."

She knew her eyes must be shining with happiness. "Oh yes, I believe you. You proved that most satisfactorily."

Caleb kissed her with sated tenderness, then drew her back down to rest her head on his shoulder. "Next time we'll take it slowly," he murmured. "I want to explore every inch of your beautiful body, and I want you to know mine. Even the scars, if you're willing."

She sighed with pleasure, knowing that if he were able to share those with her she was truly special to him. "Of course I'm willing. I don't want you to keep anything hidden from me. I want to be a part of you, just as you are a part of me."

His hands gently explored her bare buttocks. "My sweet little angel of mercy." His voice quivered with emotion. "You've given me a gift beyond price, the gift of yourself, freely and without reservation. How could I give you less? I didn't want to love you, but I wasn't given a choice. You reached out and touched my soul and taught me to live again. In the process you became as necessary to me as my heart."

Nancy was too choked up to speak. Instead she raised her face to his and let her kiss tell him the depth of her love, then snuggled contentedly against him and within minutes they were both sound asleep.

* * *

Caleb woke slowly, but even as he floated toward consciousness he knew that for the first time in more than two years all was right with his world. How could it not be with Nancy, soft and relaxed, snuggled against him?

He was curled around her with her back against his chest and belly, and her warm bottom fitted into his pelvis. His hand cupped one high, firm breast and one of his thighs rested between both of hers. Heaven.

It was getting light, and he could see the creamy smoothness of her skin as he rubbed his lips against her shoulders, then pushed aside her chestnut curls to plant small, moist kisses on her nape. In spite of their frenzied lovemaking earlier she smelled sweet and clean, like spring flowers touched with dew.

She sighed in her sleep and wiggled closer, igniting a pleasurable stirring in his groin. He'd spoken the truth when he'd told her he had never experienced anything like the incendiary lovemaking they'd shared earlier. He'd had a few teenage tussles that were more frustrating than satisfying, and he had married young. He'd been faithful to Alina and their union had been satisfactory, but certainly not earthshaking.

After the divorce he'd had too many other things on his mind to be especially bothered by his celibate state, and then after the explosion . . .

Nancy stirred against him once more as his hand moved from her breast to slowly explore her delicate rib cage and the indentation of her navel. His swelling hardness grew and pressed against the firm roundness of her derriere, and he took a deep breath in an effort to control himself. This time he was determined to keep command of the situation, and not let his needs overrule his wants.

He fitted his large palm over the softness of her flat stomach, and she exhaled in a low ripple of approval as she moved her hand to his bare hip. She was beginning to waken, and again he kissed her nape while his fingers moved caressingly over her abdomen. He felt her muscles contract and inched his hand slowly but surely lower until it tangled with the thick curls he'd been seeking.

She clutched at him and brought her knees up in a defensive gesture as though to protect her most intimate recess. "Caleb," she murmured sleepily, "you're taking advantage of me when I'm most vulnerable."

He nibbled at her earlobe. "Yes, I know," he whispered, as his fingers moved into the warm cleft of her femininity. "I can't help it. When I woke up and found myself curved around your luscious nude body I couldn't make my hands behave."

She made a purring sound in her throat and clenched both thighs around his intruding leg as his fingers probed farther. She wasn't ready yet, but he knew that if he kept this up she would be very soon. He didn't want to excite her too quickly, and he removed his hand and put it back on her stomach as he strung little kisses down her arm.

"Turn onto your back," he ordered tenderly, and when she did he leaned over her and took one rosy nipple in his mouth. She tasted ripe and sweet and her textures were dizzying, harder and a little rough at the nipple, but firm and soft as he opened farther to take in more of her breast.

She was stroking his nape and the back of his head, and he had to fight the urge to devour her as he withdrew and moved on to rim her navel with his tongue. She gasped and arched against his face. He clasped her around her hips and trailed small but intense kisses downward, causing her to writhe in his arms and clench her fists in his hair.

"Caleb! Oh my God," she implored in a tone made up of equal parts of ecstasy and urgency.

His loins were throbbing forcefully with the compelling need to possess her wholly, but he was determined to introduce her to the most exquisite pleasure possible.

He raised his head and lowered himself to stroke the sensitive inside of her thighs, then, with his lips, followed the path of his hands moving slowly upward. She was whimpering softly as her hands clutched the sheet and her head moved back and forth on the pillow.

He could feel the heat he had built in her emanating from her womanhood, and the sharp insistence in his groin told him he'd reached the limit of his endurance. He raised himself up and cried out her name as he thrust deeply and joined their bodies in a convulsion that shook him to the very core.

Chapter Five

Nancy left Caleb early that morning to go home, change into her uniform and be at her office in the clinic in time for her first appointment. He'd made her promise to come back when she was finished for the day, and she'd agreed gladly.

She felt as if she'd been reborn, and wondered why phrases such as "the grass seemed greener," and "the sky looked bluer" had always sounded so trite before. The air *was* fresher, the sun *was* brighter, and Nancy Lloyd had never been happier in her life.

She floated through the day, and her cheerful smile and optimistic attitude seemed to be catching. Most of her patients left in a more pleasant frame of mind than when they'd arrived. Dagmar, who'd been given the task of checking the telephone answering machine the night before, watched Nancy slyly but her only comment was, "It's truly amazing how much ten hours of uninterrupted sleep can do for one." It was delivered in a broad drawl.

Nancy was too content to be embarrassed and she spoke in an equally droll tone. "Really? I'll have to try it sometime."

They locked up after the last scheduled patient left at four-thirty, and Nancy raced upstairs to shower and change. She debated whether to pack a bag. If she did she could spend more time with Caleb in the morning, but something held her back. He hadn't invited her to bring her clothes over.

The evening followed the same general pattern of the night before, but the experience was even more wonderfully stimulating and satisfying because tonight there was no quarrel to mar the fairy-tale quality. By ten o'clock they were both light-headed and sated from their feverish lovemaking. Nancy clasped Caleb's dark head against the damp valley between her glistening breasts. His skin was even moister than hers, and his shoulders and back felt slippery beneath her caressing palm.

He held her loosely around the waist and one of his legs was thrown over both of hers. He was totally relaxed as she kissed the top of his head and murmured sleepily, "I could die right this minute and know that I had experienced the greatest blessing life has to offer."

Caleb's muscles tensed, and his arms tightened around her. "Don't ever talk about dying!" It was an order barked in a taut and angry tone.

Nancy was too surprised to protest as he rolled away from her and sat up. "You haven't the vaguest idea of what you're talking about. You haven't even started to live yet."

He swung his legs off the side of the bed and sat with his back to her. "Don't ever take life for granted, Nancy, or good health, either. They can end in an instant, and nothing can restore them."

The harshness in his voice had increased with each sentence, and he sat hunched on the side of the bed in an attitude of despair.

Nancy quickly slid over and knelt on her knees behind him. She put her arms around his shoulders and buried her face in his back. "Darling, I'm sorry. It was insensitive of me to say a thing like that to you. I should have realized . . . but it was only a figure of speech. I just wanted to tell you in the most dramatic way possible how much you please me."

She trailed open-mouthed kisses on his nape, and he covered her crossed hands with his and placed them on his chest. "It's all right," he said, his tone contrite. "I'm the one who should apologize. I overreacted, but I wasn't the only one hurt in that accident. Two other innocent and unsuspecting people were nearly killed, and none of us was ready to die. It was only by the grace of God that we didn't."

He turned sideways and pulled her across his lap. "Just please don't tempt fate by talking so glibly about death. The thought of anything happening to you is more than I can bear."

He lowered his head and took her mouth in an almost frantic kiss. Wrapping her arms around his neck she responded with all the fire he was demanding, but she knew that the erratic pounding of his heart against her chest wasn't from passion but fear. Fear for her.

Why should Caleb be afraid for her safety? She was strong and healthy, she had no enemies and she wasn't engaged in a hazardous occupation. Apparently this irrational terror was an aftermath of his own severe trauma.

A low moan of protest escaped her when he reluctantly raised his head and broke off their incipient lovemaking. "I don't want to stop either, sweetheart," he whispered against her ear, "but it's getting late and I don't want you going home alone in the middle of the night."

Nancy's marvelous contentment immediately evaporated. "Going home?" She slid off his lap and sat up beside him. "You don't want me to spend the night?"

Where had everything suddenly gone wrong? She'd shied away from bringing a suitcase, but it had never occurred to her that she wouldn't stay with Caleb and leave in time for work the next morning.

He put his hand on her bare thigh. "Of course I want you to spend the night," he said softly. "Do you think I'm going to enjoy sleeping alone after having you in my bed? But, honey, this is a small, close-knit island. Its few permanent residents are older, and they have strong moral convictions about sex and marriage."

He squeezed her knee, then stood and walked away from her. The room was dark, but the moonlight flooding in through the uncovered window provided enough light to see. "For the time being we're a very visible part of the community. Me because I'm the stranger, the mystery man with a limp, and you because you're the sole medical practitioner and they rely heavily on your skill and good judgment. We're not going to outrage their sense of decency by openly living together without benefit of clergy."

Nancy suddenly realized that she was naked, exposed and vulnerable. She reached for the top sheet at the foot of the bed and pulled it around her. "Are you telling me we aren't going to make love anymore?" She cursed the way her voice sounded, like that of a child who was being scolded.

Caleb turned to face her, but it was too dark to see his expression from where she sat. "Good Lord, no." His voice was harsh and loud in the stillness. "There's a limit to how much I'm prepared to sacrifice to public opinion. I'm just saying that you can't be seen leaving for work every morning from my place without offending these people."

He came to her and pulled her up and into his arms, dislodging the sheet. His hands roamed over her, and he spoke again, sadly. "I've hurt you, and that was never my intention. It would be so easy to move in together and spend the summer in the exquisite abandon of loving, but you're a very young professional in your field. You need the trust and respect of these islanders, otherwise they won't allow you to treat them. They'll go to the mainland instead, and that can kill your hopes of a career before it ever gets started."

He put his hand under her chin and tipped her face up to his. "Your reputation is all you've got right now. If you're branded incompetent by the people who should be your patients here, no doctor is going to want you working with him."

Nancy knew that what he was saying was true, but it only made her feel worse. This conversation was being conducted backward. *He* should be the one urging her to stay, and *she* should be the cool voice of reason.

Why did her love for this man drive her so impatiently? Why did she feel compelled to push their relationship along instead of letting it proceed at its own pace? It was true Caleb had imposed a deadline, but she still had two months in which to make him realize that he needed her with him always, that life apart would be impossible for both of them. If she weren't careful she'd drive him away with her childish, clinging behavior.

She put her palm to his cheek and brushed her thumb across his lips. "You're right," she said softly. "I'm sorry. I can only plead temporary insanity. That's what you do to me, you know."

He started to lean toward her, but she deflected the kiss she knew was coming by standing up. "My, it is getting late." She realized she sounded like a flustered spinster as she picked up the clothes she'd draped over the back of a chair. "I'll be dressed and out of here in just a few minutes."

Nancy got through the next day by sheer determination. Whereas yesterday she'd been on a high that no drug could have induced, today she was in the depths of despondency. She'd never experienced these severe mood swings until she met Caleb Winters, and they were frightening.

She had always managed to roll with the punches before, which was a blessing since her childhood had been full of almost constant changes of residence and foster parents. Because she had always appeared to adjust well she had been moved more often than most foster children in order to make room for those who were less adaptable.

She had always managed to hide her pain and make the best of her situation until Caleb came into her life. Now she had a feeling of impending doom, as if they had to move along quickly or their relationship would disintegrate.

Nancy knew she simply had to shake off her fears and slow down, let Caleb coax her a little instead of being two steps ahead of him. So when he had told her goodbye the night before and said he'd see her at dinner this evening she had been noncommittal. She'd murmured something about not being sure she was free and hurried off.

As the day progressed she became more certain that she should put a little distance between them. Too much togetherness seemed to make him less inclined to want a future with her instead of more so. Reluctantly she decided to call him after the last patient left and tell him she had important paperwork to catch up on and wouldn't be over that evening.

Dagmar had taken off early to keep a dental appointment on the mainland so Nancy was alone after her last patient left. She stepped into the bathroom to wash her hands. She was tired, but knew it was more from her mental turmoil than her busy day. If she didn't get her emotions on a more even keel her work would suffer.

The front door opened and the bell rang. With a sigh she tossed the wet paper towel into the hamper. Now what? Someone must have decided to chance getting in without an appointment.

She rebuttoned her white lab coat and walked out into the waiting room. It wasn't necessary to look twice to recognize the slender man dressed in brown slacks and a beige sport coat. It was Caleb, and his unexpected appearance left her momentarily breathless.

"Caleb." Her eyes widened with surprise. "What are you doing here? Is something the matter?"

His expression was troubled and serious. "Yes, I suspect something is wrong. You weren't going to come to me tonight, were you?"

Nancy's eyes widened. How on earth had he known? "Well, I do have a lot of paperwork to catch up on and..."

He reached out and put his finger to her lips, then pulled her into his arms. "Don't lie to me, love." He rocked her gently in his embrace, and her resistance fled. "I'm sorry if I was clumsy with my reasoning last night. It never oc-

curred to me that you would doubt how much I want you.
How badly I need you.''

He rubbed his face in the softness of her hair. "I'm only
trying to protect your reputation, but not at the risk of
erecting a wall between us. I'm not that noble.''

Nancy loved the way he cuddled her against him and
stroked all her fears away. She put her arms around his
waist and breathed in the musky scent of shaving lotion.
It was different from the scent he usually wore. It had an
elusive, male quality that heightened her senses and made
her heart rate speed up.

Caleb was getting stronger every day, and the hours he
spent soaking up the sun had nearly obliterated the gray
indoor pallor he'd had less than two weeks ago. He was
slowly putting on weight, and there was sure nothing
wrong with his sexual vigor. By the end of the summer he
would be completely recovered and would never again need
her with the same vulnerable intensity that he did at this
stage. She wasn't going to let foolish pride part him from
her now.

She kissed the side of his neck. "I just don't want to
seem to be too clinging, too demanding. I'll understand if
you don't want to see me every night.''

His hand strayed below her waist to caress her firm
round bottom. "Don't talk nonsense,'' he murmured.
"You could never cling tightly enough. I'm the one who's
demanding. I want you to spend every second of your
spare time with me.''

He patted her gently on the part he'd been caressing.
"Now, are you going to show me where you live? I thought
we could go to the Captain's Table for dinner, then come
back here.''

The Captain's Table was a seafood restaurant in the island's only luxury hotel, and catered mostly to the affluent tourist trade.

"I'd love to show you my apartment," she assured him happily, "but the stairs..."

He kept his arm around her and started walking toward the staircase. "I can manage," he said, indicating his cane. "I can do almost anything I set my mind to, it just takes me longer than anyone else."

Caleb was right. It was clearly slow agony for him to move his stiff leg from step to step, clutching the railing with his left hand and moving his cane with the other, but he reached the top without asking for help. Not that Nancy wouldn't have been happy to offer it, but she knew it was important to him to do it himself.

He was perspiring and out of breath, but the wide grin of achievement that lit his face made her glad she'd climbed along beside him in silent encouragement instead of voicing her fears.

Nancy seated him on the couch in the blue and gray living room and helped him prop his leg up on an ottoman. Caleb glanced around with obvious appreciation at the thick carpet, heavy draperies and comfortable furniture. "This is nice," he said.

She nodded. "Yes, and so convenient with the clinic downstairs. It's furnished rent-free to the nurse practitioner in charge. I just moved in when Zelda Kelly and her husband left on their round-the-world jaunt. All I had to bring were my own personal things."

She unbuttoned her lab coat. "May I bring you a drink before I get under the shower?"

"Better not," he said. "I still have to get down those steps. You go ahead and get ready, I'll just sit here and admire the view of the harbor."

Nancy leaned over and kissed him, then hurried to shower and change.

Ten minutes later she turned off the water and reached for a large, thick towel. When she was dry she wrapped the towel turban-style around her still damp hair, belted her white terry-cloth robe around her slender waist and walked barefoot back into the living room.

Caleb looked up from the medical journal he was thumbing through and smiled. He wondered if Nancy had any idea how incredibly sexy she was. Even wrapped from the top of her head to her ankles she radiated a seductive electricity that sent a shock through his system. Just the glimpse of her small bare feet aroused him more quickly than any other woman could if she stripped.

He held out his arms to her, and she dropped down beside him and snuggled into his embrace. His whole body came alive, and he sent up a silent prayer of thanks for this responsive young woman who gave so generously of herself to him. Was he being blessed by having her for this one summer of paradise, or was he laying himself wide open for an eternity in hell when the summer was over and she was gone?

Her robe fell apart, exposing her long slender legs and enticing his eager hand to explore.

"Nancy," he murmured huskily. "Are you deliberately tormenting me, or aren't you interested in eating?"

"Both," she whispered. "Why don't we have dinner here? I have steaks in the freezer." She put her hand on the inside of his thigh.

He shivered as she gently kneaded the receptive area, and he unknotted her belt and stroked her soft curves. Her flesh was warm and damp, almost steamy to the touch as he cupped her full breast in his palm and brushed her nipple with his finger.

"I'd planned to take you out tonight." His voice broke as her thumb probed slowly upward on his leg. "Do you realize we've never been out together?"

"I hadn't given it any thought," she answered softly as her wayward thumb continued its tantalizing trek. "I'd rather stay here alone with you."

Her seeking hand reached its target, and he groaned as she slowly slid her fingers over the bulge in his trousers and fumbled with his belt buckle. "Do you still want to go to a restaurant?" she asked with wide-eyed innocence.

He pulled her hard against him in an effort to relieve some of the pressure she'd built. "That's a moot question now. I'm in no condition to go out in public."

He slipped the towel off her head and released her flower-scented hair, then found the sensitive spot behind her ear with his lips. She had moved her hand from his belt to his chest and was unbuttoning his shirt. His self-control rapidly evaporated. He'd wanted to tell her about the plan he had worked out so they could be together without being obvious about it, but when she looked up at him with passion-filled hazel eyes he couldn't remember what it was.

She ran the tip of her patrician nose along his collar bone, then kissed him at the base of the throat. By the time her fingers reached his zipper he didn't care about anything but taking her with him on the wild ride to ecstasy.

The month of July flew by, and Nancy was busy, happy and almost content. She and Caleb met part of the week at his house and part of the week at hers where they made love with tender abandon. They spent weekends together, and when Dagmar was on call for the clinic, they left the island and explored the Door County peninsula, a narrow thumb that extended seventy miles out into Lake Michigan. Swept by water-freshened breezes from both directions, the peninsula had gained fame as a naturally air-conditioned summer retreat. It was dotted with resorts as well as with the dairy farms, with their red barns and cylindrical silos, and cherry orchards of the permanent residents.

Caleb and Nancy chose picturesque motels in secluded spots that offered privacy as well as breathtaking views. Hand in hand they wandered through tiny lakeside towns named Ephraim, Sister Bay and Egg Harbor. In the little village of Fish Creek they attended a performance at the professional summer stock theater, and made plans to return in August for the Peninsula Music Festival.

The only cloud on Nancy's horizon was the turning of the days into weeks, and the weeks were on a collision course with the first Monday in September when her contract would expire and she would have to leave the island. Neither she nor Caleb ever mentioned it, but it lay like a pall between them to be ignored in the hope that it would go away.

On the first Tuesday in August Nancy had arranged her schedule so that she could spend the morning at the hospital in Ellison Bay assisting Dr. Gunther with a cesarean section. Not that she'd be doing one, or any other major surgery, but she felt it was important to have a working knowledge of how they were performed. She'd observed various surgical procedures during her training, but she liked to jog her memory every so often and keep her ideas current.

She also had another reason for wanting to see Dr. Gunther, and when they'd finished in the operating room and were scrubbing up she said, "Doctor, could you give me a few minutes for a professional consultation?"

His bushy eyebrows rose questioningly. "Anything wrong?"

She shrugged. "I don't know. That's what I want you to tell me."

He reached for a towel. "I'll meet you in my office in ten minutes."

An hour later Nancy was again dressed and sitting in the comfortable chair in front of the desk nervously tapping her fingers on the arm when Arnie came in and closed the door. He walked over to the desk, then seated himself in the oversized executive chair and leaned back.

"Did you find the problem?" Nancy asked.

Arnie's gaze searched her face. "Nancy, you're a damn good nurse practitioner. Are you honestly telling me that you don't know what's causing your symptoms?"

Her breath caught in surprise. "No, I don't know. I've always been regular within a day or two. I've never been over two weeks late before."

The doctor sat up straight and shook his head. "That's because you've never been pregnant before."

Nancy sat bolt upright, a wave of shock making her tingle. "Pregnant?"

"Come on, Nancy, you deal with pregnancies all the time," he said impatiently. "Surely you recognized the—"

"Well, of course it occurred to me," she interrupted, "but it's not possible in this case!"

He looked at her as if she'd lost her mind. "What do you mean it's not possible? You told me before I examined you that you'd had sexual contact in the past month. If you're saying that you took precautions that doesn't rule out a pregnancy. The only one hundred percent safe birth control is abstinence."

She clutched the arms of the chair and fought to keep her voice down. "Abstinence and sterility," she said grimly.

Arnie still looked puzzled. "Okay, I agree, but you've still got all the equipment it takes to conceive a baby."

Nancy was too shocked to understand why she wasn't getting through to Arnie. "I know that, but Caleb's had a vasectomy and it tested safe!"

Now it was Arnie's turn to look stunned. "Caleb? Caleb Winters? Is he the father?"

"Of course not." There was a tinge of hysteria in her tone. "He's physically incapable of fathering children. It's written right in his medical record. You've read it and so have I. I can't possibly be pregnant!"

Arnie frowned. "I assume he's been your only partner."

The look Nancy turned on him was so filled with scorn that he dropped his gaze and cleared his throat. "Sorry, but I had to ask. All right, we'll run the test again, but I'm telling you that there's been no mistake."

Half an hour later he confirmed the accuracy of his prediction. "I'm sorry, Nancy, but you definitely are pregnant, and if Caleb Winters was your only partner then he's the father."

She'd had time to calm down while they were rerunning the test, and now she felt numb and confused. "But how is that possible? The surgery..."

"It's highly unusual but not unknown. You must have read about cases like this in the medical journals. It's very rare, but once in a great while even though the tests come back negative there's still a slipup. It's been known to wreck marriages when the husband is suspicious that his wife's been playing around."

The numbness Nancy had been feeling was suddenly replaced by terror. My God! How was she ever going to convince Caleb that this was indeed his child? And if she got past that hurdle how would he react to the news that he was going to be a father? After all, he must have had a very good reason for having the vasectomy in the first place.

Chapter Six

Nancy sat in her car on the ferry ride back to Washington Island and tried to sort out her chaotic thoughts. Why was she pregnant? The odds against it were overwhelming. It must have occurred during the first time they'd made love, after each of them had been celibate for a long time. She would have thought they would at least need a little practice for something as momentous as making a baby against such enormous odds.

The wind off the lake blowing in the open windows whipped her deep brown hair around her face and she pushed it back, then rolled up the glass next to her. How was she going to tell Caleb? And, even more worrisome, how was he going to react?

Was there any chance he might be pleased? He'd told her that he had had a past marriage that was childless, but in that case why had he submitted to the surgery that was intended to make fathering children impossible?

If he wasn't happy, or if he refused to believe that the baby was his, then this was going to change the whole course of Nancy's life. Even though she loved children and hoped someday to marry and have a family she would never have deliberately chosen to become a single mother.

Gingerly Nancy rested her palm against her abdomen. A baby. Her baby and Caleb's. If she remembered her textbooks correctly, at this stage of development it was little more than a large dot, about one-fifth of an inch long and shaped a little like a fat, elongated question mark.

She smiled. Other people's babies, maybe, but not hers and Caleb's. Theirs would be beautiful even as it was forming.

Shocked at what she'd been thinking, she sat up straight and gripped the steering wheel. Dear God, she'd only known about this pregnancy for less than two hours and already she was looking forward to being a mother. Obviously this child was going to be very important to her, but would it ever know its father's love as well? It was time to stop dreaming and face reality.

A sharp jolt alerted Nancy to the fact that the ferry had reached its destination. She'd have to find a way to tell Caleb that his solitary existence was about to be invaded by a child he hadn't expected and probably didn't want.

A near-drowning off one of the beaches shortly after lunch kept Nancy busy the rest of the afternoon. By the time the patient had been transported by helicopter to the hospital on the mainland and the clinic appointments rescheduled, Nancy barely had time to shower and dress before Caleb picked her up to take her out to dinner.

She'd had no time to think about her personal dilemma, but now she dressed with care. Deliberately she chose her most seductive satin and lace underwear, the expensive perfume that was supposed to drive men wild, and a flamingo pink silk dress with a dropped waist and pleated skirt that Caleb hadn't seen before. It rustled sensuously when she walked, and the color brought a rosy glow to her complexion that was a startling contrast to the cloud of dark hair that swirled softly to her shoulders. Deciding against panty hose in favor of her tanned bare legs, she slipped her feet into white high-heeled sandals.

The Captain's Table restaurant was located on the top floor of the hotel, and Nancy and Caleb were seated by a window with a colorful view of the sunset over the vast expanse of Lake Michigan. Caleb seemed to be relishing his fresh grilled salmon, but both the view and her spicy shrimp creole were lost on Nancy.

She tried to keep her attention focused on Caleb and their conversation, but it was a losing battle. She had to tell him about the baby tonight, but she couldn't do it here in a public place while they were eating. It was only reasonable to wait until they got back to Caleb's house where they would at least have some privacy. What would he say? What would he do? How on earth could she ever make him understand what had happened?

She met his gaze across the table and smiled. He looked so distinguished in his slacks and sport coat. Tonight he had even worn a tie, and he'd had his hair trimmed so that it hung above his collar. There was love and admiration for her in his eyes. Would it still be there tomorrow?

After leaving the restaurant Caleb drove along the seaside road until he came to a bluff overlooking Rock Island and the lighthouse. It was serene and peaceful in the twilight with the sound of water splashing on the rocks below.

Caleb put his arm around Nancy and pulled her close. "Did I tell you how beautiful you look tonight?" he whispered against her ear.

She snuggled into his embrace. "Yes, but I don't mind hearing it again. Especially from such a handsome man."

"Flattery will get you almost anything," he teased and gently rubbed his hand over her silk-covered bosom.

For the first time she was aware that her breasts were more tender than usual, and his touch caused a slight discomfort. Soon they would fill out and become even more sensitive as her body prepared itself to nourish their child.

She took a deep breath and asked the question that had been nagging at her. "Caleb, why did you have a vasectomy? Did it have something to do with your injuries?"

His whole body tensed, and she held her breath. However, in spite of a long pause his voice was calm when he answered. "No, I was fortunate that there was no damage in that area from the blast. I decided on the surgery because it will be a long time before I'm in condition to take on the responsibilities of being a father, and by then I'll be too old to raise babies."

"But—?"

He tipped her chin up and brought her face close to his. "Hey, enjoy." His lips brushed hers lightly. "We can have all the excitement of making love without worrying about the consequences."

Nancy caught her breath. Now was the time to tell him about her pregnancy. He'd just given her the perfect opening, but then his mouth claimed hers and she gratefully accepted the distraction. Later. She would tell him later when they got back to the house.

After a few minutes he reluctantly held her away from him and started the engine. His voice was slightly slurred as he spoke. "One of the many advantages of no longer being teenagers is that we don't have to neck in the car."

He backed up and maneuvered the Mustang onto the two-lane road again. "Instead, we can go home and enjoy being together in comfort and privacy."

Back at the house Caleb turned the radio to the classical music station and pulled Nancy across his lap on the sofa. The melody was soft and romantic as she put her arms around his neck and laid her head on his shoulder. They'd turned off the lights, but the full moon cut a swath of bright beams across the lake and shone through the extensive glass of the front windows. The sky was aglow with stars, and here and there a firefly flickered like a Christmas tree bulb.

He clasped her ankle lightly, then moved his hand slowly up her calf to her knee. She loved it when he aroused her with slow, gentle caresses, and she nibbled on his earlobe and sighed. "Caleb, you never talk about your childhood. Did you always live in Baltimore?"

His finger explored the bend at the back of her knee. "Baltimore? Oh, yeah, I was born and raised there." His hand inched its way up the outside of her thigh, and she could feel the stirring of his awakening desire against her other hip.

He'd loosened his tie, and she worked his collar button open as she continued her questions. "What did your dad and mother do?"

"Do? They raised me." His finger crept beneath the lacy edge of her panties. "Mmm, you feel silky all over." His voice was little more than a whisper.

"Don't change the subject," she said, trying to hold on to her sanity long enough to get some answers from him. "You know what I mean. What *work* did they do?"

He chuckled. "Raising me was work, don't ever think it wasn't, but Dad was an insurance agent and Mom ran the office." His seeking finger moved inward, and she shivered.

There were other things she wanted to ask him, but all her attention was now centered on what his finger was doing. She finished unbuttoning his shirt and bent her head to circle his flat nipple with her tongue.

He cupped her intimately with his hand, and she tightened her thigh muscles around his fingers. Caleb was an experienced lover. He knew exactly where and how to touch her to drive her to the brink, and then how to keep her waiting until she was mindless with rapture. Tonight she wanted to give him back some of the exhilaration he gave so freely to her.

She gently sucked on his nipple, eliciting a low moan from deep in his throat. "Sweetheart, we'd better move into the bedroom."

They walked hand in hand through the small moonlit house and slowly undressed each other before falling onto the bed in a tangle of arms and legs. Caleb lay partially across Nancy and caught her mouth in a long, intimate seduction of lips and tongues and whispered endearments.

She could feel the rigidity of his need pressing against her abdomen and she knew he wouldn't be able to wait much longer unless she distracted him. She put her hands on his shoulders and pushed lightly. "Roll over on your back, darling," she murmured. "Tonight I want to make love to you."

"You make love to me every time you touch me," he said huskily, but did as she asked, taking her with him so that she was lying on top of him.

"Am I too heavy for you?" she asked, anxious not to cause him discomfort.

He rubbed his palms over her bare buttocks. "You're just right for me. We fit together as if we'd been designed for each other. Now, what did you have in mind?" She heard amusement as well as ardor in his tone.

"Oh, I thought I'd do this..." She tenderly nipped at his lower lip with her teeth, then with her tongue, explored the cavern of his mouth, which was faintly scented with whiskey.

"And this..." She brought her lips to the side of his neck and sucked deeply, causing him to clutch at the hips he'd been caressing and arch his engorged hardness against the cradle of her femininity.

She moved sensuously against him, but when he tried to turn them over she resisted. "Don't be impatient," she whispered, blowing gently in his ear.

"Impatient!" he rasped. "You're driving me crazy."

"And you love every minute of it," she teased as she slid her lower body off him and moved downward to nuzzle his navel with her tongue.

She buried her face in his flat belly and stroked his thigh. Slowly she trailed kisses downward until a dark coarse patch of hair scratched her cheek. Then she moved quickly to pleasure him in a way she'd never done before. He gasped and clutched at her head with both hands as he arched his back and thrust.

"Oh, my God!" he groaned, and she, too, was aroused to the point of being only vaguely aware that he'd grabbed fists full of her hair and was tugging at it as he writhed beneath her.

With uncharacteristically rough haste he broke her hold and rolled her over, then covered her with his urgently throbbing body and filled her with his overwhelming need.

Seconds later the eruption was as hot and fiery as a volcanic explosion, and they were lost in the shimmering scarlet flames of the conflagration.

They fell asleep, exhausted, but still united in body as well as soul. When Nancy woke several hours later they were lying face-to-face securely locked in each other's arms.

The mournful dirge of a foghorn from a buoy off the harbor reminded her what had wakened her, and she rolled onto her back. Caleb, though still asleep, followed her and lay with his head on her chest. She pulled the sheet and light blanket over his bare back, then put her arms under it and caressed the roughness of his scarred shoulders.

It was still dark, and she knew it must be very late. She hadn't intended to fall asleep. Her plan had been to tell Caleb about her pregnancy as soon as they got back to the house, but, as usual, they got caught up in the sweet urgency of their loving and nothing else mattered.

She smiled dreamily and raised her head to kiss the top of his. She hadn't expected her unrestrained lovemaking to release such a torrent of passion. She had obviously taken Caleb by surprise and shattered his precarious control. Never had she experienced anything like their shared convulsive wantonness, and she was certain that it hadn't happened to him all that often either.

Caleb heard the foghorn through the haze of sleep, and he tightened his hold on Nancy's slender waist. She was warm and soft, and her hands lovingly caressed the scars that most women would have found repellent. What had he ever done to deserve such an angel?

Then he remembered their most recent union, and in spite of his sated condition his body stirred and he chuckled silently. Angel, hell! She was an enchantress who stole his power of control and literally blew his mind. He'd never had a reaction as violently erotic as the one she'd seduced from him with her potent magic. She was that special blend of innocent and hussy that he had dreamed of but never found until now.

He rubbed his face against one breast and kissed the other one as her arms clasped him tighter. Dear God, how was he ever going to let her go in just one more month? And what had he done to her? After last night he could no longer doubt the depth of her love.

He should never have let this thing between them happen. He should have been stronger and left the island when he first realized the extent of his feelings for her, of hers for him. How could he love her so deeply and yet selfishly give in to his own overwhelming needs and set her up for the heartbreak that was inevitable?

He had known all along that there was no future for them, that he couldn't keep her with him. She couldn't live the way he had to, and he couldn't give her the children she wanted. She would soon grow to hate him, but overriding every other objection was her personal safety. He couldn't, wouldn't expose her to the danger of being his wife.

Nancy knew that Caleb was awake. When he'd stirred a few minutes ago he had been marvelously relaxed against her, but then he'd begun to grow tense and now he was moving restlessly. She stroked his head. "What's the matter, darling? Can you tell me what's bothering you?"

He rested his face against her throat. "How could anything be wrong when I'm in bed with Aphrodite, the goddess of sensual love?"

"You like?" Her voice was husky with remembered passion.

"Oh yes, I like." He kissed her throat, making her shiver.

"So do I." She sighed contentedly and held him close.

Now was the time to tell him her secret. Now, while they were so intimately attuned to one another. She hadn't planned to seduce him first and then tell him when he was relaxed and sated and happy, but she was glad it had worked out that way. She would never find him in a better mood.

"Caleb." Her voice was thin, wispy, and she cleared her throat. "There's something I need to tell you."

Her heartbeat speeded up and she felt her muscles tense. *Please, God, help me to do this right.*

"I'm listening." He trailed tiny, moist kisses to the valley between her breasts.

She stroked the back of his neck. "I don't think you're giving me your full attention."

"Oh, but I am," he said huskily, and continued to kiss her.

She could feel his manhood awakening against her leg, but maybe it was just as well that he was distracted. If he were partially aroused he might take her news more calmly.

She took a deep breath. "I—I saw Dr. Gunther today."

"I know, you told me." His tongue toyed with her nipple.

She tried again. "No, I mean he examined me."

"Mmm. That's nice." His hand moved from her hip to the inside of her thigh, and she realized that the meaning of her words was totally lost to him.

Apparently she was going to have to tell him straight out with no protective cushioning.

"Caleb, please listen to me." Her tone was louder and sounded a little frantic. "The doctor says I'm pregnant."

It seemed to her that the words boomed into the silent room, sonorous and penetrating as they vibrated off the walls and the ceiling.

Caleb froze in her arms and seemed to become a solid, icy block of resistance. If Nancy hadn't been tuned into his every nuance she wouldn't have heard the harsh but almost silent "No!" that sounded as though it were torn from his very soul.

For a moment he didn't move. Then he pushed away from her and sat up, laboriously, as though he might break into pieces if he weren't careful. Nancy made no effort to hold on to him, but she felt like part of her was being torn away.

He stood and switched on the bedside lamp, then turned his back to her and put on the slacks he'd discarded so hurriedly a few hours before. "How far along are you?" His voice was toneless.

For the second time in her relationship with Caleb she was aware of being naked and exposed, and she sat up and pulled the sheet across her chest. "About a month." Her mouth was dry and she couldn't swallow.

Caleb was so totally off balance that his movements were jerky as he zipped his pants and fastened his belt. *It's not true. I just heard her wrong. Nancy wouldn't lie and cheat.*

He walked barefoot over to the window and leaned against the frame with his back to the room. His head was reeling and he felt sick. A month. Either she had been pregnant when she came to him or he hadn't been the only man in her life since.

The agony that swept over him was almost as agonizing as the physical pain he had suffered for so long before it was brought under control. How much more was he expected to endure? *Not Nancy. Dear Lord, not Nancy. She wouldn't do this to me.*

He closed his eyes. But apparently she had done this to him. They both knew that it couldn't be his child, and someone had impregnated her.

The chilling coldness that had invaded him was slowly being warmed with anger as he adjusted to the shock. Dammit, why had she felt compelled to tell him about this? In another month they would have gone their separate ways and he would never have known about her duplicity. The Nancy he thought he knew would have been kinder but, then, the Nancy he thought he knew and loved would never have gotten into this predicament.

What did she want from him, for God's sake?

He clenched his fists and his voice shook as he spoke. "Tell me, were you pregnant before you gave yourself to me, or have you been cheating on me since we began sleeping together?"

He heard the springs creak and the sound of Nancy's footsteps. "Darling, you don't understand..."

He looked at her then, standing beside him, pale and anxious. Just minutes ago they had been snuggled together in bed loving each other without restraint. Now he felt like a eunuch, and he wondered if he would ever recover from the blow he'd received.

"Put your clothes on," he said coldly and walked toward the door. "I'll wait in the other room."

Nancy's hands trembled so badly that she had trouble dressing. This was going to be even worse than she had imagined. The anger in Caleb's voice had been bad enough, but the agony that looked out of his eyes was almost more than she could bear. She had to make him listen to her and believe what she had to say.

She could hear him banging cabinet doors, and she figured he was pouring himself a drink. Probably straight whiskey. She couldn't blame him. She knew with a clear insight the torment she would suffer if she thought he had been seeing another woman during the time he'd been making such passionate love with her.

Oh, Caleb, my darling, please listen to me with an open mind and believe what I have to tell you.

By the time she reached the front room he had turned on the lights and was standing at the kitchen sink staring out the window into the dark. The mantel clock told her it was twenty-two minutes after midnight.

She went over to stand beside Caleb and put her hand on his arm. He moved quickly away, and she bit her lip to keep from crying out.

"Caleb." She struggled to keep her voice under control. "I told you the truth when I said I hadn't slept with a man since I was in college. I wasn't pregnant when we first became intimate, and I haven't been unfaithful to you. This baby I'm carrying is yours."

All the blood seemed to drain from his face, and then with an oath he hurled the glass he was holding across the room. Nancy cringed as it shattered against the refrigerator, splinters flew in all directions while liquor ran down onto the linoleum.

He glared at her. "What kind of stupid imbecile do you think I am?" he demanded in a tone that was now vibrating with fury. "I told you before I ever touched you that I couldn't father children. The fact is documented in hospital records and my medical report, so don't try to con me."

Nancy half turned and gripped the edge of the sink. A wave of nausea rolled through her, and she was afraid she was going to be ill. For some reason she hadn't anticipated this violent rage. Not from her gentle, loving Caleb. She'd expected him to be angry but amenable and willing to discuss it calmly.

She tried again to get his attention. "Caleb, if you'll just be quiet for a minute and listen to me—"

"I've heard about all I can stand." Some of the rage in his voice had been replaced with anguish. "For God's sake get out of here before I say or do something I'll be sorry for later. Just stay away from me for the rest of the time you're on the island."

Another wave of nausea hit, and this time there was no holding it back. She clapped her hand across her mouth and ran to the bathroom where she sank to her knees and retched while tears poured down her face.

It seemed like hours before the upheaval in her stomach finally subsided. She had been aware of Caleb's big hands holding her head and keeping her hair out of the way. Now, without saying a word, he handed her a warm, wet washcloth to wash her face and a glass of water to rinse her mouth. She thanked him, but was too ashamed of her weakness and the fact that he had witnessed it to look up.

When she'd finished with the cloth and the glass she handed them back to him. He set them on the sink, then reached down and lifted her to her feet. Somehow she wound up sobbing against his chest while he held her, gently but without emotion.

After several minutes he took tissues from the box on the water tank and tipped her face up so he could wipe her eyes, then he held one to her nose.

When she was done, he tossed the crumpled ball into the wastebasket, then brushed her damp, tangled hair off her face. "I'm sorry," he said. "I should have known better than to upset you so. After all, there's a baby to consider, too."

Tears spilled down her cheeks again. He was concerned about her baby, even though he was absolutely certain that it wasn't his! Maybe there was a chance that she could convince him after all.

He reached for the box of tissues and gave them to her, then with his arm around her waist he led her back to the front room and seated her on the couch. When he had settled himself in the lounge chair he pushed it back so that the foot rest came up to support his stiff leg. "All right," he said wearily, "what is it you've been trying to tell me?"

Nancy drew a ragged breath and stifled a sob. "This morning when Dr. Gunther told me I was pregnant I was almost as shocked as you were just now. I had assumed it was a hormonal imbalance of some kind. I told him you were my only lover and therefore I couldn't possibly be having a child."

She paused to blow her nose again. Caleb looked blankly off into space and said nothing.

"Arnie reminded me that there is a small percentage of failures when a vasectomy is performed. A few men have fathered babies even after all tests were negative."

Caleb lowered the foot rest with a loud bang and sat up, his disbelieving gaze pinning her to the sofa, his mouth open to argue.

Nancy held up her hands to stop him and rushed on before he could speak. "No, please, let me finish. He even gave me a recent copy of a medical journal that has an article about it."

She jumped off the sofa. "I left it in your car. I'll get it," she said and ran out the front door.

Quickly she grabbed the prestigious magazine off the back seat and hurried back into the house.

She stopped beside Caleb's chair and opened the periodical to the place she'd marked, then held it out to him. "Here, please read it. It explains everything."

For a moment she was afraid he wasn't going to take it, but finally he did. Nancy went back to the sofa and sank down to wait.

She fidgeted as the minutes went by and finally curled into a ball with her arms around her shins and her face buried in her upraised knees. It was so quiet that she could hear the clock ticking on the mantel, and her nerves twitched with tension.

Would he be reasonable and at least have the test done over again, or would he continue to insist that she was trying to stick him with another man's child? She couldn't blame him if he did. One of the most respected urologists in the country had performed the surgery and assured him that it had been successful. Why should he take her word that there had been a mistake?

She heard each time he turned a page of the magazine. It was a long, technical article written in medical terms for doctors, but she had no doubt that Caleb would understand it. He had never discussed his schooling with her, but it had long been evident to her that he was bright and well-educated.

She was about ready to scream with the strain of waiting when he finally closed the magazine. When he didn't immediately say anything she looked up and saw that he'd leaned his head back and closed his eyes.

She spoke hesitantly. "Caleb?"

He looked at her, but his expression was grim and she felt the nausea rising in her knotted stomach again.

"I know this journal wouldn't publish an article that hadn't been thoroughly researched, so I have to believe that the author knows what he's talking about." His tone was as grim as his expression. "Does Dr. Gunther want me to go in for more tests?"

He didn't look or sound at all relieved that her story had been confirmed, but at least he was willing to give her the benefit of the doubt.

She nodded. "Yes, tomorrow if possible. I—I hope you'll also talk to the urologist at Walter Reed."

She uncurled herself and put her feet on the floor. "Believe me, Caleb, I'm not trying to force you into anything. I just want you to know without a doubt that I'm not lying to you. There's absolutely no possibility that any other man could have fathered this child."

Caleb nodded and stood. "I'll do whatever's necessary to clear this up, but I'd like to be alone now." He dug in his pocket and handed her the keys to his car. "Do you mind driving yourself home? I'll send someone for the car tomorrow. May I keep the magazine?"

He was politely but firmly telling her to leave. It hurt, but at least this time he wasn't shouting at her.

She took the keys and retrieved her purse from the table. "By all means keep the magazine," she said and started to leave.

He opened the door for her and stood back. His shoulders were stooped, and his face was white and drawn. His beautiful brown eyes had an empty, haunted look that tore at her heart.

She reached out her hand, but stopped short of touching him. "Will…will you be all right? You look so…so…"

"I'm a grown man, Nancy." There was no warmth in his tone. "I don't need a keeper."

With a strangled sob she turned and rushed out of the house.

Caleb shut the door and leaned against it. Nice going, you ungrateful son of a bitch, he castigated himself. She tells you she's carrying your child, and you treat her like dirt.

He limped over to the sofa and sank down in the spot where Nancy had been sitting. The cushion was still warm from her body heat, and her presence seemed to surround him with an odd sense of comfort coupled with a regret too deep to comprehend.

Now that he'd survived the shock and calmed down, he knew the child was his. He might not have known Nancy long, but he knew her well. She wasn't capable of the deceitful hypocrisy he'd accused her of. The suspicion that she had been involved with another man had shattered his reason, and it had taken a while to regain his sanity.

He stared vacantly into space and groaned. How much longer was he going to be punished for his original sin of hard-headed pride? All he had demanded two years ago was justice, and instead he'd brought down the wrath of God.

No, he couldn't blame God. The choices had been his own. He could have paid the price, pretended the extortion was just a business expense and gone about his comfortable, upper-middle-class existence, but no. He had to be the mighty avenger who liberated the oppressed single-handedly.

After the explosion he could have died. It would have been so easy. All he would have had to do was sink into that soft valley of tranquility between the peaks of excruciating pain and let the black peace of oblivion wipe out the torment. There were times when he had wanted to let go, but again his stubborn pride wouldn't admit defeat. The specter of death was too great a challenge.

Any other person would have learned a lesson after that experience, but not Caleb Winters, the man who finally emerged from that hellhole of a hospital. He had known that it would be years before he could safely form an ongoing relationship with a woman. Marriage was out of the question. He'd known it and accepted it, but then he'd met Nancy Lloyd. Nancy, the angel of mercy, who soothed his pain, filled his aching loneliness and drove him mad with wanting.

That's when he had committed the greatest sin of all. Instead of beating a quick retreat and relocating somewhere else he'd told himself that he could handle it, that he didn't have a breaking point like lesser men. By the time he realized that he was as mortal as everyone else it was too late to stop himself from making her his, and inadvertently compounding the transgression by creating yet another victim of his pride.

Caleb groaned and dropped his head into his hands. A baby! A tiny defenseless son or daughter who, along with its mother, was already in danger just because it belonged to him.

A cry of anguish escaped his tight control and his shoulders shook with wrenching, bitter sobs that could no longer be held back.

Chapter Seven

For the rest of the night Nancy succumbed to the sleep of total mental and physical exhaustion, but she woke the next morning anxious and still nauseous. It must be morning sickness catching up with me, she decided, as she munched on a salty cracker and sipped strong, hot tea.

Her first thought was to call Caleb. She wanted to hear his voice, make sure he was all right. Last night he had looked so shattered, and he still had a long way to go before he was completely strong and well again.

He'd told her he didn't need a keeper, but he was her patient. Surely she could justify her concern on that basis.

She reached for the phone, but then drew back. No, it was early yet. He might still be sleeping, and she didn't want to wake him if he was.

Midmorning, one of the mechanics from the garage came for the keys and drove Caleb's car away. Nancy finally called during the noon break, but although she let the phone ring a long time, there was no answer. He had agreed to see Dr. Gunther to have the test redone. Probably he was at the doctor's office on the mainland.

She tried again about three, but there was still no answer and her anxiety increased.

Finally the last patient left, and Dagmar appeared in the open doorway to the bathroom where Nancy was washing her hands. "Caleb came in while you were with Hilda," she said. "He asked me to tell you he'd wait upstairs."

The joy that surged through Nancy left her weak, and she leaned against the wall to steady herself. Caleb had come to her!

She left Dagmar to close up and rushed upstairs to her apartment. Caleb was standing at the window looking out at the harbor, and he turned as she entered the living room.

She started to go to him, but stopped when she saw his bleak expression. Their eyes met, and the torment in his was almost more than she could bear.

His limp was even more pronounced than usual as he walked toward her, and she knew the painful ache in his leg had escalated again. She stood still as he reached out and cupped her cheek with his hand. "Can you ever forgive me?" he asked, his tone filled with remorse.

She wet her dry lips. "You...you've had the test again?"

"Yes, and this time it was positive. I talked to the urologist in Washington, too, and he confirmed everything Dr. Gunther said, but I knew long before I talked to him or had the test that the things I'd accused you of weren't true. I don't expect you to believe me after the way I behaved, but it's the truth. I went a little crazy when I thought you had lied to me and were having another man's baby."

She turned her head and kissed his palm. "I can understand that. I would have reacted the same way if I'd thought you had fathered another woman's child."

With a sigh of relief he put his arms around her and cradled her close. For a few minutes they just stood there holding each other, but gradually Nancy realized that something was wrong. Well, not wrong exactly, but different. The sensual tension that had shimmered between them every time they were together was absent. There was warmth and concern, but it was more like being held by a brother or father than a lover. The passion they had always aroused so easily in each other was missing.

At least it was in Caleb. She knew it would take only a few strokes and a murmured endearment to excite her, but neither was forthcoming. She felt bereft, and small tentacles of apprehension tugged at her.

The silence suddenly seemed foreboding, and she felt the need to fill it with talk. "What would you like to eat?" she asked, her voice brittle. "I have pork chops. I can cook them with rice pilaf and stir up a cherry cobbler for dessert."

His hold on her relaxed. "Maybe later," he said and stepped back. "First we have to talk. Nancy, how do you feel about this pregnancy?"

She blinked. "Well, I . . . surprised, certainly. No, more than surprised. Shocked. I was absolutely dumbfounded when Arnie told me. Of course I recognized the symptoms, but at this early stage there are any number of other reasons . . ."

Caleb interrupted. "No, that's not what I mean. What I need to know is do you want the baby?"

"Want the baby?" That was an odd question under the circumstances. "I wouldn't have planned for it to happen, if that's what you mean. I had always expected to be well settled into a marriage before I started a family, but I don't have that option now."

"But you do." He moved his hands to cup her shoulders. "There's a legal alternative. Would you consider it?"

Nancy stared at him, stunned. "You mean you want me to..."

She found that she couldn't finish the sentence.

She saw the pain that twisted Caleb's features before he turned away and ran his fingers through his hair. When he spoke it was with a heavy sadness. "Two years ago I would have considered myself truly blessed to have you carrying my child, but I'm no longer the same man I was then. I mean that literally. In the past twenty months my whole life has changed."

He walked back to the window. "Bringing a child of mine into the world at this time is unthinkable. I'm still recuperating from my injuries, I don't know when I'll be able to go back to work, and my future is uncertain at best. I'm only now learning how to take care of myself again and I can't possibly be responsible for an infant."

Nancy twisted her fingers together nervously. "That's not a problem, Caleb. I have a good income, and during the months I've been here my expenses have been practically nil. I've saved enough money to keep us until I can find another job after I leave here. Nurse practitioners are in demand, so it won't take long."

He slapped his palm against the wall and turned to face her, his features twisted in anger. "What kind of a man do you think I am?" he demanded. "I don't accept charity. I take care of my own."

"Charity!" Nancy's own temper was heating up. "It's my baby, too, and you're its father. Where is it written down that I can't support the three of us until you're able to work once more?"

He ran his hand through his hair again. "People have no right bringing a child into the world if they can't take care of it. A baby needs a mother to nurture it, and a father to support it."

She couldn't believe what she was hearing. "And just what's wrong with the father attending to its needs and the mother supporting it? Men can be just as good at nurturing children as women can, and a child needs both parents, regardless of which role they're playing."

The fight drained out of Caleb, and he seemed to age before her eyes. His shoulders slumped and defeat crept into his voice. "You've put your finger on the focal point of this argument, love. A child needs both parents, but as I've told you before, I'm not free to marry you and take on the responsibility of a family."

Nancy's eyes widened, and she felt a chill. "Not free? But you insisted you weren't married."

He nodded. "That's right. I'm not, but I have other pressing obligations. That's why I had the vasectomy, so I would never be put in this position."

"Tell me what your obligations are. Surely we can find a way to honor them and still be together."

He drew a ragged breath. "I can't. It involves other people whose confidentiality I can't breach."

His words were like a slap in the face, and all her hopes and dreams vanished. "You just plain don't want this baby, do you." It was a statement, not a question.

He closed his eyes, and she saw a muscle twitch beneath his clenched jaw. "It's not a question of what I want, but what has to be. I honestly have no choice, sweetheart."

He opened his eyes, and she saw the pain that lodged there. "Please, think about the way out that's available to us. I won't pressure you anymore. Take all the time you need, then let me know what you decide."

Leaning heavily on his cane he limped out of the room, then made his slow, tortuous way down the stairs and out the door, shutting it quietly behind him.

Nancy realized that he hadn't even kissed her.

She slept little that night, and she had trouble concentrating on her patients' problems the next day. She tried hard to view the situation from Caleb's perspective and to understand why he felt so strongly that it was impossible.

Ultimately, however, she had to wrestle with her own feelings and moral values. She made phone calls to the obstetrician and the psychiatrist who had been her teachers when she was doing her hospital training, and she spent a long time just thinking.

After a second restless soul-searching night she finally faced the truth she'd known all along. No matter what the law said was legal, or what other bright and thoughtful people did in similar situations, Nancy knew she would have this baby that she and Caleb had conceived in the heat of passion and the tenderness of love. It had already stirred her strong maternal yearnings and filled the empty corner of her heart. For her there was no alternative.

She called Caleb early that morning, knowing he had been as anxious and upset as she was. When he answered the phone and she heard his voice she had a strong urge to weep. "Is it all right if I come to see you after office hours?" It took all her control to keep her voice from breaking.

"You know you don't have to ask," he said huskily. "I'll be waiting."

He hadn't even questioned her about her decision. She hadn't wanted to discuss it on the phone, but she knew she wouldn't have had that much patience if she'd been in his position.

The day seemed to drag on forever, and by the time she closed the office the strain had set her nerves on edge. She didn't bother to shower or to change from the white slacks and pastel print blouse that she'd worn under her lab coat.

She got to the small house earlier than usual, but Caleb was waiting for her just inside the door and he took her in his arms. She lifted her face and his mouth captured hers, softly, sweetly. "I was awake most of the past two nights wishing I could go back to you and collect that," he murmured.

"I was waiting for you," she said and stroked an errant lock of black hair off his forehead. "Why didn't you come?"

He kissed her again. "You know why. I couldn't. I promised I wouldn't try to influence you. Have you reached a decision?"

She backed out of his embrace. "Yes, I have."

Hand in hand they walked across the room and sat down together on the couch. She put his hand to her mouth and kissed the palm, then held it to her cheek. "I'm going to have the baby," she said, her gaze searching his face.

When she found no change of expression she continued, "I've given your arguments long and careful consideration. In fact, I've hardly been able to think of anything else, but they just aren't good enough, Caleb. You haven't convinced me that there's a compelling reason to take the drastic measure you've suggested."

There was still no reaction from him. He didn't even blink; he just sat there quietly listening to her.

"I want your child. Oh, as I told you before I wouldn't have deliberately conceived it, but now that it's a part of me I can't give it up."

This time he opened his mouth to speak, but she put her fingers across his lips. "I respect your feelings, even though I don't understand them. I don't expect anything from you. It'll be my baby, and you won't need to concern yourself about it.''

He frowned and put his hand down. ''Do I really come across to you as being so unfeeling?''

Nancy looked away. ''I don't know. Certainly you didn't until I convinced you I was pregnant with your child. Now... I think you must be, otherwise you couldn't have asked what you did of me. I guess we're what you could call intimate strangers. I just don't know you very well.''

Caleb reached out and gathered her into his embrace. ''You're not a stranger to me,'' he said into her hair. ''I knew you would decide what you did. One of the things I love most about you is your strongly maternal nature, but I've also been aware that it, among other things, could make a permanent relationship between us impossible.''

For a long time they sat there silently clinging to each other. There didn't seem to be anything else to say. There was no possible compromise. It had to be either her way or his, but neither of them could accept the way the other wished to resolve the situation.

It was her body and therefore he had to abide by her decision, but what price were they both going to have to pay for this impasse?

After a while Caleb stirred and put her away from him, then stood and walked over to the fireplace. It was still too warm for a fire, and the fireplace was cold and sterile without even the ashes of a former flame.

Nancy shivered as the analogy registered. For all of Caleb's tenderness since she'd arrived less than an hour ago his kisses and caresses were still without passion, or even the remnants of a former blaze.

''I can't think straight when I'm with you,'' he said as he turned to face her across the distance he'd put between them. "This can have serious repercussions, and I need more time alone to sort things out. Will you give it to me, sweetheart?"

The chill that had passed through her deepened. For the third time in twenty-four hours he was retreating into himself, closing her out. How could they hope to find a solution to this mess if he wouldn't let her get close to him?

Even if his passion for her had burned itself out, how could he be so uncaring about his own child?

She stood up. "All right, Caleb," she said, and her tone was harsher than she'd intended. "I'll go, and this time you can call me when you've reached a decision, but please don't take too long. I have to start planning for my future."

She picked up her purse and left without a backward glance.

Caleb leaned wearily against the back of the couch and rubbed his temples with his fingers.

His head was pounding, and it seemed to him that every muscle and bone in his body ached. If he didn't get some sleep he was going to be sick. Then Nancy would come with her gentle hands and her healing ministrations to make him well, and he would agree to anything just to keep her with him.

His mind rebelled. Would that really be so bad? Surely he was entitled to a little happiness. He'd been given a second chance at a wife and family, so why not grab it? They could go to the West Coast and start life all over again. Others did, why not him?

He covered his face with his hands and heaved a shuddering sigh. No, he couldn't afford the luxury of giving in to the love he felt for Nancy and the joy he couldn't entirely suppress when he thought of her carrying his baby.

He had to act rationally, and he could only do that if he could sort out his chaotic thoughts.

For the first time since leaving the hospital he took one of the sleeping pills the doctors had prescribed for him and then went to bed before the sun set.

He slept deeply for almost twelve hours and woke the next morning at six feeling a little groggy but rested. Miraculously, his subconscious must have continued working while he slept, because he now knew what he had to do.

He fixed coffee in the old-fashioned percolator, then went to the phone and dialed a long-distance number. The voice that answered sounded sleep-drugged and definitely antisocial. Only then did Caleb remember that it was early Saturday morning in Washington, D.C.

"Barry," he said tersely, "this is Caleb."

There was a moment's hesitation on the other end of the line, then the voice spoke again, clearly and concisely. "What's wrong?"

"I have to see you."

"Is anyone following you?"

"No, it's not that. It's personal."

Another short silence. "Can we talk about it on the phone?"

"No. There's been a foul-up and now there's hell to pay. Sorry, but this can't be handled long-distance."

Another pause, longer this time, and Caleb could hear drawers opening and closing. "Okay," the voice finally said, "I'll meet you in Chicago tomorrow afternoon. There's a suite available for our use at the Marriott hotel on Michigan Avenue. I'll call and tell them you'll be checking in. Wait for me there, and, Caleb, this had damn well better be important."

"Believe me, I wouldn't put you to all this trouble if it weren't. See you tomorrow and . . . thanks, friend."

After breakfast Caleb took out his suitcase and started to pack. He didn't know how long he would be gone, and since he had so few clothes and personal possessions he just dumped them all in the bag rather than sort them out.

He started to call Nancy, but then decided to write her a note instead. She had been hurt and angry when he'd sent her away last night, and he knew she wouldn't take kindly to being told that he was leaving the island and wasn't sure when he'd be back. If he talked to her in person and she demanded an explanation he would cancel the trip rather than upset her further.

No, it was better to send her a letter and hope she would understand. He would be more able to cope with her anger and feelings of rejection after he'd talked to Barry.

His hand shook as he scribbled the short missive:

My darling,
I have to seek advice and sort out a number of things in my mind and I can't be objective with you so near. I've made an appointment to get some counseling in Chicago, and I'm leaving as soon as I finish this letter. I'll be at the Marriott hotel on Michigan Avenue if you need to get in touch with me.

I won't be gone long. A few days, a week or two at the most, but I'll miss you every minute of the time we're apart.

I'm deeply sorry for the anguish I've put you through. I can't expect you to understand, but I hope you'll trust me and give me the time I need.

I love you, Nancy. Don't ever doubt that.

He reread it and knew he hadn't come close to expressing his feelings or to saying all he wanted to say, but it was the best he could do for now.

He signed it and put it in an envelope addressed to Nancy, then picked up his suitcase. He felt closed in here, buffeted by forces bent on destroying him, and he was desperate to get away.

When he stepped outside he realized that the sky was as black as his mood. A summer squall was imminent. He dropped his suitcase in the trunk of the car and drove out to the road where he hurriedly shoved the letter in the mailbox and put up the flag before heading for the ferry.

It was late Sunday afternoon before Barry arrived at the hotel suite in Chicago. Caleb greeted him warmly. Barry was probably the closest thing to family Caleb had left, even though they'd only known each other a year and their relationship was strictly professional.

Barry was amazed by Caleb's appearance and said so. "You're looking great, Caleb. If I'd met you on the street I wouldn't have known you. You're walking much more easily, you've got a tan I'd kill for and you've put on weight. At least ten pounds, I'd judge."

Caleb grinned. "That's what lolling around in the sun and eating good food will do for you. You ought to try it sometime."

Barry rolled his eyes upward. "In D.C.! I'd get sunstroke in the summer and frostbite in the winter, and who's got time to eat?"

They had a lot of catching up to do, and it was a relief to Caleb to be able to talk freely and without reservation once more. By mutual consent they postponed the discussion that was the reason for their meeting until the next day.

The following morning they ordered breakfast from room service, and when they'd eaten the last of the pancakes, eggs, bacon, fruit juice and coffee Barry pushed his chair away from the table and stretched. "I'm afraid it's time to get on with the business we came here for," he said. "Do you want to tell me what's happened?"

Caleb got up and walked over to the thickly upholstered chair where he could sit comfortably with his stiff leg propped up on the ottoman. He started his story with his wood-chopping accident and his first meeting with Nancy and told Barry everything.

It took a long time as Caleb attempted to explain his feelings and thoughts as well as the facts. Several times while he was talking about Nancy's pregnancy he had to stop and get his voice under control before he could go on.

"Under other circumstances I would get on my knees and thank God for blessing me with Nancy and our baby," he concluded sorrowfully. "But instead it's become a nightmare, and I can't find a way to resolve it. I know now that I should have asked you to relocate me as soon as I realized I was falling in love with her, but by then it was too late. I had to be with her."

He propped his elbows on his knees and, with a shuddering sigh, dropped his face into his hands.

Barry went over to the bar and poured generous portions of brandy into two snifters, then handed Caleb one. "Here, drink this," he said. "Maybe it'll help ease the pain for a little while."

He sat down on the couch across from Caleb. "Damn those bumbling, incompetent doctors to hell," he muttered.

Caleb leaned back again. "It's not the doctor's fault. Apparently the human body works very hard to repair itself, and sometimes the tubes that were clipped grow back

spontaneously. It's not something the doctors can fore-
see, and it's too rare to worry about, except for the occasional poor sucker who thought he was safe.''

"Yeah, I suppose you're right," Barry agreed, "but I
feel so helpless. There's not a thing I can do except remind you that if you tell Nancy the truth there are others
close to you who will be put at risk. You sure as hell don't
want to hear that.''

Caleb took a long, burning swallow of his brandy.
"That's a fact of life that I live with twenty-four hours a
day. I don't need to be reminded of it.''

"It's an intolerable situation," Barry said, "and I wish
I had the answer, but I don't. My advice to you is to stay
here, away from Nancy, for a couple of weeks and think
about it. I have to leave tomorrow, but I'll make arrangements for you to use the suite. You've been out of the
mainstream of life for over a year. Get back in. I can get
you tickets to some of the Cubs games. Take in a show or
two, spend time in the bars, meet other women.''

Caleb grimaced at the last suggestion, and Barry
shrugged. "Yeah, I know. You don't want any other
woman, but try to understand that Nancy was the first and
only one you've had contact with since leaving the hospital. You were ripe, man, and she was sweet and warm and
willing—''

Caleb slammed his glass down on the lamp table. "It
wasn't like that, dammit!" he roared. "You make it sound
like a one-night stand.''

Barry held up his hand. "Hey, I'm sorry. I didn't mean
it that way. I'm only saying that you should weigh all your
options, examine your feelings for this woman closely and
make sure that she's as important to you as you think she
is. If so, then try to come to terms with the fact of the child
and marry her. Hell, Caleb, nobody said you had to live

the life of a monk. Just keep your mouth shut about the past and stay away from the East Coast."

Caleb shook his head. "It's not that simple and you know it. If I keep Nancy with me then I'll be putting her and the baby in danger, too."

Barry shrugged. "They'll be safe as long as you don't breach your identity. It's unlikely that will happen unless you talk too much."

Chapter Eight

Nancy didn't hear from Caleb all weekend, and when he still hadn't contacted her by Tuesday her patience gave way to anger. What was taking him so long, for heaven's sake? For that matter what was he trying to decide anyway? She was having his baby, that was a fact he no longer disputed, so why couldn't he relax and be happy about it?

This wasn't turning out at all the way it should. In her adolescent daydreams she'd planned the way she would tell her adoring husband they were going to be parents. He would take her in his arms, kiss her tenderly and maybe even shed a few discreet tears of joy as he told her how proud he was, how happy she'd made him, how he worshiped her for giving him this magnificent gift of their love.

She scattered the magazines she'd been attempting to straighten on the table in the waiting room. Yeah, sure. Nice dream, little girl, but in grown-up reality she wasn't married to the father of her child, and her announcement had gotten her a scene where she was yelled at, accused of unfaithfulness and told that bringing a child of his into the world was "unthinkable."

She choked back a sob and left the magazines in disarray to hurry upstairs. Office hours were over for the day, and she was through waiting while Caleb did nothing. As soon as she changed her clothes she was going over there to confront him.

When she turned into Caleb's driveway Nancy noticed that his car wasn't parked in its usual spot beside the house. Did that mean he was gone, or had he simply put the car in the garage?

When she walked around to the front of the house she noticed that the drapes were pulled across the glass wall. Odd. Caleb almost never closed them since the windows faced the lake and it was unlikely that anyone would see in.

She knocked on the closed door, and when there was no answer she tried it only to find it locked.

Obviously he wasn't at home. Nancy knew he was something of a recluse and didn't go out much on his own. He was always polite to the islanders, but didn't encourage friendly overtures. To the best of her knowledge he didn't see anyone else but her on a regular basis.

A quick check of the garage failed to produce the Mustang, and she opened her purse and took out the key he'd given her, then hesitated. She had never used it because he was always there when she arrived. Of course, those other times he'd been expecting her, and she hated to invade his privacy.

She banged on the door again and called, "Caleb, it's Nancy." When there was still no answer she went ahead and opened it. He'd probably gone to the grocery store and would be back any minute.

The front room was dim without the light from the windows. Even the one over the kitchen sink had the blind pulled, and the air had a slightly musty smell.

Nancy fought back the apprehension that tightened her muscles. Again she called, "Caleb, it's Nancy. Where are you?" The silence was eerie, and she was startled by the sound of her footsteps on the wooden floor as she crossed to the hall and looked in the bedroom. The bed was made up in Caleb's usual haphazard manner, but the window in there was covered, too.

She turned around and peered into the bathroom. A towel and washcloth hung on the towel rack and everything seemed normal, except that again, the blind was pulled down.

The apprehension increased and again she fought it down. Don't be silly, she told herself. He probably went to the mainland for some reason and shut the house up before he left. He may have decided to have dinner at a café over there before coming back. Relax and go get yourself something to eat. No doubt he'll be here when you return.

Reluctantly Nancy locked the door and left. She drove to a small rustic restaurant on the wharf where she could see the ferry when it docked. After taking a seat by the window, she gave her order to the teenage waiter and chatted with the owner who stood a few feet away behind the counter.

Two ferries docked while she deliberately lingered over her fried chicken dinner, but Caleb's Mustang wasn't on either of them. Maybe she'd been wrong, and he'd just gone for groceries after all.

She hurried back to Caleb's house. The car was still gone and the house shut up. Tiny prickles of fear crept up her spine and gripped the nerves at the back of her neck. Where was Caleb?

She got back in her own car and drove slowly around the island, but there was no sign of his car anywhere. When she returned to the house it was still empty, and she again used her key to go in.

This time she opened the draperies and turned on the television in a determined effort to relieve the gloom of the chillingly empty cottage. Nancy opened the windows to let in the fresh air, then settled down in Caleb's lounge chair to watch a movie while she waited for him to come home.

An hour later it was over, the sky was starting to get dark and Caleb still wasn't back. Her unease escalated and she fought against the steadily increasing nausea that usually plagued her only in the mornings. Where on earth was he?

Her nerves were wound tight with tension, and as she cast around in her mind for an answer to her question it occurred to her that if she knew how he was dressed it might shed some light on what he was doing.

It was nearly dark when she went into the bedroom, and she turned on the light. She opened the closet door and stared. Her heart lurched, and she clutched at the edge of the door. *The closet was vacant.*

She knew Caleb didn't have many clothes. He'd explained that after a forty-pound weight loss during his long stay in the hospital nothing he owned fit, and he had to buy everything new. Since he would be gaining most of the weight back, he had purchased only what he needed to get by, mostly jeans and shirts, and then a pair of slacks and a sport coat for dress. Now there was nothing in the closet but bare hangers!

She rushed across the room and opened the dresser drawers. They were all empty. Where once there had been small stacks of underwear and socks, now there was nothing. A frantic search of the bathroom confirmed that his grooming items and medication were missing, too.

In the kitchen the refrigerator was empty, but there were still a couple of TV dinners in the small freezer. Nancy's stomach constricted and her knees gave way as she sank down on one of the hard, straight-backed chairs. Her whole body was bathed in perspiration, and she took a deep breath and swallowed to combat the bile that rose in her throat.

Caleb was gone! Not just away but *gone*, along with all his clothes and toiletries. He'd rented the cottage completely furnished, including linens and cooking utensils, so all he had to take with him when he left were his personal things.

Her head began to swim, and she clutched the table to steady herself. There had to be some explanation. Caleb wouldn't just take off for good without even saying goodbye.

A note. Maybe he had been called away suddenly but had left a note.

She got up gingerly and began searching, but except for a grocery list on top of the refrigerator there was nothing. And if he ever received mail there was no trace of it, either.

Mail. Maybe there was mail in his box. She ran out to the road and opened the door on the box, but there was nothing inside.

Nancy trudged back to the house and sat down on the rough, wooden front step. Dear Lord, what had happened to him? Caleb Winters wasn't the type of man to simply walk away and leave her all alone to bear and raise his child.

Or was he? She suddenly realized just how little she knew about him. Somehow in their conversations they had talked a lot about her background and dreams for the future, but he was amazingly adroit at changing the subject when it got around to him.

She stood and went into the house. No, she mustn't think like that. There was no need to panic. Wherever Caleb was he had had a good reason for leaving without telling her where he was going. When he came back he would explain everything.

Nancy spent a restless night, and early the next morning she drove to the house again. Caleb still wasn't there, so she went back to her apartment and called Dr. Gunther. "Arnie," she said when he answered the phone, "have you seen Caleb since he was retested last Wednesday?"

"Nope. No need to. The test came back positive, and we had a long talk. I explained what had happened and he seemed to accept it. Why? Is anything wrong?"

Nancy's hopes plummeted. She had counted on Arnie knowing where Caleb was. "I . . . I'm not sure. I haven't seen or heard from him since Friday night, and he's not at his house. Even his clothes are gone."

There was a pause at the other end of the line. "Didn't he leave a note?"

She clutched the phone tighter. "Not that I can find, and I've looked everywhere."

Again the pause. "Did you two have a quarrel? He acknowledged that your baby was his, and I thought he took it pretty calmly."

Nancy sighed. "So did I. We didn't quarrel, but he did send me away from him Friday night. He said he had to be alone for a while to think, but I didn't get the impression that he meant he was going to leave the island." She went on to tell him about finding Caleb gone the night before.

Arnie listened patiently until she was finished. "Why don't you check at the post office and find out if he left a forwarding address," he suggested. "I really don't think you have anything to worry about. He probably just went off by himself for a few days. This has all been pretty much of a shock to him, but he doesn't strike me as the sort of guy who would duck out on his responsibilities. Meanwhile, I'll make some inquiries, too.''

As soon as Nancy got off the phone she hurried over to the post office. The woman in charge knew everybody on the island and didn't even have to check to answer Nancy's question.

''Near as I can remember Caleb Winters seldom got mail, but if he's moved away he didn't leave a forwarding address. Was one problem, though. Remember that storm we had Friday with all the wind and rain? Well, the next morning the flag was up on Winters's mailbox and when the carrier stopped he found the door to the box wide open and a sopping wet letter inside. It had been addressed in ink which ran together and made the writing illegible. The carrier brought it in, but all we can do is send it to the dead letter office. We've tried to call Mr. Winters, but he don't answer the phone. If you see him tell him to get in touch with us, will you?''

Nancy sifted this information through her confused thoughts. Who had Caleb written to? Was the letter for her? No, that was absurd. If he had wanted to tell her where he was going it would have been much quicker and easier to either phone or stop by to see her. If he had left the island, and apparently he had, then he'd had to drive past the clinic to get to the ferry.

Determinedly she shoved the disturbing thoughts out of her mind. Caleb loved her. He had told her and shown her that in so many different ways, and she believed him. She'd been hurt and disappointed by his reaction to her pregnancy, but the justifications he had given for not wanting a baby made sense. They weren't insurmountable, but she'd known women who hadn't wanted a family for less important reasons and she'd always felt that it was their decision to make and should be respected. Why hadn't she been able to extend Caleb the same courtesy?

The answer to that was obvious. It was her baby, too, and she was perfectly capable of both raising and supporting it. Still, she should have been more sensitive to Caleb's objections. If she had only insisted on more time to explore the situation with him. To make him see that there was nothing unmanly about letting her take care of him and the child until he was well enough to accept his share of the responsibility.

He would be an ideal father, gentle and patient, and she was so sure that once he got used to the idea of having a son or daughter he would change his mind. But Caleb's doubts had been more overwhelming than she'd realized. Without ever meaning to, she had apparently presented him with an intolerable dilemma, and now she would just have to wait until he worked his way through it and came back to her.

For the next few days Nancy haunted the mailbox and the dock, hoping for a letter or the sight of Caleb's familiar blue Mustang driving off the ferry. Neither materialized, but on Friday she received a letter from the Sisters of Mercy in Dallas, who ran a clinic for the indigent in the poorer section of the city.

Shortly after arriving on Washington Island, Nancy had answered an advertisement in one of the medical journals for a nurse practitioner to take over the Dallas clinic. She'd heard nothing from them and had thought no more about it until today.

She ripped open the envelope and scanned the contents. A Dr. Phillip Ingram, the physician in charge, wrote that she was the top contender for the post, but they couldn't offer it to her without a personal interview. He set a date two weeks away, adding that if she didn't confirm the appointment within a week he would assume she wasn't interested.

Nancy was thrown into a quandary. Her present contract didn't expire until the first of September, two weeks after she would have to leave for Texas.

She could probably come to an agreement with Dr. Gunther on that, but what about Caleb? Where was he? When would he return? She had to give Dr. Ingram an answer within six days, but she couldn't do that until she'd talked to Caleb.

For three more days Nancy stewed, her concern turning to anger. There was still no word from Caleb. Finally, on Monday evening, she took the ferry to the mainland and confronted Dr. Gunther in his office.

He was sitting at his desk when she knocked and walked in. Without smiling, he indicated the chair on the other side of the desk and she sat down.

"You sounded upset when you called to say you wanted to see me," he said. "I gather you haven't heard from Caleb yet?"

Nancy was seething. "No, and I'm not sure I even want to anymore. I'm afraid I just have to face the fact that my charismatic mystery man who survived against seemingly hopeless odds is just a flawed human being after all. When things didn't go the way he wanted them to, when he was faced with a difficult decision, he solved it by disappearing."

Arnie frowned. "I'll admit it looks that way, but don't forget he's still recovering from injuries that should have killed him. He's not always thinking straight. Give him a little more time—"

Nancy clutched the arms of the chair. "I don't have more time. I've had an offer of a position, and I have to let them know in three more days if I want to accept it. Since I'm apparently going to be the sole parent of my baby I've got to support it. I don't have its father's leisure to 'find myself' and 'get my head together.' I know who I am and what I want, and I'm through waiting around for Caleb Winters to decide whether his child and I are important enough to him to acknowledge us."

Dr. Gunther started to rise. "Nancy, that's not—"

"Please stay seated, doctor," she said, "and we'll change the subject. I didn't come here to talk about my relationship with Caleb. I want to discuss the contract I have with the clinic. If I accept this new position I'll have to leave here at the end of the week. Would it be possible for me to be released from my contract two weeks early?"

Arnie settled back in his chair. "I had an inquiry about you a couple of weeks ago from a medical group in Detroit. Is that the practice you've been offered?"

She had applied there, but when she opened her mouth to tell him that wasn't where she meant she was amazed to hear herself saying, "Yes."

She blinked and closed her mouth. Why was she lying to him?

Before she could pursue the question in her mind Arnie spoke again. "Surely they'll give you a couple of weeks to wind up your business here."

Nancy laced her fingers together in indecision. She was quite sure that the Sisters of Mercy in Dallas would agree to a reasonable amount of time to resettle, but now she realized that she didn't want to finish out her obligation here.

She had already lied to this man once, and she wasn't ready to retract it. But neither was she willing to compound that falsehood with another.

"They probably would, Arnie," she said, "but to be honest I want to get away from here as soon as possible. I'll go crazy waiting around for a man who doesn't want me and has no intention of coming back."

This time Arnie did get up. "You don't know that, dammit! Caleb knows you're committed here until the first of September. He'll return by then. I would bet on it."

He came around the desk and stood, leaning against it, in front of her.

She looked up at him and shook her head sadly. "It wouldn't matter now if he did. Maybe I'm an incurable romantic and expect too much, but I don't want a man who needs weeks to decide whether or not he cares enough about me to share his future with me. If he loved me he wouldn't have to think about it, and if he doesn't I'd prefer to raise my child by myself."

Her voice broke, and she took a deep breath. "Could Dagmar possibly run things here on a limited basis until Zelda returns? I know it's asking a lot, but . . ."

Arnie sighed. "If it's that important to you I'll make arrangements for you to leave next week, but don't let your pride get in the way of your good sense. If you haven't heard from Caleb by the first of September, then it will be reasonable to assume he's abandoned you, and I'll be the first to admit that he's a first-class bastard. On the other hand, if he does come back between now and then, and I'm betting that he will, you should be here to listen to what he has to say. You can still tell him to get lost, but at least you'll know for sure why he left and what he decided."

Nancy pushed her chair back and stood. "You're probably right, but I really need this job that's been offered. I have to get started working as soon as possible in order to qualify for time off when the baby's born. I didn't know I was pregnant when I sent in the application, and I suspect my new employer isn't going to be thrilled with that piece of news.''

Arnie took her arm and walked with her to the door. ''In that case I'll be in touch as soon as I've talked to the board of directors. I don't think there'll be any problem about your leaving early. Dagmar can handle the first-aid cases, and the rest can come to my office here. Take care, now, and try not to get yourself all worked up.''

The next morning Nancy called Dr. Ingram in Dallas to tell him she was still interested in the position and would be there for the interview at the date and time he'd requested. She also informed him that if hired she would be free to start work immediately.

For the next four days Nancy spent long hours preparing to leave Washington Island. She wrote a letter to her patients telling them she had been called away earlier than expected and explaining the new clinic services.

Her evenings were spent bringing her records up to date and writing personal reports for Zelda on patients who had non-medical problems that Nancy felt Zelda should know about. Leaving a practice, even a short-term one such as this, was a wrenching experience, and although she was anxious to get away it was hard to say goodbye to her patients.

No one but Dr. Gunther and Dagmar knew Nancy was pregnant, and she hadn't told anyone, even those two, of her real destination. She wanted it to be a clean break. Caleb mustn't know where she was. Not that she believed he would actually come back, or look for her if he did, but she wasn't willing to take the chance.

Her love for Caleb Winters had been too deeply rooted. He had killed the respect and empathy she'd had for him, but her love was more difficult to destroy. She wasn't ready yet to put herself through the anguish of examining her feelings, but she knew that even if that love still flourished under the pain and disillusionment, she could never share her life, or her child, with a man who had treated her so shabbily.

No, these nice islanders who had become friends as well as co-workers and patients would be lost to her once she left. She knew the feeling of loss well. She had made friends so often during her childhood, only to leave them behind when she was uprooted and sent to yet another foster home or orphanage.

Nancy was no stranger to adversity, but that fact didn't make it any easier to overcome.

Early Saturday morning Nancy was on the dock waiting for the first ferry of the day. Her suitcases were packed and stored in her car trunk, and her maps, the routes through each state marked for easy reading, were on the seat beside her, along with a box of saltines.

She nibbled on one of the crackers while she waited, trying to appease the nausea that was stronger than usual this morning because of an all but sleepless night. Probably more emotional than physical, she thought as the line of cars finally began to move.

She drove to the front of the boat and sat staring straight ahead until the Wisconsin shoreline came into view. Not once did she look back. That episode of her life was finished. From now on she would only look ahead.

It was 7:40 a.m. on Saturday, August 13th.

Caleb woke to the sound of incessant, heavy traffic, and for a minute he was disoriented. Where was he? This drab little room sure as hell wasn't the Marriott hotel.

Then he remembered and relaxed once more. No, of course it wasn't. It was a cut-rate motel beside the freeway on the outskirts of Milwaukee.

He stretched and rolled over on his back with his hands behind his head. He felt rested, and excitement tugged at him. After two interminable weeks away from Nancy he had been too impatient to wait any longer and had checked out of the hotel at eight o'clock the night before to start the trip back to Washington Island. Unfortunately he had overestimated his uncertain strength as well as the strain of driving through Chicago traffic, and by the time he'd approached Milwaukee his flagging energy had reached the danger point. He'd had the good sense not to push himself any further and had stopped at the first motel he'd come to.

He put his left arm down and looked at his watch. Good Lord, it was almost ten o'clock! He really must have been exhausted to have overslept. He would just grab a quick shower and a cup of coffee, then get back on the road. He'd taken Barry's advice and resisted the temptation to call Nancy while he was running around Chicago doing all the things Barry had suggested to put her out of his mind, but nothing had worked. He'd just missed her more each day until he couldn't stand it any longer.

He rolled off the bed and headed for the bathroom. He needed the shower, but he would skip the coffee. He wasn't going to waste any more time getting home to the woman he now knew meant more to him than life itself.

By midafternoon Caleb was sitting in his car on the Washington Island ferry straining for the first glimpse of the shoreline. In a few more minutes Nancy would be in his arms, the arms that had been so empty and aching without her.

How could he ever have thought he could say goodbye and walk away from her at the end of the summer? Even without the added bonus of the baby he could never have let her go. He had been lying to himself.

Barry had been right, he did need some time alone, not to forget her but to finally understand just how deeply entwined in his life she had become. She was truly one with him. He couldn't separate himself from her without tearing out his heart and soul.

His eyes searched the horizon, finding the speck that grew larger until it became an island. Caleb's excitement reached fever pitch. He and Nancy were about to become a family, to be joined later by a small son or daughter. He had been given a second chance at happiness, and this time he would make sure to hold on to it, to cherish his wife and child and protect them from harm.

This time he would know better than to put them in danger.

As the boat swayed into the dock Caleb started the engine of his car. For the first time in over a year he was looking forward to the future with great anticipation.

It was 3:30 p.m. on Saturday, August 13th.

Chapter Nine

Thursday, June 23. Ten months later.

Nancy Lloyd hopped off the city bus as she did every weekday morning and walked a block and a half through dirty, littered streets in Dallas's slum area to the battered front door of Mercy Clinic. She unlocked the door and greeted the tall, dark, muscular man inside, who was setting up for their day's activity.

"Good morning, Ricardo," she said with a smile as she shut and relocked the door.

Ricardo Gutierrez was a registered nurse who acted as Nancy's assistant and self-appointed bodyguard. He was thirty years old and built like a boxer. Although it wasn't part of his duties, he insisted on arriving before her each morning to make sure the run-down old building was free of alcoholics, mentally ill homeless, or drug addicts who might have broken in during the night.

In the ten months that she had been in charge of the clinic she had never been accosted by the street people in the area, but the small supply of drugs kept for treatment purposes was a potential target for anyone desperate for a fix, and she was grateful for Ricardo's protection.

"You're early," he answered, eyeing her suspiciously. "I'll bet you skipped breakfast again."

She sniffed the air. "I knew you'd have fresh coffee waiting so I saw no reason to waste time making a pot at home." She held up the white paper sack she was carrying. "I stopped at the neighborhood bakery on my way to the bus stop and picked up some Danish pastries. If we hurry we can eat before the line starts forming."

Nancy wasn't being facetious. Every morning except Sunday patients began lining up in front of the door at eight o'clock and filled the small area inside until the clinic closed, hopefully at five but often later.

In the tiny office area that held a beat-up desk and chair, a filing cabinet and a TV tray table, Ricardo poured coffee into earthenware mugs while Nancy donned a white lab coat over her faded jeans and blue T-shirt.

"Have you heard from Maya?" Nancy asked. "She's not planning to drive all the way from Mexico in one day, is she?"

Maya, Ricardo's pretty young wife, was also a nurse. She worked in the emergency room at Baylor University Medical Center, where Ricardo and Nancy sent their patients who needed to be hospitalized.

With a quick, jerky movement Ricardo added powdered cream to one of the cups of coffee. "She's not coming back tomorrow after all," he said angrily. "She insists her parents still need her, and she's arranged to take another week off work, this time without pay."

Nancy took two pastries out of the sack and put each on a paper napkin before answering. "Is there a problem with the way her father's fractured leg is healing?" she asked cautiously.

She could see that Ricardo was upset, and she didn't want to appear to take sides in a family argument.

"Not that I'm aware of. The old man's strong as a bull." He handed Nancy the cup with the cream and picked up one of the Danishes. "I was afraid this would happen when she went down there after his accident two weeks ago. Dammit, we've been married three years and I still haven't managed to wean Maya away from that family of hers."

Nancy took a sip of the coffee and enjoyed the warm feel of it sliding down her throat. She never really felt awake until she'd had her first cup in the morning.

"Maya was born and raised in that small farming community," Nancy reminded him. "The only time she was ever away from it was when she took her nurse's training in Monterrey, and even then it was close enough so that she could go home every time she had a few days' break. Then you married her and brought her up here to a big city in a strange country. It's no wonder she's homesick a lot of the time."

Ricardo sighed. "Yeah, I know you're right, but that doesn't make it any easier. I'm her husband, so why can't she think of me as her family now?"

Before Nancy could respond, a loud banging and shouting sent both of them running for the front of the building. The door swung back as soon as it was unlocked, and a young woman carrying a small child in the throes of a convulsion stumbled wildly into the clinic, screaming in panic. The woman was followed by the long line of patients who had been waiting outside.

The day had begun at Mercy Free Rescue Clinic.

* * *

The heat and humidity built together as the hours passed, and at quitting time Nancy felt as if she'd been rushing around in a sauna. She had discovered last year that the Texas heat was almost tropical in its intensity, and she'd had trouble adjusting—especially after the summer spent in the springlike climate of Washington Island.

In the absence of air-conditioning the diocese had provided large, strategically placed fans which helped a little, but mostly just moved the hot air around. The odor of unwashed bodies and fetid wounds hung in the muggy air even though the place was thoroughly scrubbed each night by the volunteer janitors.

Nancy was nearly finished suturing a long but fairly shallow knife wound when Ricardo came into the treatment room. "There's a guy out there who wants to see you," he said. "He's well dressed, not a patient, but won't give his name or state his business. Should I tell him to get lost?"

She tied the last knot and reached for the scissors. "Better not. It's probably someone from yet another government agency wanting to check our permits and licenses. If the city would spend as much money helping their indigent as they do putting obstacles in everyone's way there wouldn't be any need for our services. Is there anyone else waiting?"

"No, I locked the door. It's six o'clock, we can't stay here all night."

Nancy chuckled. "Okay, tell him I'll be out in a minute." She wiped the sweat off her forehead with the back of her arm. "God, but it's muggy. I'd sell my soul right now for an air conditioner."

"Dream on," he muttered and withdrew.

She quickly bandaged the clean arm that in no way matched the rest of the dirty, disheveled man sitting on the treatment table. "There you are," she said as she applied the last piece of tape. "Keep the bandage dry and come back day after tomorrow. That's Saturday, but I'll be here all morning."

She assisted him in getting off the table. "Are you all right?" she asked anxiously when he seemed to totter on his feet.

"I'm okay." He didn't look at her as he started to move away.

She took his arm to steady him and walked along beside him. "If the pain is bad tomorrow, come back and I'll give you another pill."

Nancy knew better than to give these patients drugs for future use. They either sold them, or lost them or overdosed on them.

"If you're hungry there's a food kitchen around the corner," she said as they entered the outer area.

She was aware of Ricardo sitting at the scarred table that served as a reception desk, and of another man standing off to the side, but her attention was centered on the patient. She led him to the door and took her key from her pocket. "Now remember," she told him as she unlocked the door, "you're to come back Saturday morning. It's very important that we change the bandage and have another look at your arm."

He nodded and thanked her as he stepped out onto the sidewalk.

She closed and locked the door, then leaned against it and fanned the air with her hand in an attempt to stir up a little breeze. She didn't really expect to see the patient again. Few returned for follow-up treatment unless they were in pain and needed drugs. When that happened it was usually because they were users and were looking for an easy fix, and then she had trouble getting rid of them.

Ricardo got up and came around the table. "Nancy, this man has been waiting to see you."

She straightened and started toward the figure still leaning against the wall. "I'm sorry to keep you waiting, sir—"

As she moved closer she felt a chill at the back of her neck, as though a cold breeze had blown gently across her raw nerve endings. Ricardo had turned off the powerful fluorescent light on the ceiling and the room was dim, but there was a magnetism that flowed between her and the man in the shadow that sent little shocks through her system.

"Hello, Nancy," he said and took a step closer so that she could see him more clearly.

All the little shocks converged into a mighty detonation that shattered her and left her rigid and unable to move as she stared into the face that still haunted her dreams.

"Caleb!"

It sounded more like a cry of anguish than a greeting, and the room began to spin around her as she reached out for something to hold on to.

"What the hell?" It was Ricardo's voice, and it was his arms that caught her as she fell.

Effortlessly he picked her up and carried her to one of the mismatched chairs that were scattered around the room. "Put your head down," he ordered and guided her shoulders as she bent forward and rested her forehead against her knees.

"Now you," he said, obviously talking to Caleb who was standing next to them, "I'll give you two minutes to leave before I throw you out."

"I wouldn't advise you to try it." Caleb's voice was strong and determined. "I'm not going anywhere until I've talked to Nancy, and I would appreciate it if you'd leave us. I'm not going to harm her."

Ricardo straightened to his full towering height. "Your two minutes are up."

Nancy heard the quick rage in his voice, and she knew what he was capable of. She had seen him handle belligerent punks who had wandered into the clinic intent on stirring up trouble. Her only thought was that Caleb wasn't strong enough to tangle with Ricardo, and he would be hurt.

"No," she screamed and sat up just in time to see Ricardo's large, muscular body go flying through the air and land with a loud thud on the floor a few feet away.

It was Ricardo on the floor, not Caleb! Caleb had apparently decked him with a martial arts maneuver.

Nancy jumped up just as Ricardo leaped to his feet, and she planted herself between the two angry men. "Stop it," she yelled and put her hands firmly on Ricardo's chest. "It's all right, Ric. Caleb's not threatening me. I just wasn't expecting him, and I guess the shock, plus the heat, got to me for a minute."

Ricardo eyed her doubtfully. "Are you sure?"

"I'm sure, believe me. You can go on home, I'll close up."

"No way," he said, glaring at Caleb. "Go ahead and talk to him if you want to, but I'm staying. I'll wait in the office. If you need me, just holler." He turned and walked across the room to disappear around the partition that separated the small office from the rest of the clinic.

"The man's very protective of you," Caleb said from directly behind her.

She heard the barely controlled anger in his tone, the unspoken accusation, and to her relief her confused feelings for him slipped back into the notch she'd relegated them to almost a year ago.

She tensed and turned to face him, and saw him clearly for the first time. He had aged. Oh, he was more physically fit than he had been ten months ago, but he still looked older than his thirty-seven years. His dark hair was liberally sprinkled with gray, and he had gained at least fifteen pounds. Weight that he had desperately needed, but instead of making him look younger it had added to his maturity.

"That's none of your business," she informed him tartly. "What are you doing here, Caleb? How did you find me?"

They were standing almost toe-to-toe. Too close. She could hardly breathe. She backed up a few steps. "No, I guess what I really want to know is why did you bother to look for me?"

She could actually see the anger drain out of him leaving him looking stunned. "Why did I bother to look for you?" He sounded as if the question didn't make sense. "Because I went back to Washington Island and found you gone. Why didn't you wait for me, Nancy? Just a few more hours and this misunderstanding would never have happened."

She gasped. "Misunderstanding!" Damn him, did he think he could convince her that his desertion was just a misunderstanding?

"You disappeared first, remember?" She forced her voice to remain low and taut. "You simply drove away without a word to me or anybody else. I needed you then, but you ran away so I took care of myself. I don't need you anymore, I'll never need anyone again. You can get on with your life with a clear conscience, just please, stay out of mine.''

She whirled and hurried to the office where she picked up her purse and asked Ricardo if he would lock up.

When she came back out into the waiting room Caleb was still there. She walked past him and was almost to the door when he called to her. The agony in his voice stopped her as effectively as if he'd held her in place. ''Yes?'' she said, but didn't turn.

''I . . .'' For a moment there was silence, then he started over. ''Tell me about the child.'' It was spoken in little more than a whisper, but every word penetrated her soul.

So that's why he had gone to the trouble of finding her. It was his child he was concerned about. After abandoning her to shift for herself and face what followed later alone, he'd finally taken an interest in the baby. Well, she would tell him. This was one piece of knowledge he deserved to hear.

She turned slowly and walked back a few paces until they were less than a foot apart. Through the film of tears that clouded her eyes she noticed that he looked haggard and tense, but there seemed to be a demon inside of her driving her on.

''Two months after I came here I lost my baby,'' she said flatly. ''It was a girl, and she died when nature saw fit to expel her into the world much too early. You got what you wanted, Caleb. There is no child.''

The blood drained from his face and instinctively she reached out her hand, but although he stumbled he righted himself, and she put her arm down without touching him.

He didn't say anything, just stood there looking as if she'd shoved a knife into a vital spot. Nancy knew she should do something to help him bear the blow she'd just delivered, but she couldn't. Her own pain was too great. She couldn't accept his, too.

With a cry of anguish she turned and ran.

At the small studio apartment that she called home she paced the floor. She had tried cooking, eating, watching television and reading, but nothing could drive Caleb Winters from her mind. She was right back where she'd started ten months ago.

At that time, with persistence and the knowledge that her emotional state could adversely affect her baby, she had managed to conquer her torment and calm down. It had also helped that she'd had the baby to look forward to. She'd been able to dissolve her bitterness toward Caleb because he'd given her a child. By then it hadn't mattered that he didn't want it. She did, and that was enough.

Then she lost her tiny daughter, and for a while she'd truly feared that her sanity was threatened. It was the Sisters of Mercy who arranged for counseling and, even though she wasn't Catholic, they were always there when she needed someone to help her bear the burden.

With their friendship and the professional counseling she'd finally managed to put the whole episode of Caleb Winters behind her, except for the dreams that haunted her sleep. They consisted of nebulous images and half-formed feelings that were never clear when she woke up crying. She dismissed them and tried to bury them deep in her subconscious.

But the Caleb Winters who appeared to her today, in the flesh and seemingly determined to torture her, couldn't be dismissed or buried. He had a voice and demanded to be heard, but she wasn't sure she was strong enough to battle with him.

At dawn the next morning, after a sleepless night, she placed a call to Ricardo. The sleepy snarl in his voice reminded her that it was still very early. "Sorry, Ric, I didn't mean to wake you, but did the man who came to see me at the clinic yesterday afternoon tell you where he was staying?"

"Gonna give him another whack at you, huh?" Ric's tone was heavy with sarcasm.

Ricardo and Maya had helped her through the horror of her miscarriage, so it was no surprise that he had guessed Caleb was the lover who had walked out on her. Even so, she was tired and edgy and in no mood for his disapproval.

"I'm not asking for advice, just for an address," she snapped.

"Yes, ma'am." He fairly barked the words. "Pardon me for being concerned. Before he left he told me to tell you that he's staying at the Fairmont Hotel." Ricardo slammed down the phone before she could reply.

Half an hour later she'd had a long, revitalizing shower, a fresh cup of coffee and a chance to calm down. She was glad now that Ric had cut the connection before she could respond to his anger with her own heated temper. He'd earned the right to try to protect her. He and his sweet and compassionate wife had been her confidants during those nightmare months when she first arrived in Dallas, pregnant, abandoned and heartbroken. They and the Sisters had saved her sanity, and she owed them more than she could ever repay.

Unfortunately, she had finally come to the conclusion that she also owed Caleb something—an explanation. Even though he'd been the first to disappear he'd obviously gone to a great deal of trouble and expense to find her. He must have been concerned.

Nancy was ashamed of the vicious way she had told him about losing the baby. She'd let her shock and suppressed rage override her good sense and her natural compassion. She had regretted it as soon as the words were spoken. He'd looked so stunned, as though she'd staggered him with a physical blow.

She would never have been so brutal to a patient, or even to a stranger, so why had she felt justified in attacking the one man who could provoke her to such violence?

Was it because you had to feel deeply in order to hurt someone that badly? She didn't hate Caleb. She disliked him because of his attitude toward her pregnancy, but she'd never hated him, so why had she struck out so cruelly?

With a sigh she reached for the phone and dialed the number of the Fairmont Hotel.

Caleb paced the thickly carpeted floor of his room in the elegant, twin towered hotel. He had long since adjusted to the awkward gait necessary with a knee that wouldn't bend, and it no longer frustrated him.

The enormous window of his eighteenth-floor room provided him with a sweeping view of awesome glass buildings that blazed in the sunlight and seemed to stretch upward as far as the heavens. He had never been in Dallas before except to change planes at the air terminal, but he'd always thought of it as a sprawling, provincial town. He wasn't prepared for the dazzling skyline of towering, mirrored skyscrapers that rose out of the Blackland prairies and dwarfed the older, smaller buildings which not too many years ago had comprised the heart of the city.

At another time he would have enjoyed exploring the huge, bustling metropolis, but now all he could think of was his disastrous encounter with Nancy the evening before. He was still badly shaken.

He'd been apprehensive, of course, about how she would react to seeing him again, but he couldn't wait until he had more facts before approaching her. He'd suffered through almost eleven months without her and it was killing him. He had to see her, had to plead with her to forgive him for his many mistakes.

Dr. Gunther had told him she'd never received the letter he'd written to her so he expected her to be angry at first, but he'd never envisioned the venomous reception he'd received. In his worst nightmares it had never occurred to him that she might have lost the baby!

Why hadn't the operatives told him there was no child? They knew they were looking for a pregnant woman. At least in the beginning they had been.

He stopped pacing and absently rubbed at his throbbing leg. He hadn't really given them time for an in-depth report. As soon as he'd received the news that Nancy had been located he'd dropped everything and headed for Dallas on the first flight out of Salt Lake City. The only information he'd had was her work and home addresses.

The telephone rang, and Caleb jumped. Who could that be? Nobody knew where he was staying. He had rented a car and bought a map at the airport when he got in yesterday, then picked a hotel that was close to both the clinic and Nancy's apartment before rushing on to see her. After the encounter with her he'd been too shattered to remember anything. He hadn't even contacted Barry yet.

Apprehensively he picked up the receiver and answered, then nearly dropped the phone when he heard the dearly familiar voice.

"Caleb, this is Nancy."

His head whirled and he tried to say something but no sound came.

"It's important that I see you," she continued, as cool as though she were speaking to a business acquaintance. "May I come over for a few minutes?"

Could she come over? Sweet Lord, didn't she know he'd give up the rest of his life just to spend a few precious minutes with her?

He swallowed, and this time managed to speak. "It's important that I see you, too." His voice sounded rusty. "Please come, and . . . could you hurry?"

Nancy strode into the large, plush lobby of the Fairmont Hotel and was immediately cooled by the comfortable, temperature-controlled atmosphere. Even at seven-thirty in the morning the air outside was hot and humid. She'd dressed for work, and her white nurse's oxfords sank into the thick carpeting as she made her way to the elevators.

At another time she would have appreciated the luxury around her, but her heart was thumping so hard that she was sure the expensively dressed woman who stood waiting beside her could hear it. Nancy's tension had been mounting steadily ever since her short conversation with Caleb less than an hour before.

The ascent to the eighteenth floor was quick, and long before Nancy was ready she was standing outside the door to Caleb's room. Her hands trembled, and even with the air-conditioning she could feel drops of perspiration rolling down between her breasts.

Damn. Where was that celebrated composure she'd prided herself on achieving? She had been so sure that she'd finally relegated Caleb to the past where he belonged, but when she saw him yesterday she'd literally fallen apart.

She'd promised herself that he would never hurt her again, but now here she was in agony at the prospect of seeing him once more and talking to him.

Quickly she made a decision. She wasn't going to put herself through this. Maybe she owed him an apology for the way she'd treated him yesterday, but he'd sinned against her, too. Surely one canceled out the other. She would go to the clinic and ask Ricardo to call Caleb and tell him she wouldn't be able to see him after all.

She turned away and had taken one step when the door opened behind her. Her first instinct was to run, but her pride stopped her. She wasn't a quitter, and now that she'd been caught she would finish what she'd started.

Turning around she saw Caleb standing in the doorway watching her. He was wearing blue dress slacks and a blue plaid, short sleeved shirt open at the throat. His graying hair was neatly combed, and she could smell the musky scent of his shaving lotion. She stifled a moan and cursed herself for not staying as far away from him as she could get.

"Come in, Nancy," he said and put out his hand to her.

She ignored it as she stepped past him and into the room. It was light and spacious with a king-size bed, a dark, ornate dresser and a grouping of comfortable chairs.

Caleb shut the door, and suddenly the room was too small. "How did you know I was out there?" she asked in an effort to break the tension-filled silence.

"I don't know." His tone was low. "I just felt that I had to open the door quickly or I'd miss you."

Nancy wasn't surprised at his allegation. She'd always known that the attraction between them was strong enough to penetrate any barrier.

She didn't attempt to deny it. "This is difficult for me, Caleb. I've suffered enough. I don't want any more pain."

He was looking at her, and again he put out his hand, this time to touch her lightly on the head. "You've cut your hair." She caught the note of disapproval in his voice.

Stepping away she unconsciously put her hand up to the short, feathery dark cap. "Yes, we have a problem with head lice at the clinic."

A look of revulsion twisted Caleb's features. "Dammit, Nancy, why do you work in a place like that? You're a highly trained nurse. You could..."

Her hands clenched. How dare he criticize her! "I didn't exactly have the leisure to be choosy about the job I took," she said heatedly. "I was pregnant and expected to have to support my child. I jumped at the first practice offered."

Caleb closed his eyes for a moment and shook his head as if trying to clear it. "I'm sorry," he said brokenly and turned away from her. "I want so desperately to make things right between us, but instead I manage to offend you even more grievously every time I open my mouth. It tore me apart to see you in that stinking slum yesterday, and to know that you've cut your beautiful hair because of..." He choked and for a moment stopped trying to speak. Then with a muttered, "Excuse me," he strode into the bathroom and closed the door.

Nancy's knees began to tremble, and she sank down on one of the two upholstered chairs. This was the first time she'd actually seen Caleb walk, and he still had a noticeable limp. Did his leg continue to hurt? Would he have to live with pain for the rest of his life?

She clutched her hands in her lap. It was a mistake to have come here. She should have apologized on the phone and let it go at that.

Closing her eyes she leaned back against the thickly padded chair, exhausted from tension and lack of sleep. Her weary body and the comfortable chair seemed to be made for each other. Her curves blended into the soft upholstery and she felt herself relaxing. She was vaguely aware of water running in the bathroom as her head rolled to one side. Maybe a few minutes of total relaxation would refresh her enough to think clearly.

She took a deep breath and willed the tension to drain from her clenched muscles.

Caleb doused his face with cold water, then again, and again. Would the time ever come when he could once more get a good strong grip on his emotions and be able to control them? He was functioning normally now in every other area, but just the thought of Nancy left him weak. Being in the same room with her scrambled his ability to reason, and when she was angry at him he broke down completely.

It was not only unwise but downright dangerous for a man to let a woman become that important to him.

Let her! Ha! He'd never had a choice in the matter. He'd been like a starving man reaching for sustenance when she came into his life, and she'd filled his every need—for comfort, for companionship, for love. Even his great desire for a child.

He groaned aloud and reached for a towel, then buried his face in it.

In his surprise and shock and fear, he'd bungled everything and driven her out of his life, when all he'd wanted was to come to terms with what was happening and do what was best for her.

He threw the towel down on the counter and looked at himself in the big mirror. *Come off it, quit lying to your-*

self. If you'd really wanted what was best for her you would never have gotten involved with her in the first place.

He picked up a comb and ran it through his hair. *Quit hiding in the bathroom like an adolescent kid and go back in there. Whatever she wants to dish out you've got coming to you, if for no other reason than your monumental stupidity.*

Chapter Ten

Caleb opened the bathroom door and walked out, prepared to apologize for taking so long, but Nancy was curled up in the chair looking relaxed in sleep. The thick carpeting made no noise as he went over and stood beside her.

Her eyes were closed, and the lines of strain that had bracketed them and her mouth were miraculously gone. He hated the fact that he'd been the one to put those lines there.

He cupped her cheek gently with his hand and got an incredible jolt of pleasure when her mouth turned up in a little smile. It was the first time she had smiled since he'd found her. Was she thinking of him, or was it that hulking assistant who now filled her dreams?

The pleasure turned to a sharp pain, but he determinedly banished it. None of that! He had no right to be jealous, and he had a great need to touch her while he could.

He sat down on the arm of the chair and carefully threaded his fingers through her cropped hair. It had shocked him at first, but now that he was more used to it he liked it. She looked like a pixie with the layered cut, and the hair that was left was still soft and silky and shining with good health.

He leaned over and kissed her moist temple. She had the sweet, clean fragrance of shampoo and moisturizing cream. Her only makeup was a pink lipstick, and she looked very sweet and vulnerable.

She was obviously exhausted. Probably she hadn't slept any more than he had last night. Would he wake her if he carried her over to the bed? It was worth a try, she wouldn't nap long in that awkward position.

He went over to the bed and pulled back the covers. The maid hadn't been around to make it up yet, so it was still rumpled.

He returned to the chair and carefully picked Nancy up. While they were on Washington Island he couldn't have done so, but now he was able to carry her with little strain.

She wound her arms around his neck and pressed her face in his shoulder. The sheer joy of her embrace made him shiver even though he realized she wasn't aware of what she was doing.

It had been so long since he'd held her, and he'd wanted her so badly. He had ached with needing her, and not just sexually. He knew that if she never let him in her bed again he would still want her with him. He could adjust to anything but losing her completely.

He sat down on the side of the mattress and cradled her on his lap, careful not to wake her. If the only time he could hold her, touch her, was when she slept then he would accept the limitation. It was a million times better than not touching or caressing her at all.

After a while the pressure of her weight on his legs became too painful to continue, and he tenderly laid her down on the bed, then walked around it and stretched out beside her. God, but it was good to lie next to her again.

He put out his hand and rested it on her thigh. The heat in his loins was immediate and powerful, and he quickly drew the hand back. No. He wouldn't do that to her. Caressing her face and hair while she slept was acceptable, but he wasn't going to violate her.

When, or if, he seduced Nancy he wanted her wide awake and cooperating. He wouldn't steal her passion or her love. He wanted her to give it to him willingly and without reserve as she had done in the beginning.

He lifted himself up and brushed his lips lightly across hers, then lay back down and closed his eyes. He hadn't slept for more than two or three hours in the past forty-eight. He would doze until she wakened. Maybe then she'd let him tell her, and show her, how deeply he loved her.

Nancy stirred and snuggled into the firm but oh-so-comfortable mattress. Odd. Her sofa bed was lumpy and too soft. Her own pillow was hard and flat, but this one was pure heaven, soft but supportive.

She opened her eyes and stared at a huge window that was partially covered at either end by heavy beige drapes. It had a view of the tops of some of Dallas's gleaming skyscrapers. Her windows at home were small and had blinds under the tattered, age-dulled white curtains.

Good grief, where was she?

She jerked upright and for a few seconds felt totally disoriented. Then she saw the man sleeping beside her on the bed and her heart slammed against her chest. She was in Caleb's hotel room, but how had she gotten into bed with him?

She drew her knees up and discovered that she was fully dressed. So was Caleb, and he was sleeping soundly, lying on his side facing her with his hands tucked under his pillow.

Familiar feelings of tenderness swamped her, and without thinking she reached out to touch him. She caught herself in time and wrapped her arms around her legs instead. Why was she in bed with Caleb? That was the last thing she would have done voluntarily. Why didn't she remember?

She had come to his room to apologize, but they'd quarreled instead. She remembered him going into the bathroom, and her sitting down in the chair to wait, but after that her mind was a blank.

She must have fallen asleep. Had Caleb carried her to the bed? He must have, but how was that possible? She weighed 120 pounds and he walked on legs that had had most of the bones in them broken and pinned together again. He shouldn't carry that much weight.

She buried her face in her knees. Why had he risked crippling himself even more by putting her in his bed instead of waking her and sending her away so he could catch up on the rest he apparently needed badly?

She raised her head and looked at him lying so peacefully beside her, then fought the overwhelming urge to stroke his cheek and kiss his closed eyelids. Even when he was relaxed there were deep lines etched in his maturely handsome face.

He had endured so much and still had lived through it. She'd had patients, who hadn't been hurt nearly as badly as Caleb, who survived, to be bitter and resentful, but not him. He had borne the agony and fought death with every bit of strength in him and without a trace of self-pity. He'd scaled insurmountable heights and won, so why did the conception of a tiny baby panic him into such uncharacteristic behavior as rejection and flight?

Unable to resist the burning impulse any longer Nancy shifted on the bed and leaned over the man who had brought her so much joy and caused her such pain. Cautiously she brushed the graying hair off his forehead, then bent down and kissed the exposed side of his throat.

Before she could move away his arms caught her, and he rolled onto his back. Her face landed in the hollow of his shoulder. For a moment she thought he had wakened, but then she realized that his action was just a reflex. Still, he held her close and murmured something unintelligible before he started to relax again.

Nancy lay in his embrace, unable for a moment to summon the strength to break away. *Oh, Caleb, Caleb, why did you track me down and come after me? If you don't want me why didn't you leave me alone? I was just beginning to pick up the pieces of my life, and now you've scattered them all to hell again.*

It took all the willpower she could gather to slip carefully and silently out of his arms and off the bed. As she left she took the DO NOT DISTURB sign and hung it outside so the maid wouldn't wake him when she came to clean the room, then cursed herself as a fool for caring.

It was almost eleven o'clock by the time Nancy got to the clinic. Ricardo was swamped with patients and in a grouchy mood. She quickly washed her hands, then pitched in to help while apologizing for being so late. He grumbled something she was glad she didn't hear and ignored her.

By midafternoon Ric's snit had become a full-blown tantrum and he began snapping at the patients. Finally, Nancy had to take him into the office and remind him that he was being unprofessional and that his behavior wouldn't be tolerated.

He crossed his arms over his massive chest and lowered his head. "Sorry," he muttered. "You're right, I shouldn't take my foul mood out on you and the patients."

Nancy hesitated. There was still a room full of people to treat, but Ric needed to get something off his chest. He was entitled to her help, too.

"What's the matter, Ric?" she asked. "Did I wake you too early with that phone call this morning?"

He sighed. "No, I'd only just dozed off. I don't sleep worth a damn without Maya. I guess that's what's wrong with me—I miss her like crazy. I was looking forward so eagerly to her coming home today, and now it'll be another whole week." He uttered an expletive and ran his fingers through his black, curly hair. "I'm her husband, doesn't that entitle me to some rights?"

So that was it. Nancy could certainly sympathize with anyone missing a lover. She'd been in purgatory for months, and now that Caleb was here it was even worse.

"Look," she said gently. "I can manage tomorrow morning without you. Why don't you fly down there for the weekend? Take Monday, too."

Ricardo's expression softened as he looked at her. "You're some lady, you know that?" There was gratitude in his tone, but then it turned to hopelessness. "Thank you for the gesture, but I can't afford plane fare down there and back. I'm not overpaid at this job, you know. Neither are you, and Maya will be docked a week's salary for taking leave after her vacation time ran out."

He looked so miserable that Nancy would gladly have loaned him the money except that she didn't have any to spare, either.

She threw up her hands. "Okay, then take a week of your vacation starting tomorrow and drive down. You're not going to be much use to me in your frustrated state. Go to your wife and get it out of your system..."

She stopped and felt the hot blush as she realized that what she had just said had a double meaning.

Ric roared with laughter at her unintentionally bawdy suggestion. "Boss lady, I hate to tell you this, but I never 'get it out of my system' with Maya. Each time just gets hotter than the last, but I promise you we'll give it one hell of a good try."

He grabbed her and kissed her on the cheek. "Did I ever tell you that next to Maya I love you best of all?"

The sunshine of the morning had been swallowed up by clouds during the afternoon, and as Nancy stepped off the bus at the stop near her apartment a rumble of thunder in the distance warned of an imminent shower. With a quick glance at the rapidly darkening sky she scurried into the small, independent grocery store on the corner. Maybe if it rained the air would cool down a little, but she hoped the storm would hold off until she got home.

It didn't. By the time she had gathered up the items she needed and paid for them it was sprinkling, and when she was a block from her ancient apartment building the clouds opened up and poured. She clutched her paper bag and ran. When she got to the front door someone called to her.

She turned to see Caleb getting out of a car parked at the curb a few yards up the street. By the time he reached her she had the door open. When she stepped inside he was right behind her.

He glared at her as he took the soggy bag out of her arms. "Why are you walking in this weather?" His tone was impatient and critical.

"Because it's the only way I can get home from the bus stop," she snapped as she hurried across the linoleum-covered floor and punched the button for the rickety elevator. "How did you know where I lived?"

The elevator door opened, and they walked inside. "The same way I knew where you worked. Fourth floor, isn't it?" he growled, then punched the right button without waiting for an answer. "Why aren't you driving? Is something wrong with your car?"

Dammit, what was he so hot about? It was none of his business how she got to and from work. Still, she didn't want to quarrel. For some reason even when she won her battles with him she still lost the war.

She took a deep breath in an effort to control her rising ire. "I hope not. When I sold it it was in good working condition."

"Sold it!"

The lumbering old elevator stopped with a jolt, and Caleb followed her down the hall. "Do you mean you don't own a car anymore?"

Nancy halted in front of one of the look-alike white doors that had yellowed with age and infrequent scrubbings. She selected a key from her ring and inserted it in the lock. "That's right, I take the bus. It's cheaper, easier and it gets me anywhere I want to go."

She swung open the door, then turned to face him, blocking the entrance. "If I don't invite you in will you go away?"

His eyebrows lifted, and a reluctant smile tugged at the corners of his mouth. "No."

She sighed. "That's what I was afraid of."

Turning again, she walked inside and he followed. "The kitchen is behind the folding door over there. Just set the groceries on the counter. I'm going to get out of these wet clothes."

She walked across the room to the corner she called the bedroom and rummaged through the closet. After sliding a wheat-colored linen caftan off the hanger she opened a drawer in the dresser and took out clean underwear, then headed for the bathroom.

"You'd better turn on the air conditioner in the side window. It's stuffy in here," she said to Caleb just before she shut the bathroom door and locked it.

Caleb opened the folding door and stared. Kitchen, hell! It was a shallow closet with a Formica counter that held a tiny sink and a two-burner stovetop. There was a cupboard above and an oven, short refrigerator and two shallow drawers below.

He set down the groceries and turned to inspect the rest of the apartment. It consisted of one room plus a bathroom that offered little privacy since he could hear everything going on through the thin walls.

The hardwood floor was strong but badly in need of refinishing, and the furniture was shabby. Since there was no bed he assumed the faded brown sofa pulled out into one, and the cheap, walnut-veneer end tables and matching coffee table were right out of the 1950s.

The place was clean and neat, but the only evidence of Nancy's touch was a new brick-colored swivel rocker and a small, portable television that sat on one end of a rickety, yellow Formica kitchen table. The table was placed along the front wall with two matching chairs tucked under it.

Caleb realized that he was sweating and he went over to turn on the small air conditioner mounted in one window. The cool breeze felt good, but the racket it made was distracting. It sounded as if it needed a general overhaul.

He went back to the kitchen and found a can of coffee and an electric percolator. He could hear the shower running in the bathroom as he filled the pot and plugged it in, and in his mind he could see Nancy standing nude under the stream of water as clearly as if there were no wall between them.

His heart pounded, and he banged on the counter with his fist in a useless gesture of frustration. In the name of all that was holy, why was she living in a place like this? If she was trying to punish him, she was succeeding beyond her wildest imaginings—but he knew it wasn't that. She'd done everything she could to make sure he never found her, and he never would have if he hadn't had the clout to force the government to find her for him.

Was it possible that this was all she could afford? Was she having trouble making ends meet? But she'd told him once that nurse practitioners were well paid, and that she had money saved.

Nancy turned off the shower and reached for a thick new bath towel. She had rented the apartment furnished, but she'd had to supply her own linens and dishes.

She wondered if Caleb was still waiting as she hurriedly dried herself. She'd been startled but not really surprised when he had appeared at her doorstep. He was probably wondering what she had wanted to talk to him about this morning. They'd started quarreling before she had even stepped inside his room and she'd never gotten to the apology.

The humidity in the air, plus the steam in the hot little bathroom, had her dripping before she finished putting on her bra and panties.

They had quarreled again this evening when he had berated her for walking in the rain. Where did he get off criticizing her and telling her what to do? He'd forfeited any rights he might have had when he walked out on her almost a year ago.

She swiped at the mirror over the sink with one end of the towel, but it fogged over again before she could get the cap off her lipstick.

Abandoning any thought of applying makeup, she pulled the caftan over her head and picked up the brush before opening the door and escaping into the relative coolness of the other room. She was determined to settle things with Caleb right now and send him on his way.

The aroma of fresh-brewed coffee permeated the air, and Caleb stood at the counter with the percolator in his hand. He raised it and looked at her. "Want some?"

When she had rented this shabby little studio she'd never expected to see him here. It was good enough for her, all she needed was somewhere to crash after working ten or more hours a day, but Caleb was out of place.

In the shock and confusion of seeing him again it hadn't registered with her earlier, but his bearing had changed in the months they'd been apart. There was an air of authority about him, a self-sufficiency that he hadn't had when he had first come to Washington Island. He no longer needed her strength, he had plenty of his own again. Why wasn't she glad instead of feeling so empty?

"Nancy, I asked if you wanted some coffee." He was looking at her strangely, and she pulled her errant thoughts back into line.

"Yes, thanks. There's cream in the refrigerator under the counter."

He filled two mugs and bent down to open the refrigerator. "I was going to make you a drink, but I couldn't find your liquor."

"I don't have any," she murmured absently and ran the brush through her short, disheveled hair.

He straightened and poured cream into both cups. "If I'd known I would have brought some with me."

She shook her head as she picked up one of the mugs. "I'm glad you didn't," she said. "I don't drink. When I first came here I was pregnant and couldn't, then after..." Her voice broke. Even after all these months she could hardly talk about it. "After the miscarriage...I was afraid I would rely on a few drinks to dull the pain so I quit buying or drinking liquor."

Caleb's face was drained of color, and his features had hardened into a mask of anguish. Hot coffee sloshed from his mug and ran over his hand, but he didn't seem to notice as he set it back on the counter.

"Nancy, sweetheart..." His voice was raspy as he reached out to her, but she moved away before he could touch her.

"No, Caleb, let me talk. I went to your room this morning to apologize for the brutal way I told you about losing the baby. It was unforgivable."

She put her cup down, too, and ran her fingers through the hair she'd just brushed. "I can't even claim that I didn't know what I was saying because I did. I wanted to hurt you. I wanted you to feel some of the agony I'd experienced, and I'm ashamed to say that I was willing to go to any length to inflict it on you."

A sob shook her, and then she was in his arms.

He held her close while the tears she'd hoped had finally dried up flowed unchecked onto the shoulder of his sport coat. She thought he was just comforting her until she felt the sobs that shook his own body, and then she knew he was seeking comfort from her as well.

She put her arms around his neck and tried to give him, with caresses and broken words of understanding, the solace he so desperately needed.

For a long time they stood there clinging to each other, but eventually the sobs stopped and the tears ran dry. Nancy was the first to pull away, but Caleb made no effort to restrain her.

She reached for a paper napkin on the counter and used it to wipe her face and blow her nose. Caleb took a handkerchief from his back pocket and did the same. She leaned against the kitchen door frame and watched him as he slowly straightened his shoulders and raised his head before he turned to face her.

She was shaken by the depth of his grief. He had made it plain that he didn't want the baby, had left her rather than accept responsibility for it, so why was he so heartbroken? His face was white and ravaged, his eyes dark with anguish.

When he spoke his voice was ragged. "Why didn't you make an effort to get in touch with me when you lost the baby?"

Get in touch with him! How dare he even suggest that she was in any way at fault!

He must have seen the spark of rage that flared in her because he held up his hand and continued quickly, "I know you thought I'd deserted you, but you could at least have dropped a note to Dr. Gunther. He's been worried about you, too. You promised to keep in touch with him."

Again her temper started to ignite, but he hurried on, "I didn't run out on you, sweetheart. Such a thing never occurred to me. I knew I was behaving badly and hurting you by my inability to accept the idea of a child. That's why I arranged for counseling and spent two weeks in Chicago.

"I wrote you a letter, Nancy. I know you never received it, Dr. Gunther told me so, but I swear with God as my witness that I wrote it and put it in the mailbox before I left the island."

His gaze caught hers and held it. "You and I both know what happened to it." His tone was determined. "In my unhappy and confused state I forgot to close the door to the box, and the letter was ruined by the rainstorm later that day. When I inquired at the post office the postmistress told me. She also said she'd told you about it."

The letter! Nancy remembered wondering if it could have been for her, but she had rejected the idea as implausible. There had been no reason for him to write to her when he could more easily have picked up the phone or dropped by the clinic and told her in person.

She straightened up and jutted out her chin. "That doesn't prove a thing. It's convenient now to say the letter was to me, but in fact it could have been written to anyone. The writing was illegible, and you're not going to convince me that if you really were just planning to be away temporarily you wouldn't have discussed it with me personally. I was only a few blocks away, and you knew I was waiting to hear from you."

He ran his fingers through his hair. "I took the coward's way out. I never seem to say the right words when I'm trying to explain something to you. Look at the way I've messed up today. This morning when I caught you trying to leave instead of coming into my room I was so upset to think that I might have missed you that I growled at you and we quarreled. Tonight I did the same thing when I saw you walking in the pouring rain carrying that heavy grocery sack. It's almost more than I can stand to see you working so hard, living in this crowded closet and having to walk or take a bus everywhere you go.''

He jammed his hands in his pockets and moved away from her. ''I had hoped that by writing to you I could better make you understand why it was necessary for me to be away from you for a little while. You can't possibly know what a shock it was when you convinced me that you were pregnant with my child. The decision to have a vasectomy was not one I made lightly, but the circumstances were such that I felt it was necessary.''

He turned again and looked at her. ''In spite of my behavior I did care about the child. I wanted to do what was right, and I'm as capable of grief as any father.''

Nancy was bewildered and frightened by the familiar feelings of tenderness and compassion that Caleb so easily aroused in her. The same emotions that had been her undoing before. He pleaded his case so eloquently. If he wasn't a lawyer he should have been. Even his most outrageous behavior seemed logical when he explained it to her, but that could be just one more reason to distrust him. A silver tongue seldom spoke the truth. It just sprinkled a few facts in with the fiction to make the tale more believable.

She'd had ample proof that she couldn't trust her instincts where he was concerned, and she didn't know whether to believe there was a letter or not.

''I don't question your grief, Caleb,'' she said gently, ''but I am confused by it. I thought you'd be relieved. You made it plain that you didn't want the baby.''

He winced. ''Oh, I wanted the baby, but I was sick with the knowledge that bringing it into the world would be a selfish mistake. We can't always have what we want, my darling. Sometimes we have to make decisions that are heartbreaking. For me this was one of those times."

Nancy fought against the overpowering need to give in to her intuition and believe him. If he would only give her a strong reason for his inflexible attitude toward his own child. One that she could accept and understand.

"Why, Caleb?" she pleaded. "Tell me why it would have been selfish for us to have our baby? Is there a genetic problem? A disease that's handed down in your family from generation to generation?"

She'd considered that often since she'd left Washington Island. If he was afraid that the child might be born only to die an early death, or go through life badly impaired she could certainly sympathize with his fears.

For a long moment he hesitated, as though weighing an answer in his mind. She found herself actually wishing he would confirm her suspicion.

Instead, when he finally spoke he dashed her last hope. "I wish I could lie to you and say yes, but I won't. There's nothing like that in my family line."

He was toying with her again. Asking her to believe him but giving her no reason to. Well, dammit, she was entitled to some answers.

"Just tell me one thing," she said, and her tone betrayed the anger that was once more building in her, "and I want the truth. No evasions and no lies. Why did you go back to Washington Island? What decision did you come to while you were gone?"

This time he didn't pause but looked directly at her as he spoke. "I decided that life without you wasn't worth living, and I went back to tell you that I wanted the baby and to ask you to marry me."

Something exploded inside Nancy, and the anger of a moment ago turned to fury. "You bastard," she hissed. "Are you telling me that after almost three weeks of making me feel like a slut because I was pregnant with your child you were going to waltz back into my life and tell me that you had finally decided to do the right thing and marry me?"

Caleb gasped, and if possible he went even whiter as he opened his mouth to speak, but she was in no mood to listen. "Am I just supposed to ignore the fact that it took all that time to decide you wanted me after all and be delighted that you finally condescended to accept your own daughter?"

Too wrought up to stand still she began to walk up and down. "Well, I hate to disillusion you, Prince Charming, but that doesn't sound like undying love to me. All summer you'd been telling me that you loved me but wouldn't marry me, that you wanted me but when you left the island you wouldn't take me with you."

"Nancy!" Caleb's voice boomed in the small space, but she paid no attention.

"Okay, I'll admit I was a dope. You see, I still believed in fairy tales. I actually thought that by September you would love me too much to walk away from me. I was your naive Cinderella who went right on spinning fantasies about love and marriage and happy ever after, but it wasn't my fault I got pregnant. There's no way you're going to dump your load of guilt on me by telling me that if I'd just waited around like a good little girl you would have eventually come back and married me."

Caleb grabbed her arms and stopped her pacing. "Dammit, Nancy, be quiet and listen to me—"

With strength born of her rage she wrenched away from him and stood by the door. "I'm through listening to you,

Caleb. You speak lovingly, but you tell me half-truths. You twist facts to disguise the fact that you're actually saying only what you know I want to hear without giving me any insight at all into who you are, what you want and why you won't level with me.''

She put her hand on the doorknob. ''If you're telling the truth and you really do love me then why did it take you so long to decide to marry me? Why didn't you rejoice with me when I told you about the baby instead of suggesting I take the 'legal' way out?''

With a twist of her wrist she pulled the door open. ''On the other hand, if you're lying, if you were just amusing yourself with me last summer, then I hope you roast in hell.''

Caleb moved across the room to stand in front of her. ''That's what I've been doing for ten months now, love,'' he said softly and walked out the door and down the hall.

Chapter Eleven

Caleb spent another sleepless night pacing the floor and drinking. First whiskey, then coffee, and finally coffee laced with whiskey.

Dammit to hell, what was he doing wrong? Why was it that every time he spoke to Nancy he made her even madder at him?

He poured another half mug of coffee and filled it with liquor. If he faced facts he would admit that there was no way he was going to be able to convince Nancy that he could love her desperately but still not feel free to marry her unless he was willing to tell her everything about himself. He owed it to her and he owed it to himself, but could he do that without endangering the safety of others dear to him?

It had been nearly two years since he'd come close to dying in that explosion, and everything had been quiet. No unexpected incidents to cause worry.

He'd lived a lonely existence since Nancy had left, yearning for her, wondering about the child, never allowing himself to form close friendships. Surely after all this time the danger was past!

He sank down on the bed and rubbed his throbbing leg. But if it wasn't? This new Nancy Lloyd was different from the trusting, naive girl who had given herself to him so completely. She was harder, more suspicious, and she was filled with rage at him.

He couldn't blame her, but could he trust her with his secret? One thing was becoming certain. He would have to if he wanted to keep her with him, and the thought of losing her again was unbearable. He'd given up too much already, he had to have Nancy.

He stretched out on the bed, hoping to ease his aching leg and maybe get some sleep, but doubts continued to nag at him. When he'd agreed to this way of life it had never occurred to him that he might fall in love. He'd been half out of his mind with pain and the drugs that were supposed to relieve it, but even so his ego had insisted that he could control his emotions.

Caleb sighed and shifted to find a more comfortable position. The problem was that at that time he'd never known a woman like Nancy. Also, he'd never known the bone-chilling loneliness of not being able to trust anyone. Nor had he known how much physical agony the human body could endure. Put the three together and he had been a perfect setup for what happened when he got out of the hospital.

He looked at his watch. It was four-thirty a.m. Five-thirty in Washington. He would call Barry and talk to him about confiding in Nancy. Besides, he should have called him when he first arrived in Dallas. Caleb was supposed to check in if he changed location for more than a day.

Barry's reaction to the sound of Caleb's voice was immediate and angry. "Where in hell have you been? We've tried for days to contact you."

Apprehension clutched at Caleb's gut. What had gone wrong?

"I'm in Dallas," he said. "We finally found Nancy. She's down here working in a charity clinic. Sorry I didn't let you know sooner, but—"

"Texas? You're in Texas?" Barry sounded relieved. "Is Nancy okay? Which do you have, a son or a daughter?"

"Nancy's fine, but she lost the baby shortly after she got here." Caleb swallowed in an effort to keep his voice steady.

"Oh, hey, I'm sorry."

"Yeah, so am I." He didn't want to dwell on that fact, and he quickly changed the subject. "Look, Nancy's understandably mad as hell. She thinks I deserted her, and there's no way I can convince her that wasn't my intention without telling her the whole truth about me—"

"Don't do that!" Barry's tone brooked no argument.

Caleb argued anyway. "I've got to. Dammit, Barry, I'm thirty-seven years old. I could live another forty or fifty years and I'm not going to live them alone. I need Nancy. Hell, you're the one who told me I wasn't expected to behave like a monk."

"If you'll calm down and shut up for a few minutes I'll explain. Two days ago Tony Durante broke out of prison."

Caleb's whole body went rigid with shock, and he uttered an expletive he seldom used. "Danny and Luke. Are they—?"

"They're fine. We've got them and Alina under twenty-four-hour surveillance, but they're in no danger as long as the Durantes think you're dead. That's why I don't want you to take any chances right now. Wait until Tony's captured. It shouldn't take long. The government wants him locked up just as badly as you do. They've pulled out all the stops on this one. Tony doesn't have a chance of remaining free. Meanwhile Dallas is a good place for you. Where are you staying?''

Caleb was so shaken that for a moment he couldn't remember the name of the hotel. ''The Fairmont,'' he finally said.

Barry muttered a succinct oath. ''Probably the most expensive hotel in the city. I don't suppose you ever heard of Motel 6?'' His tone was sarcastic. ''Oh, well, we'll pick up the tab. It will give Uncle Sam another incentive to catch up with Tony Durante in a hurry. Just keep in touch and don't go wandering off again without letting me know where you are.''

Caleb relaxed a little. ''Thanks, Barry. I'd intended to stay here anyway until I get things settled with Nancy. There's just one more thing. My job . . .''

Barry sighed. ''I'll take care of it. It'll be there when you get back, and, Caleb, good luck with Nancy. I'm sorry I can't help you.''

It was a long weekend. Nancy spent it alternately wishing that Caleb would come back and hoping he wouldn't. She managed to keep busy on Saturday, because with Ricardo gone, even though she closed the door to the clinic at noon, it took her several more hours to finish with the patients who had come in the morning.

On Sunday she did all the usual things, cleaned house, did the laundry, went shopping, but she was constantly on edge, wondering if Caleb would call or come over.

As the day wore on and she hadn't heard from him she fought a restless urge to go to his hotel. In all the shock and confusion of his sudden appearance, plus their almost constant quarreling, she'd neglected to find out where he had been for the past ten months, what kind of work he did and where he lived. If he left Dallas without seeing her once more she would lose all contact with him.

On the other hand her good sense told her that Caleb Winters was well out of her life and that she should stay as far away from him as she could get.

By noon on Monday Nancy knew it had been a mistake to give Ricardo the week off without asking for a temporary helper to replace him. She couldn't take care of the desk work and treat the patients, plus handling all the interruptions, without falling further and further behind. At this rate she would be here until midnight.

As soon as she could find the time to take a break she'd phone Sister Mary Margaret and ask for help. Not that it would do any good, she admitted ruefully. There was a shortage of trained caregivers and those who wanted to work already had jobs that paid a lot better than this one. The few private-duty nurses were priced way out of the Sisters of Mercy's budget.

Nancy washed up after finishing with a patient and hurried into the waiting room to admit another one. Keeping track of the order in which the patients should be admitted was Ricardo's job, and she was hopelessly confused without him. She had no way of knowing which ones came in first, or who needed treatment most urgently so it was more or less a matter of making an educated guess. She could pretty much tell by looking at them which ones were sickest.

Her gaze swept the room and stopped abruptly at a familiar figure standing in the corner. It was Caleb. A wave of relief washed over her, but she forced her attention to the other patients until she saw a teenage boy with a discolored lump on his forehead. She beckoned to him, then looked at Caleb. "I'll see you, too," she said and led them both into the examining room.

She had the boy lie down on the table, then got a basin of hot, soapy water and washed the wound while Caleb stood just inside the closed door. Her pulse was racing at his nearness, but she determinedly ignored him and spoke to the young man.

"What happened?"

"I got hit," he mumbled.

"What with?" She examined his head and checked his eyes.

"A baseball bat."

"Did you lose consciousness? Black out?" She checked his ears and nose for internal bleeding.

"Nah. I got a hard head."

"Do you want to tell me about it?"

He shrugged. "Nothin' to tell. It was an accident."

Nancy knew better than to pry further. He wouldn't tell her what happened. Since he didn't have a concussion or any other signs of serious injury all she could do was give him a couple of aspirins and some instructions on how to care for himself. She picked up a record sheet. "What's your name?"

"John Jones."

She sighed. If they weren't going to give their right names, which most of them didn't, she wished they would at least think of something original.

"Age?"

"Eighteen."

Yeah, and so am I, she thought. He couldn't be more than fifteen, but these streetwise kids knew they would be badgered for the true stories of their injuries if they admitted to being underage.

She questioned him on his medical history and hoped that at least on this subject he was being truthful.

When she'd finished she helped him to sit up and slide off the table, all the time watching for signs of dizziness or nausea. His color was good and he didn't stagger so she let him leave with an admonition to come back in, or go to a hospital emergency room, if he didn't feel better by the next day.

When he'd gone she turned to Caleb. "Now, what can I do for you?"

He grinned. "Don't ask, sweetheart, I might tell you."

She wasn't in any mood to be teased after spending the past two days terrified that he might have dropped out of her life again, and cursing herself for not rejoicing at the prospect.

He saw her scowl and was immediately serious. "I came to take you to lunch."

She shook her head reluctantly. "I'm not going to have time for lunch today. Ricardo's gone to Mexico and I'm swamped here alone."

Caleb frowned. "Why don't you have help? You can't be expected to man this place all by yourself."

Nancy explained about Ricardo's problem with his wife, and her own impulsive suggestion that he take the week off and go after Maya. Also about the nurse shortage and the improbability of getting competent assistance on such short notice. "Maybe I can at least get someone to act as a receptionist and control the traffic."

Caleb grunted impatiently and unbuttoned his sport coat. "I'll help you," he said and took off the jacket. "Tell me what you want me to do."

Nancy stared at him. "But...but you're not qualified."

"Look, honey, anyone can sort out patients. I also happen to have been a medic in 'Nam, to say nothing of spending more time on the receiving end of the profession than any doctor. My first-aid credentials are all in order, so if you'll just tell me what you want me to do maybe we can get out of here before dark."

It took less than an hour for Caleb to catch on to the routine, and after that they worked smoothly together. They shared the tuna fish sandwich and orange she'd brought for lunch, eating on the run between patients.

Nancy was surprised at how competent he was, better than any nurse's aide she'd worked with. He had a way of calming the patients with a tender word, a distracting story or a warning scowl, and he was as skillful at applying bandages as Ricardo.

By seven o'clock they were finished, and Nancy wearily hoisted herself up on the examining table and sighed. "I don't think I've been off my feet all day," she said and swung her legs to loosen her aching muscles.

Caleb removed the lab coat he'd been wearing, then reached over and tugged hers off, putting them both in the hamper. "Lie down on your stomach," he said, and she obeyed without question, then jumped when he put his hands on her back.

"Just relax." His tone was soothing as he began to massage her shoulders, lightly at first, then gradually increasing the pressure until he was kneading muscles and sinew deep inside her. The tension that had kept her going all day began to lessen, and she buried her face in her folded arms and gave herself over to his ministrations.

Oh, it felt so good. Not just the expert massage, but the familiar, sensual caress of Caleb's hands roaming over her back. Would she ever get over wanting him? After she had lost the baby she had felt numb, and for a while she'd been lulled into thinking her feelings for Caleb had died, too, but then he came back.

She knew she should put a stop to this but she didn't have the strength. His touch was like a narcotic. She'd become addicted and couldn't free herself of the craving for it. He only had to look at her with that repressed hunger in his dark eyes or touch her with tender concern, as he was doing now, and she melted.

Nancy dozed and when she wakened Caleb was sprawled in a straight chair beside the examining table watching her. She sat up and rubbed her eyes. "Your massages are better than sleeping pills," she said and smiled. "How long have I been asleep? You should have wakened me."

He smiled back and stood. "Only about half an hour," he answered. "I didn't disturb you because I like to watch you sleep. I used to wake up early just so I could look at you lying in bed beside me, so warm and peaceful."

His voice was husky and made her shiver with the need to move off the table and into his arms. "Don't talk like that, Caleb," she said harshly and sidestepped him as she stood up. "We'd better get out of here. The clean-up man will be arriving soon."

"I put things away and straightened up," he said and shrugged into his sport coat. "I'm starved. Come on and I'll take you to dinner, since we weren't able to get away for lunch."

She looked down at her jeans and cotton T-shirt. "I'm not dressed to go out to dinner." She couldn't disguise her disappointment. "No self-respecting restaurant would let me in."

He looked her over slowly, starting with her cropped haircut and full, rosy lips, past the firm, high breasts that strained her shirt, her slender waist and flaring hips, and continued from her denim-clad thighs down to her white running shoes. "You look beautiful," he said simply. "But if you would rather, we can pick up fried chicken to go and take it to your place."

She'd been caught in a trap of her own making. It was folly to be alone with him in a place as intimate as her apartment or his hotel room, but the only alternative was to refuse to eat with him at all, and she couldn't bring herself to do that.

They ate their chicken, mashed potatoes and gravy, cole slaw and biscuits at her yellow Formica table and talked about the clinic.

"We get Dallas's human eyesores," Nancy said. "The orphans, homeless women and children, alcoholics and mentally ill, who beg for food and sleep in the alleys. The two hundred-plus patients who stream through the clinic each week suffer cat, rat and dog bites; infections caused by intravenous drug use with dirty needles; bullet wounds and cuts; broken limbs; hepatitis; pneumonia; and severe drug problems."

"But there are hospital emergency areas in the city," Caleb protested. "Why don't they go there?"

"There're a lot of them," she said scornfully, "but because most of our patients have little or no money they're basically excluded from care at established hospitals. When they get sick they come to me because they know I won't demand payment. Neither do I hand them over to the police unless I'm dealing with a gunshot wound or something else that the law requires I report."

When they'd finished dinner they took their banana cream pie and coffee over to the lumpy sofa. Nancy noticed that he winced with each step. "Sit at the end and stretch your legs out in front of you on the cushions," she suggested.

He looked at the sofa, then back at her. "But then there won't be room for you."

The plaintive note in his voice made her knees turn to jelly, but she tried to ignore it. "That's all right, I'll sit over there in the rocker."

He put his arm around her waist and drew her against him and she was lost. "I want you right here with me," he said against her hair.

It was like coming home at last, and she was powerless to move out of the embrace she'd longed for. "Caleb, please..."

He put his other arm around her and held her full length against him. "Please what?" He sounded breathless.

Her palms were against his chest, but she didn't have the strength to push him away. "Please don't do this." She was breathless, too. "You know you're taking unfair advantage of my feelings for you. I've never denied them, but you haven't given me much reason to trust you." She rubbed her face against the soft cotton of his shirt. "If you really do care for me, then give me more time. Don't overwhelm me."

For a moment his arms tightened, as if he wouldn't, couldn't, let her go. "Will you sit next to me on the couch?"

She answered him with another question. "Your legs hurt, don't they?"

"Yes, but they usually do. It's no big deal."

She snuggled closer. "It is to me. You've been on them far too much today. I'll sit on the sofa with you, and you can put your feet in my lap."

"That's not what I had in mind," he muttered.

"I know, but it's the best you're going to get. Agreed?"

He sighed. "If you say so, but can we stand here like this a little while longer?"

She was achingly aware of his aroused manhood pressing into the lower part of her stomach, and it was driving her crazy with the desire to sheathe him in her throbbing core. To once more be one with this man who seemed destined to become the other half of her.

If she didn't break away from him right now she wouldn't be able to, but then she still wasn't sure that he wouldn't leave her again when the going got rough. She took a deep breath and pushed her hands against his chest. "No, Caleb. Sit down, and you can put your legs up."

Reluctantly he released her, and she helped him stretch out on the couch, then sat down at the other end and put his feet in her lap. "Better?" she asked.

"That depends on what part of my anatomy you're talking about," he grumbled. "I should have taken off my shoes, they're too heavy on your legs."

He started to raise his feet, but Nancy captured them in her hands. "I'll do it," she said and untied his right shoe and removed it and his sock, then did the same with the left.

She settled his bare feet against her thighs and massaged them. They were long and narrow and well formed. Apparently they'd been spared the fate of his legs in the blast, since they had no scars or broken bones.

He shifted slightly, and she looked up. "Am I tickling you? I didn't mean to."

"No," he said lazily. "I like it. I didn't know feet were an erogenous zone."

Her hands stilled and she stared at him. "You're kidding!"

He grinned. "If you come up here I'll prove it."

His tone had an enticing quality that made her blush, and she dropped her hands to her sides. "I'm sorry. I didn't mean..."

He was instantly contrite. "No, I'm the one who's sorry. I hoped you knew what you were doing, but please, don't stop."

Nancy looked away, embarrassed. "I'm not going to tease you—"

"Honey, it's not teasing when you're only doing what I ask. I understand that it won't go any further, and I promise to behave myself. I love it when you touch me."

She closed her eyes and stifled a groan. She loved to touch him. Just having his feet in her lap, so close to the heat he was building in her, was ecstasy. If he understood that she wasn't just leading him on, surely it couldn't do any harm to give in to his request.

She opened her eyes and brought her hands back up to wrap them both around his right foot, then began to knead it using enough pressure so it wouldn't tickle. In an effort to neutralize the sensual tension she started to talk. "You haven't told me where you're living now or what you're doing. Have you been able to go back to work?"

"I work in finance and accounting at Tooele Army Depot in Salt Lake City," he said. "When I got back to Washington Island and found you gone I immediately started looking for you. You'd told Dr. Gunther that you were going to Detroit, but when we checked with the medical group there they hadn't contacted you since they were still processing applications. Why in God's name did you lie to Arnie, Nancy? He was nearly as frantic as I was when we found out you'd simply disappeared."

She pressed her lips together. "I—I didn't exactly lie. He asked me if that was where I was going and I didn't deny it."

"You didn't exactly tell the truth, either. You assured him that you would write as soon as you were settled, but you never did. If you honestly thought that I wasn't coming back why didn't you keep in touch with Arnie? He didn't know where I was, so if you didn't want me to know where you were he couldn't have told me."

Nancy didn't like the turn the conversation had taken. Caleb was right. If she'd truly believed that he'd disappeared for good she would have confided in the doctor. Why hadn't she?

"I wasn't thinking straight," she explained hesitantly. "I'd had three severe shocks in about ten days. First, the discovery that I was pregnant. Second, your negative reaction, and third, your disappearance. All I knew was that you didn't want either me or the baby, and I had to get away. I couldn't sit around waiting and wondering and hoping that you might come back someday."

She realized that she was practically pummeling his foot and moved her hands to the other one. "It's easy for you to say now that you wanted me and our child all along, but at the time you told me you had no intention of marrying and raising a family. That's exactly what you said, Caleb, and don't try to deny it."

He ran both hands over his face before answering. "I know," he said wearily. "I've got a lot of nerve accusing you of lying when I've done so much of it that it's become almost second nature."

He changed position and swung his legs painfully over the side of the sofa. "I have no one but myself to blame for the shambles I've made of our relationship. You did what most resourceful women would have done under the circumstances. You took charge of your life and made the best of the cards you'd been dealt."

He reached over and took her hand. "I have an enormous amount of respect for you, Nancy. It wasn't easy to uproot yourself and start over like that. I'm just so damn sorry that you never got my letter. I should have called you from Chicago, but I'd been advised not to until I got things straightened out in my mind. That's no excuse, though. Even if you had received the letter I still should have called just to check in. I admit that I wasn't thinking straight, either.''

He turned her hand over and kissed the palm, then held it to his mouth, sending pinpricks all the way up her arm and straight to her heart. How easily he could manipulate her. A few sweet words and a little physical contact and she was practically falling at his feet and begging to be stepped on.

Her bitter thoughts shocked her. Now she was wallowing in self-pity. Caleb had never taken advantage of her or mistreated her. It was true she'd given herself to him too soon after they met, but she'd been an aggressor as well as he. He might have waited until they knew each other better, but she had been so much in love, so eager to know him intimately, to lie in his arms and prove her love, even though he had never put his desire for her on that basis.

He stood and pulled her up with him. "I'm going to leave now," he said. "It's been a long day and we're both tired."

He put his arm around her waist and led her to the door with him. "Thank you for helping out today, Caleb," she said. "I would never have been able to manage by myself."

They stopped and he turned to her. "What time do you want me to pick you up in the morning?"

"Pick me up?"

"As long as I'll be driving I might as well swing around and take you, too."

Her eyes widened. "You mean you're going to help at the clinic tomorrow, too?" She had planned to call Sister

Mary Margaret tonight and ask if one of the nuns could come over for a few hours.

He smiled. "You said Ricardo was going to be gone all week, didn't you?"

She nodded. "Yes, but—"

"Then I'll work with you until he comes back."

The idea was too appealing for her to even consider it. How could she distance herself from him when he was working beside her every day?

"Caleb, you can't do that. Your legs would never hold out, and I doubt if there's any money in the budget to pay you."

He took her face in his hands and brushed a short strand of brown hair back with his fingers. "I'll stay off my legs as much as possible, and I don't remember asking to be paid. I'll be here at seven and take you out for breakfast. There's a coffee shop in my hotel and the food's great."

He leaned down and brushed his lips across hers. "Good night, my love," he whispered, and then he was gone.

Caleb eased himself into the hot tub and settled down in a comfortable position. Since going back to work he had come to rely on the warm swirling water of the Jacuzzi to soothe the knotted muscles and raw nerves in his legs at the end of the day. There was a spa in his apartment complex in Salt Lake City, and he only stayed in hotels that provided them when he traveled.

He leaned back and let the healing waters do their magic. If only he could persuade Nancy to come here and enjoy it with him. She worked so hard. He hadn't totally comprehended the grueling physical demands her profession made on her until he'd worked with her this afternoon. She never quit, or even sat down, but paced from one end of that clinic to the other attending to patients, dealing with belligerent bystanders, answering the phone and reassuring frightened children.

He had felt so inadequate even though he'd been busy all the time, too. The place was woefully understaffed, and no matter how hard he and Nancy had worked they were always behind. It was obvious that she felt good about what she was doing, and well she might, but at this rate she would burn herself out in a few years.

He leaned back and closed his eyes. At least she wasn't romantically interested in Ricardo. Caleb had barely been able to disguise his relief when she mentioned that her assistant was married and passionately in love with his wife. No one would deny that the man was attractive, and he was certainly protective of Nancy, but apparently their relationship was nothing more than a close friendship.

As the pain in his legs slowly dissolved he relaxed, and his mind wandered back to the tattered sofa in her tiny apartment and the feel of her strong, soft hands caressing his feet. The memory brought a tightening in his groin. She'd been surprised that massaging him there would arouse him, but he got that way every time he came near her. No matter where she touched him it started a fire that built until it was out of control.

Damn, just thinking about it inflamed him!

He shifted uncomfortably and tried to think of something less volatile, but Nancy was firmly entrenched in his mind and nothing could remove her. He wasn't even going to attempt it.

He'd learned one important thing about himself in the months since she had left him. Life wasn't worth living without her, and he didn't intend to do it. He would make any other sacrifice necessary to insure the safety of those others close to him, he would even give Barry a reasonable amount of time to settle things on the East Coast, but he would do whatever had to be done to keep Nancy with him.

He had the means to make her understand and forgive his seeming indifference, his bumbling mistakes, his inability to be open with her, and he intended to use it. He wouldn't lose her again!

Chapter Twelve

The following morning Nancy dressed in a pair of new, white, tailored gabardine slacks and a mint green blouse, an outfit that was suitable for breakfast at the Fairmont and, with the addition of a lab coat, for work.

She was waiting in front of her building when Caleb arrived to pick her up, and even at that early hour it was hot and sultry. The blast of arctic air that greeted them as they stepped into the lobby of the hotel was a welcome relief, and they dined in comfort in the elegant coffee shop. It was the first time Nancy had felt pampered since leaving Washington Island.

From there on it was all down hill. Besides the usual broken bones, drug problems and infections, by early afternoon they were getting patients with sunstroke, fainting spells and food poisoning, as well as other heat-related problems. Caleb was amazingly competent. He seemed to know what to do before being told, and they worked well together.

More than well. Nancy reveled in the affinity of their minds as well as their bodies. Why couldn't it be this way in their personal relationship? At one time she had thought it was, but why did he profess to care for her when he continued to shut her out of the most important areas of his life?

By three o'clock the heat and humidity had become almost unbearable even with all the fans going at top speed. They had both shed their lab coats, and Caleb had knotted rolled up linen towels around their foreheads to keep the sweat from dripping into their eyes.

He was sitting at the table in the outer room taking medical histories, and Nancy was examining a child with tonsilitis when she heard a high-pitched scream coming from just outside the clinic. Knowing Caleb would see to it she continued what she was doing as the commotion moved into the other room.

The scream stopped abruptly, but the babble of loud voices and children crying went on as Nancy quickly picked up the little boy and handed him to his mother. "Please take him out to the other room and wait. I'm afraid we have an emergency."

As Nancy readied the table for another patient Caleb appeared in the doorway followed by a distraught man carrying a sobbing woman. Two small hysterical children clutched at the man's legs as he walked.

"Lay her down here," Nancy ordered. The woman stiffened and screamed with pain again. "Take the children out. Ask someone in the waiting room to look after them."

The man laid the woman on the table, then looked at Nancy and began to speak in Spanish. He apparently didn't understand English, and Nancy spoke only a few words of Spanish.

Caleb restrained the thrashing woman on the table and tried to calm her while Nancy repeated her instructions about the children in gestures and halting phrases. The man finally understood and hustled the two little girls out, and Nancy turned her attention to the patient.

She was obviously in the last stage of labor, and Nancy had never seen her before. Even worse, she didn't speak or understand English either, and she was too frantic to make sense of Nancy's limited Spanish.

Nancy put on a clean, white coverall apron. "Do you speak Spanish?" she asked Caleb as she positioned the squirming patient on the table and draped her. They treated a lot of Hispanic patients at the clinic, but Ricardo was the one who talked to them. He had been teaching her the rudiments of the language, but she felt hopelessly inadequate with this panic-stricken couple.

"No," Caleb answered grimly as he strapped the protesting woman to the table, "but I've read Homer in the original Greek."

"Oh, great," Nancy groaned as she pushed the woman's wet, shapeless dress up to her distended waist and pulled off her underpants. "I can conjugate verbs in French—"

She stopped speaking abruptly and drew in a sharp breath. "Oh, my God!" she whispered.

"What's wrong?" Caleb spoke softly, too, although the woman was making too much noise to hear if they had shouted.

"She's fully dilated, and it's a footling breech presentation. One foot is already out. There's no time to transport her to a hospital."

Nancy felt a moment of panic. She had never seen the patient before, had no idea of her medical history, and a breech delivery was usually done by cesarean section.

She felt Caleb's calming hand on her shoulder. "Can we deliver it?" His voice was steady, promising her his full support.

A wave of gratitude flooded her. "It looks like we'll have to, doesn't it?" she said and sat up straighter. "I'm a licensed midwife, but a breech should be delivered in a hospital."

She was back in control now. Everything depended on her remaining calm and acting fast. "Call the number that's taped to the phone and ask for Dr. Phillip Ingram, stat. Tell them it's an emergency."

The woman's husband came back in, minus the children who could be heard wailing in the other room, and went immediately to his wife. She clutched his hand and yelled as her body arched in another contraction.

The doctor answered almost immediately, and Caleb switched on the amplifier. "What's the problem, Nancy?" Dr. Ingram's deep voice boomed into the room, startling the woman and her husband into a moment of silence.

Nancy explained the situation, raising her voice as another hard contraction ripped through the woman and the screaming began again. "I don't speak the language, and there's no time to take a medical history if I did," she concluded. "You'll have to talk me through it. I've never delivered a breech before."

"I have a nurse calling the paramedics," he said. "They'll come with an ambulance and an interpreter. Meanwhile widen the area with an episiotomy and watch that the cord doesn't prolapse and interfere with circulation to the fetus."

Nancy worked swiftly, following the doctor's directions. The baby was coming fast, and it was an extremely dangerous situation. Thank God for Dr. Ingram's cool and precise instructions. He seemed to know exactly what was going on. Almost as if he were looking over her shoulder.

With one last strenuous push from the mother the infant boy slid free and Nancy held him in her hands. He was at least seven pounds and his color was good, but he hadn't drawn a breath yet. She rubbed upward on his back, then patted it and he let out a wail that rivaled those of his two siblings in the other room.

Nancy felt jubilant as she placed the child on the mother's abdomen, then tied and cut the umbilical cord. "You have a baby son, a *niño*," she said. She wrapped the baby in a towel and laid him in his mother's waiting arms just as two husky paramedics appeared in the doorway.

The mother and father wept with relief and joy as they cuddled their new son.

A glow of satisfaction engulfed Nancy as she helped the paramedics. Caleb took the father out in the other room to fill out the necessary medical history form with the help of the translator.

Nancy didn't make a habit of delivering babies. In the cities there was usually a doctor nearby to do that, but when she did she always found it an exhilarating experience. Watching a tiny human being struggle so mightily to emerge into this imperfect world always renewed her faith that everything would turn out all right after all.

From then on there was no time to compare notes or talk over the experience. They locked the door and left two hours later, and Nancy didn't protest when Caleb suggested that they go to his hotel room and have dinner sent up. She needed to talk to him about the information he'd obtained after the translator had arrived. She didn't even know her patient's name.

"You can have first crack at the shower," he said when they stepped into the room. "I'll order dinner for eight o'clock. How does prime rib sound?"

She patted her stomach. "Great. I'm starved. Do you have a robe I can put on?"

He went to the closet and handed her one in maroon silk. "Here. There's shampoo and conditioner in the basket on the counter in the bathroom." He rubbed his knuckles along her cheek. "Take your time and relax," he said huskily, "you look about done in."

The warm water combined with the flower-scented soap and shampoo washed away the sweat and grime that had collected on her during the long, busy day. As the pulsating spray relaxed her knotted muscles her mind wandered to the times she and Caleb had showered together after making love. The picture of his long, thin body, scarred but still intensely virile and masculine caused a tightening in her groin and she clenched her jaws to keep from calling to him to come and join her.

Damn! She'd known it was a mistake to come to the secluded intimacy of his hotel room with him. She was especially vulnerable now after the euphoria of delivering an infant under difficult conditions. She and Caleb together had saved that precious life. There was no doubt about it. If they hadn't been immediately available the baby would surely have died. It made up a little for not being able to carry her own child to term.

At least they'd spared that young mother from the hell Nancy had known. That made the long hours and the low pay all worthwhile. She was glad she'd stayed on at the charity clinic instead of leaving for an easier, more financially rewarding position in one of the private medical groups that served patients in bright, new, air-conditioned offices.

A few minutes later Nancy entered the bedroom with Caleb's robe belted around her waist and relinquished the bathroom to him. She couldn't bring herself to put back on the soiled rumpled clothes that she'd worn all day, but she was uncomfortable wearing nothing but Caleb's robe.

The silkiness of it felt sensual against her still damp skin and she didn't need the extra stimulation. Neither did she want to give him any ideas he might not already have, but before she could decide what to do he emerged from the bathroom dressed in clean jeans and a pullover shirt.

Nancy felt even more vulnerable, although she remembered that he always covered himself with clothing to hide his scars. Even though he'd let her see him nude when they'd made love, he had never appeared before her less than fully clothed at other times.

Her glance traveled downward to his bare feet, and the memory of holding them in her lap and massaging them made her fingers twitch. She swung her gaze upward and it collided with his. It was then that she realized she'd been staring, and that he was equally intent on scrutinizing her.

She looked away, embarrassed. "I—I guess I should get dressed," she said inanely.

He reached out and touched the side of her throat. "Please don't," he said softly. "I never realized that robe could be so sexy."

The huskiness of his voice made her tingle. "But I—"

"You don't want to tease," he finished for her. "You're not. You're just pleasing me very much. I'm a grown man, sweetheart. I can control my baser instincts. I only want what you're willing to give, freely and without regret."

What she was willing to give? Right now she was willing to give him anything he wanted, and she didn't have to guess what that was. She could see the need in his dark eyes. It matched the need he must see in hers.

Almost of its own accord her hand reached up to touch his face, but just as it made contact there was a sharp knock on the door and a muffled voice called, "Room service."

The spell was broken, and Caleb muttered something under his breath as he walked away to let the waiter in.

They ate at the small, round table in front of the huge window, and had a sweeping view of downtown Dallas at night. Straight ahead, the Flying Red Horse atop the Magnolia Building soared against the sky; slightly to the right the 72 story Interface Plaza, called the Jolly Green Giant, stood in its transparent splendor outlined in lighted green tubing; and to the far right the lighted ball, like a round full moon, seemed suspended in midair atop the fifty foot Reunion Tower.

All this luxury brought nagging doubts and questions to Nancy's mind. She couldn't help but compare Caleb's present lodgings with the tiny rented cottage on Washington Island, or his expensive clothes with the cheap jeans and T-shirts that he'd formerly worn. He had told her he was working as an accountant, but would a new employee start out at a large enough salary to afford all of this? Also, how did he get what appeared to be unlimited time off to come to Texas to see her when he'd worked for less than a year?

She cut her thick, juicy prime rib. "You have a beautiful view," she said as an opening to approach the subject, "but isn't all this very expensive? I mean, even if you had a car or entertainment club discount it would still cost a lot to stay in a place like this."

Caleb buttered a piece of warm French bread. "That's true, but I chose it because it's close to both your apartment and the clinic."

That wasn't what she'd asked, although it was possible he could have misunderstood what she was getting at. Possible, but unlikely.

"It's a far cry from the cottage you lived in when I first knew you." She made no attempt to disguise the hint of sarcasm in her tone. "You were lucky to find such a well-paying job after being out of work for so long."

He stopped eating and looked at her. "I told you that I'd received a settlement after the accident," he said carefully.

"Yes," she said and looked away. "You did."

She'd had the impression when he'd mentioned the settlement that it was just enough to cover his medical expenses and tide him over until he could start working again. Had she jumped to the wrong conclusion, or had he deliberately misled her?

"Is something bothering you, Nancy?"

It surprised her that he was giving her an opening, but she intended to use it. "Yes, something is bothering me," she said and looked back at him. "I'm wondering how come you have the money and the leisure time to run all over the country looking for me, to stay in luxury hotels, rent expensive cars and take time off from the job you've only been working at for a few months. You told me numerous times last summer that marriage was out of the question for you because you weren't even sure you could earn a living."

Her mouth began to tremble and she took a sip of her coffee. "You said we shouldn't have the baby because you weren't sure you could take on the responsibility."

Her voice broke and she jumped up, tipping over the chair, and walked across the room with Caleb right behind her.

He caught her by the shoulders and turned her around. "Sweetheart, don't," he said and folded her into his arms. "I told you, I wasn't thinking straight at that time."

He rubbed his face in her soft, clean-smelling hair. "Last summer was a year ago. I'm in far better physical shape now than I was then. I'm also much improved emotionally, except for the hell I've been going through trying to find you. I didn't know then that I was going to be capable of the things I'm doing now."

He cuddled her against him tenderly, as though she might pull away if he weren't very, very careful.

If only she could. It was madness to let him hold her, but she was mesmerized by his touch, by the husky yearning in his voice as he murmured words that sounded so truthful, so reasonable.

"That's why I needed to be away from you," he continued. "The last thing I wanted was to leave you at a time like that, but I had to. I was too shocked and confused to make a rational decision without some counseling. There were...other complications as well."

She had been willing to believe him until he uttered that last sentence. "What other complications?" she demanded, stepping out of his embrace. "You keep making vague references to other responsibilities, but you won't tell me what they are."

When he didn't answer she whirled away. "You say you needed counseling, but why didn't you tell me that? I, of all people, would have understood."

"I told you—"

"I know. You told me you wrote me a letter." Her tone was bitter. "Well, I'm sorry, but I don't believe you. Obviously you wrote to somebody, but it wasn't to me. It's just too farfetched to believe that you would go to the trouble of writing a letter when I was only a few blocks away."

They'd had this argument before, and she hated it. Hated the bitterness and suspicion that made her quarrel with him. If only he would tell her the truth...

Caleb came toward her. "Nancy, my darling, if I'd stopped to try to explain I would never have been able to leave you. Why do you find that so difficult to believe? You were angry and disappointed in me. You had every reason to be. I'd let you down."

He reached out and put his hands on either side of her waist. "I very much doubt that you would have understood, and I was terrified of losing you."

She gasped and tried to argue, but he wouldn't let her interrupt.

"No, now think about it. It would have seemed to you like yet another rejection. God knows, you would have been entitled to think that. I'd been rejecting you in one way or another all summer. Then when you told me you were pregnant I behaved like such a bastard that you would have had every right to think I was running out on you."

She had to admit that he had a point, but still...

Somehow he'd managed to get her back into his arms again and was holding her loosely. "If you'd misunderstood or had been upset about my plan to go to Chicago, I wouldn't have gone, but that wouldn't have solved anything. I really needed to get away from you and talk to someone who could help me clear up my muddled thinking."

Nancy knew all about muddled thinking. Caleb muddled hers every time he touched her, and now he was doing it again. "Oh, Caleb, I—"

He hugged her close. "Let's talk about it later. We don't want all this food to get cold. Come back to the table and I'll tell you what I found out about the Esteban family."

She sighed. Why not? This argument would never be resolved, and she was hungry. They might as well finish their dinner. Then she'd dress and go home to her own apartment.

As they ate Caleb told her what he'd learned about the parents of the child they'd delivered earlier. "Their names are Juan and Carlotta Esteban, and they're in the country illegally. They're farm laborers and she hasn't even seen a doctor during this pregnancy. They were on their way back to Mexico to have the baby, but it got in a hurry and put in an appearance a week early."

Nancy shook her head sadly. "Before I started work here I wouldn't have believed that so many people go without medical care. Now nothing surprises me. What's going to happen to them?"

"I don't know," he said thoughtfully. "They'll probably be sent back to Mexico whether they still want to go or not. They're one lucky couple even so. They somehow found you to deliver their child. You were magnificent, Ms. Lloyd."

She shivered as the afternoon replayed itself in her mind. "I hope I never have another one like that," she said, emphatically. "I was so afraid..."

He put his hand over hers on top of the table. "No one would ever have known it," he said, his voice sincere. "You were as cool and calm as if you delivered footling breeches every day."

Nancy looked up at him and smiled. "I wouldn't have been nearly as calm if you hadn't been there. Thank you, Caleb, for the assistance. Not only today, but for the whole week. There're not many men who would use most of their vacation time working for free in a sweltering charity clinic in the city's slums."

He lifted her hand and kissed the palm. His lips were firm but gentle and sent little shock waves all the way up her arm.

"I'm not on vacation, sweetheart," he murmured. "I came here to find you, and I'm going to stay until you agree to marry me."

She blinked and pulled her hand away as she bolted upright in her chair. "Marry you!" The words seemed to echo through the room. "You still want to marry me?"

His eyes widened with surprise. "Of course I want to marry you. I told you that's what I'd decided while I was away."

"B-but there's no longer a baby. You have no reason to marry me now."

Caleb stood and pulled her into his arms. "Nancy, my precious love, for someone as bright and talented as you are, you're amazingly dense at times. My decision to ask you to marry me had nothing to do with the baby you were carrying. A marriage entered into simply because we'd inadvertently conceived a child would have been a mistake for all three of us. I would have been a father to our daughter in every way you would have allowed even if we hadn't married, but I wanted, and still want, the legal commitment because I love you so much that I can't face a future without you."

Nancy felt as if she'd had the breath squooshed out of her. Caleb was telling her he loved her and wanted to marry her. Words she'd wanted so desperately to hear, but could she believe them now? He had told her before that he loved her, but then, when she'd really needed him, he wasn't there.

She tried to squirm out of his embrace, but he wouldn't let her go. Finally she stood still in the circle of his arms and looked at him. "Why did it take you so long to come to that conclusion?"

His expression was one of desolation. "That's still a raw spot with you, isn't it?" His tone was heavy with regret. "Can't you just accept the fact that I'm an imperfect man who made a mistake? Haven't you ever been wrong, Nancy?"

She winced as the question stabbed her conscience. Oh yes, she'd been wrong. She'd been wrong to fall in love with a man she'd just met. She'd been wrong to allow herself to get so emotionally involved with a patient. She'd made a grave mistake by making love with him so soon, before she knew anything about him.

Her list of errors was long, but that didn't mean she had to repeat them. Neither could she bring herself to break off the relationship completely. Her love for him was too compelling, but this time she would take it slowly, let him court her and get to know him. When he had to leave and go back to Salt Lake City they could write letters, talk to each other on the phone. They would be friends but not lovers until she was sure he wouldn't bolt again the first time something went wrong.

All her lofty intentions were shattered when his hands wandered down her hips and pressed her against his rigid shaft, sending tremors radiating from the sensitive core of her.

Her arms fastened around his narrow waist in an automatic reflex and she held him even as her brain screamed a protest. Sweet Lord, why did she have to want him so badly? She hadn't learned a thing from these long, lonely agonizing months. She was just a seething mass of hormones that refused to be weaned from Caleb Winters.

A low moan escaped from deep in her throat. "Oh, Caleb..." She lifted her face to meet his seeking lips, and the fire that had been building between them burst into a roaring flame.

They were fused together as she opened her mouth to his intimate invasion and again tasted the heady essence of him. It was an imitation of the searing union their bodies had been denied for so long, and her tongue welcomed his with eager caresses.

In an instinctive movement her hips began the rhythmic tempo of coupling. Caleb gasped and strained against her, then reluctantly but firmly lifted his head and put her away from him. "Sweetheart, I know I said I could control myself, but not if you tempt me beyond endurance."

He was breathing heavily, and his tone was ragged with frustration as he turned away and ran his hand through his hair.

Nancy's whole body quivered with an equal frustration, and she sat down on the edge of the bed to steady herself. "I—I believe you said you wanted what I was willing to give." Her voice was as raspy as his. "You couldn't possibly have thought that I wasn't willing just now."

He was standing at the window with his back to her. "Ah, yes," he said softly. "Wonderfully, passionately willing, but I also said I wanted you to come to me freely and with no regrets."

He turned to face her then, and the look of strain on his face told her what his battle to regain control had cost him. "Can you honestly say you would have had no regrets? That you wouldn't have hated me in the morning for making a promise I couldn't keep?"

She knew he was right, and she dropped her gaze and hung her head in shame. It was selfish and unrealistic of

her to expect him to exert all the self-control and then cas-
tigate him when he failed. She wanted him, but she didn't
have the guts to give herself to him and then share the
blame if it turned out to be a mistake.

"I...I'm sorry," she said, still not looking at him. "I'll
get dressed now and leave."

She stood up, but two steps put him beside her. He cradled her face with his hands and lifted it. "Please don't go,
Nancy," he said urgently. "Stay with me, at least for a
while longer. They show current movies on this television.
We can choose one and—"

Their gazes clung, and she melted at the tenderness that
shone from his beautiful brown eyes. "I don't think that's
a good idea," she whispered just before their lips came
together in a soft, sweet but short exchange.

"It's a wonderful idea." He brushed her lips with his
again and stroked his fingers through her short hair. "I'll
admit my overactive male hormones make uncomfortable
demands when we're together, but I want so much more
from you than just sex. I want you with me where I can see
you, touch you, talk to you. Go pick out the movie you
want and push the button while I fix the bed—"

Nancy's eyes widened. "The bed?"

He chuckled. "Take it easy. I'm not setting up a seduction scene. The bed is the most comfortable place to watch
television from.

"The pillows are stuffed with goose down," he said as
he began rearranging them. "They're soft but firm, and
they'll probably lull you to sleep before the movie's over."
He straightened. "There now, try that and tell me if you've
ever been more pampered."

He had turned down the sheet and quilted spread and
made a virtual nest of the six large pillows. It looked too

good to resist, and she crawled into it and settled herself with a long, contented sigh.

"Oh my, how do you ever force yourself out of this in the morning?" she asked as she grappled with the robe that had come loose and was threatening to expose more of her than was either wise or decent.

Caleb retrieved the sheet from the bottom of the bed and handed it to her. "Here," he said with a hint of amusement, "this will protect your modesty and my sanity. Besides the air conditioner is turned up high and it gets chilly when you're not moving."

She tightened the robe around her and snuggled under the sheet in decadent luxury while he went over to the television and read the list of movies to her. She chose one that starred her favorite comedian, and he touched the right button, then turned off all the lights before he climbed in and settled himself beside her in the nest of pillows.

The room was dark except for the light coming form the television screen and the skyscrapers outside the undraped window. Nancy tensed and moved as far away from him as she could. She wanted to be with him, but she knew she was playing with fire. There was nothing platonic about their feelings for each other, and they were both passionate, sexual beings with strong appetites. She didn't want to set herself up again for the anguish of unconsummated arousal. Neither did she want to do that to Caleb.

The movie had begun a few minutes before they started watching and by the time they had figured out the plot and character relationships Nancy had realized that Caleb wasn't going to make a pass at her. She relaxed and inadvertently moved closer.

The plot was hilarious, a spoof on an old-fashioned murder mystery. When the body fell out of the closet,

Nancy, taken by surprise, screamed and buried her face in Caleb's chest. He caught her in his arms and held her as they laughed at the comic antics of the fictional rookie cop who had opened the door.

Caleb laid his cheek on the top of her head and cuddled her close. She didn't protest. She couldn't. She was too content. It was madness, but she didn't care. She would pay the price later, but for now she was going to enjoy.

Apparently Caleb felt the same way. Although she was pressed against his hip and chest with her arms around his waist, and one of his hands lay on her silk-covered stomach, he made no effort to seduce her with intimate caresses or kisses. He lay quietly, and while his heartbeat under her cheek was faster than normal and she felt a fine thread of tension in him, he seemed to be relaxed and enjoying the show.

They continued to chuckle at intervals for over an hour and a half, but as it got later Nancy's eyelids got heavier until she was forced to close them. She missed some of the punch lines and knew she was dozing off now and then.

By the time the movie ended she was only partially awake. She stretched her legs and rubbed her face in Caleb's chest. She had never been so comfortable in her whole life, she realized, as she sleepily brought her knee up and positioned it across his thigh.

It was his swift intake of breath and the moan that followed that wakened her. She blinked at the darkness of the room and raised her head. Caleb had shut off the television with the remote control, and the only illumination was from the lights outside the window. "Caleb? Darling, did I hurt you?"

He chuckled and caressed her cheek with his palm. "No, love, but you're about to drive me crazy with all that wiggling around, and could you please move your knee?"

It was only then that she realized where she'd placed it, and the long, hard ridge that lay so intimately beneath her knee positively throbbed with heat even through the heavy material of his jeans.

Appalled, she pulled her leg away quickly and tried to sit up. "Oh damn, I'm sorry," she said, her tone gravelly with embarrassment. "I didn't mean...that is I...I've got to get dressed and go home."

She tried to roll off the bed, but got caught in all the pillows and the sheet, Caleb turned on his side and reached for her, then hauled her back against him. "It's not terminal," he muttered as he curled himself around her, spoon style. "Just relax and go to sleep."

She snuggled against him and again felt the hardness of his arousal, this time against her buttocks. A rush of liquid warmth signaled her body's readiness to receive him and she had to force herself not to rub against him. "Caleb." It came out as a groan. "I can't spend the night in bed with you."

He put his hand underneath the robe and cupped one aching breast. "Of course you can, my darling. You didn't really think I was going to let you leave me tonight, did you?"

She smiled and sank into the warmth of his embrace. "I hoped you wouldn't," she said softly and closed her eyes.

Chapter Thirteen

Caleb lay cuddling a sleeping Nancy in his arms. He'd untied the sash of the robe she was wearing, and one of his hands held her soft, full breast while the other rested on her firm, bare belly. Except for the turbulence in his loins he'd never been so comfortable and content in his life.

It was difficult not to shudder as he remembered the ten months when she had disappeared into the millions of faceless, nameless people who populated the country. If it hadn't been for the Justice Department's help he would never have found her, and the very thought was terrifying.

He nuzzled the warm, damp hollow at the side of her neck. She had the clean smell of soap mingled with the woman scent that was exclusively hers. It set up a tingling in his anatomy that made him grind his teeth with the effort at control, and was glad she was still sleeping. He didn't have to be on guard against doing or saying something to remind her that he had behaved like a jerk in the past.

He sighed and moved his lips to her nape. He used to have to push her shimmering hair off it before he could sample her skin's sweetness, but now the long, dark tendrils were gone and the back of her neck was bare. If only he'd been there to stop her from cutting it, to take care of her so she wouldn't have had to go to work in that lice-infested clinic.

He stifled a self-deprecating hoot. At the time he couldn't even take care of himself, how could he have hoped to look after her? It probably wouldn't have made any difference, anyway. Nancy made her own decisions, and he had to admit that she seemed to be born for the work she was now doing.

He spread the fingers of his hand caressing her stomach. Two of them tangled with the dark curls that protected the moist sheath which had encased him and driven him to the brink of madness in the past. A sharp jolt to his already engorged masculinity warned him not to proceed any further with that exploration. Besides, he didn't want to wake her.

With a concentrated effort he began relaxing his tense muscles. He wanted to stay awake all night savoring the feel, the fragrance and the warmth of the woman he held in his arms. He couldn't be sure he would ever again be allowed the privilege, but tomorrow promised to be another busy day. He had to be alert if he were to carry his share of the load, and he wanted more than anything to make things as easy for her as he could.

He would sleep well tonight, better than he had in months, because he finally had Nancy in his arms and in his bed, even if only for a few hours. The relief was indescribable.

* * *

Nancy was pulled out of a deep slumber by someone shaking her and calling her name. "Sweetheart, wake up. Breakfast will be here any minute, and then we have to go by your apartment so you can put on clean clothes before going to the clinic."

She opened her eyes and looked into Caleb's shining brown ones. "Caleb!" She sat up and then remembered where she was.

He sank down on the side of the bed and gathered her in his arms. He felt and smelled fresh and clean in his crisp cotton shirt and jeans, and she twined her arms around his neck and hugged him. "How did you get up and dress without me even hearing you?" she asked with a yawn.

"You were out for the count, honey," he replied cheerfully. "I've been trying to wake you for several minutes. You must have been exhausted last night."

"I guess I was." She leaned forward and kissed the hollow at the base of his throat. "Also, I've never slept in such a comfortable bed before." She buried her face in his shoulder. "I felt safe and secure with you beside me."

His arms tightened around her, pulling her even closer. "I hate to tell you this," he growled, "but you're not all that safe with me. Don't trust me too far."

He held her a little away from him and lowered his head. It wasn't until she felt his lips on her bare breast that she realized the robe was open and she was fully exposed. By then it was too late. She clutched at him, bringing him down with her, as he lowered her back into the pillows.

She made little mewling sounds in her throat as his tongue circled her nipple before he took it into his mouth. His suckling tugged at invisible chords deep within her and made them quiver.

He moved to the other breast and repeated his fondling until she was strung as tightly as a harp string. Her hands roamed freely over him, but the material of his shirt was an intrusion between her bare skin and his. With a strong tug she pulled the garment out of his jeans and put her hands under it.

His back wasn't as rough as she had remembered. That meant that the scars had healed and softened, but her fingers were still able to trace them in a loving caress. He shivered and nestled his face in the valley between the breasts he'd been so eagerly sensitizing.

"I missed you, Nancy," he murmured as he nibbled delicately at the warm flesh next to his mouth. "And that's the understatement of all time. There were times when I was so depressed I actually wished I hadn't fought so hard to live after the accident."

Her whole body stiffened with alarm. "Caleb, no!"

He lifted his head to look at her, puzzled, then understanding dawned. "No, love, I don't mean I was suicidal. After such a close brush with death I would never deliberately destroy something as precious as life, but without you the future looked bleak indeed."

He laid his head back down where it had been and she relaxed. "Don't ever run away from me again." There was a touch of desperation in his tone. "If you decide that you truly don't want me in your life I'll leave and not bother you, but please keep in touch. I need to know where you are, and if you're all right." His arms tightened around her. "Promise, Nancy?"

Before she could answer there was a knock on the door, and with a strong sense of déjà vu they heard a voice call, "Room service."

Caleb raised up and kissed her quickly. "Good old room service," he said ruefully and stood. "Apparently I can count on them to intrude every time I forget my promise."

He threw back the covers and helped her climb out of bed. "You go on into the bathroom and get dressed while I let him in." He pulled her robe shut and tied the sash as the knock sounded again. "Get a move on," he said with a loving pat on her bottom, "before I send him away and take up where we left off."

It was another grueling day, and at the end of it Nancy refused Caleb's invitation to dinner. "No, Caleb, not tonight. We both know how it would end, and I need more time to sort out my feelings."

She wouldn't allow him to drive her home, either, insisting on taking the bus. He was angry, but she was afraid of what was happening between them.

That night she paced the floor while her mind seethed with unresolved conflicts. Holding Caleb at arm's length became more difficult each day. He was so loving, so willing to put up with her restrictions, and so persuasive when he said he loved her, needed her in order to function.

If she could believe that, she could forgive him anything—but then she had believed him before when he had said he loved her. She'd given herself to him in every way she could, and he had berated her for insisting on having their baby, then walked out. She couldn't forget those awful weeks. She had been too badly scarred by rejection during her childhood to simply shrug off one as shattering as Caleb's had been.

She ran her hands through her already tousled hair. Still, he'd gone back to Washington Island. Surely that action indicated he was telling the truth about everything else. The obvious solution would be to give him another chance.

No relationship came with a gilt-edged guarantee. She would never know if it would work if she didn't try.

The battle with her insecurities continued, and by the time she collapsed into bed and fell asleep from pure mental exhaustion she still hadn't come to a clear-cut decision. She suspected that she would simply have to take matters one at a time and hope she wouldn't make any irreparable mistakes.

Thursday didn't dawn, it washed in on a tide of thunder, lightning and rain. Caleb insisted on picking Nancy up and driving her to work, even though she protested that she was used to catching the bus in a rainstorm.

It persisted all morning, and their patient load was light. Those who had shelters stayed in them, and those who didn't huddled under anything that would keep them reasonably dry. Nancy used the time to bring her records up to date and to work on her quarterly report to the city and the diocese, while Caleb opened boxes of supplies that had recently been delivered and put them away.

At noon they locked the door and Caleb drove the few blocks to the restored Old Town section where he parked at the curb and ushered her to the end of the block. The old wooden two-story building they entered was an Italian restaurant, rustic and unpretentious.

"I took a guided tour of the city one day while you were working," he said as they stopped at the end of the line of people waiting inside the door. "We were in the West End Historic District at lunchtime, and the bus driver recommended this place as having good food and fast service. You have to line up here to order if you want the ten-minute service."

When they came out of the restaurant half an hour later the rain had stopped. When they drove past the clinic in search of a parking space Nancy gasped and grabbed the door handle. "Caleb, someone's in there! The door's open. Stop and let me out."

Caleb clutched her arm as he continued up the street toward an empty spot at the curb. "You stay with me," he ordered. "I'm not going to let you go charging in all by yourself."

He quickly parked the car, and they ran back to the clinic. Before Caleb could restrain her Nancy pushed open the screen and rushed inside to be confronted by a grinning Ricardo and his pretty wife, Maya.

"Ricardo!" She ran into his open arms, then turned and hugged the laughing lady beside him. "Maya, I wasn't expecting you back until Sunday. Did you just arrive?"

"We did," Ric confirmed. He shook hands with Caleb and introduced his wife.

It took nearly an hour for the two couples to bring each other up to date on their activities during the week, then Ric and Maya prepared to leave. "We're going home now and unpack, but Maya and I will take care of the clinic tomorrow. You two deserve a couple of days off." He turned to Caleb. "I can't tell you how much I appreciate your helping out here while I was gone. I felt like a lowlife deserting Nancy that way." He put his arm around Maya and started toward the door. "Have fun this weekend. I'll see you on Monday, Nancy."

By two o'clock the sun was shining, the weather was hot and steamy, and the clinic was back to business as usual. Nancy's happiness at seeing Ricardo and Maya dimmed as she faced the fact that after today Caleb would no longer be working with her.

Would he stay on in Dallas, as he'd threatened, if she continued to refuse to marry him or even to make love with him? Or would he decide he'd had enough of her procrastinating and go back to Salt Lake City to look for someone more amenable to share his life and his bed?

No matter what he said she knew Caleb wasn't the type of man to sit around indefinitely waiting for her to decide to forgive him for something he insisted wasn't his fault. On the other hand, he hadn't wanted the baby when she had told him about it. He'd said as much, and even suggested that she terminate the pregnancy. Wasn't it logical for her to assume that he had simply packed up and left her?

But then why had he gone back? And why had he spent so much time and money tracking her to Dallas?

It was the same old merry-go-round that she'd been on ever since he'd found her. She hated seesawing back and forth, loving him but unable to trust him.

Unfortunately there was no middle course if she chose a future with Caleb. It would either be a dream come true, or a nightmare revisited.

They closed the clinic at five o'clock, and as they got into Caleb's car he said, "I see by the paper that Dallas has a series of summer musicals featuring Broadway touring companies. *Les Misérables* is playing this week. I can arrange for tickets from the concierge at the hotel if you would like to go tonight."

Nancy felt a surge of excitement. "I'd love to," she said. "I haven't taken in any of the nightlife here."

He reached over and took her hand as he maneuvered the car through traffic. "Haven't you dated at all?"

"The thought never occurred to me," she said. "I don't even know anyone here other than the people I work with."

He squeezed her hand. "It's the same way with me in Salt Lake City. Some of the guys at work have tried to fix

me up with women. I wasn't even tempted. I don't want
any woman but you, love. I suspect that I never will, even
if you won't..."

He didn't finish the sentence, but put her hand on his
thigh and held it there. She didn't attempt to remove it. His
leg was fleshier and more firm than it had been the last
time she'd caressed it. Besides putting on weight he had
obviously been keeping up with his exercises.

His muscles flexed under her palm, and she realized
she'd been kneading him gently. Dammit, why was she
being so stubborn? It wasn't as if she'd never made love
with him. Besides, she couldn't be any more miserable with
him than she was without him.

Deliberately now she let her fingers roam over the heavy
denim of his jeans, and again his muscles jumped. His
hand tightened on hers, pressing it harder against him, but
he was silent as they neared her apartment.

He parked in the nearest space and got out of the car.
"You don't have to see me to the door," she said as he
came around and helped her out. "Just tell me what time
you'll call for me."

He took her arm and put it through his as he walked
along beside her. "The show starts at eight-fifteen. I'll
come for you about seven. That will give us time to go
someplace and have a bite to eat first."

They reached her building and stepped into the dim
foyer. The area was empty, and Caleb led her to a shad-
owy corner away from the elevator.

He turned and took her in his arms. "If you're going to
leave me in this condition the least you can do is kiss me
and make it better," he murmured huskily and lowered his
mouth to hers.

She gave herself up to the kiss that she could no longer
deny. Her palms rubbed slowly up his arms and met be-

hind his neck to hold him and pleasure him as he was pleasuring her.

He lifted his head, but only to reposition it as his lips took hers again and again and again, until she was dizzy with swirling desire. His hands had lowered to press her against him leaving no doubt about what his "condition" was.

When they finally came up for air she buried her face in his shoulder and whispered, "Kissing doesn't usually make it better."

"Now you tell me," he moaned. "Nancy, will you come to my room after the show?"

The temptation was almost irresistible, and she had to force herself to be sensible. "I...I don't think that's a very wise idea, Caleb."

"We won't do anything you don't want to do, I promise." He shivered as he clutched her closer still. "Oh, sweetheart, if I could only make you understand how much I love you." There was a tinge of misery in his voice that tore at her.

She stroked his cheek with hers. "All right, darling," she whispered against his ear. "I know you care about me, and I love you more than I'm willing to admit even to myself. I'm just not sure that I'm ready to make a commitment yet."

The Fair Park Music Hall was packed with theatergoers thrilled at the opportunity to see the smash London and Broadway musical adapted from Victor Hugo's classic novel. Nancy finally even managed to ignore the shimmering sensual tension that radiated between Caleb and her as she became caught up in the powerful music and the fascinating story of Jean Valjean and his tormentor, Inspector Javert.

When it was over the enthusiastic audience rose to their feet and brought the actors back time after time with thundering ovations. The palms of Nancy's hands stung from clapping before the curtain was finally brought down for the last time.

She clung to Caleb's arm as they threaded their way through the crowded hall. "Didn't you just love it?" she asked. "I'm so glad you brought me."

He looked down at her and smiled. "The sparkle in your eyes is more than worth the price of admission. I'll have to remember to take you to the theater often."

"Oh yes, please do. I've never been to a live musical before, although I've seen a lot of them as movies." She was positively bubbling with exhilaration.

On the ride back to the hotel they discussed the play, but Nancy's hungry gaze kept straying to Caleb. Tonight he was wearing a dark suit with a crisp white pleated shirt and a blue paisley tie. His clothes were expensive, tailored to fit him and she had trouble associating him with the memory of the pale, gaunt, jeans-clad man she'd fallen in love with on Washington Island.

She fought back the tiny wings of fear that beat softly but insistently against her happiness. Was he the same man? If not, how had he changed? Had he ever been the man she'd fallen in love with, or had she created a mythical hero out of her dreams and his vulnerability?

At the hotel they walked across the lobby to the bank of elevators. Caleb's hand rested lightly at the small of Nancy's back, and he could feel the sway of her hips as she walked along beside him. His whole arm tingled, and he wondered if he'd ever be able to touch her without setting off sparks of electricity.

He glanced at her as they waited for the doors to open. She was breathtakingly beautiful, and tonight for the first time since he'd found her again she glowed with excitement and happiness. It had been one of the things that attracted him so strongly on Washington Island. In spite of her difficult childhood, or maybe because of it, she'd been easily pleased, and he hated himself for snatching that innocence from her. Lately it had been replaced with a wounded cynicism that tore at his conscience.

She was wearing a mint green silky dress with a modest neckline and a skirt that swirled around her shapely calves. It was conservative in design, but it hugged her full breasts and tiny waist in such a way that his hands ached to roam and cup. No matter what she wore she was one of the sexiest looking women Caleb had ever seen, and she wasn't even aware of it.

That sensuality all too often made him forget just how young she was. She'd turned twenty-six in October of last year. Twenty-six, for heaven's sake. He sometimes wondered if he'd ever been twenty-six. The last two years had aged him so that he both looked and felt older than he was. He'd never be young again, even in spirit.

They'd been joined by several other people as they waited, and when the elevator arrived it stopped at almost every floor. Caleb's anticipation heightened as he waited out the slow ascent, but he was determined to keep himself under control. He wasn't going to seduce Nancy. He'd promised to let her set the pace, and he intended to keep that promise. He'd have a snack sent up from room service. Maybe she'd like to watch another movie on television.

He almost groaned at the thought, but steeled himself not to be disappointed if she didn't want to make love. He wanted her with him whether they were lovers or not.

They finally reached the eighteenth floor, and after a short walk down the hall Caleb unlocked his door. They went into the darkened room together, and then they were in each other's arms. He didn't know which of them made the first move, but all his good intentions went up in flames along with the rest of him.

He couldn't wait. Hell, he couldn't even let loose of her long enough to turn on the light! She was so round, and so soft, and she fitted against him in all the places that had longed for her so ardently.

Lifting her face to him she opened her mouth just as his covered it. His tongue plundered the sweetness of her until she captured it and began to suck gently, sending shock waves all the way to his groin.

Her hands caressed his back and shoulders, and she moved against his hardness, making him tremble. He clutched her to him, widening his stance so he could fit her between his thighs. Instead of relieving the pressure the intimate contact made him throb all the more, and he fought to retain some semblance of control, at least until they could get undressed and into bed.

He broke off the searing kiss and moved with her toward the bed. The room was dark, but the lights from the skyscrapers gave enough illumination to move around without stumbling. The few steps to the bed gave Caleb the space he needed to stop his headlong rush to oblivion. He turned on the bedside lamp and took a deep breath as he started to loosen his tie.

"Let me do that," Nancy said and slid it over his head, then began to unbutton his shirt.

He wasn't sure how long he could stand her talented fingers making teasing forays down his chest and belly, but he was going to give it a good try.

"Just don't take too long," he warned as his hand moved to the zipper at the back of her dress.

He opened the placket, and Nancy put her arms down to allow the dress to flutter to the floor. It was lined, and she wore no slip, only a satin bra and bikini panties to which she'd added a narrow lace belt with long garters that held up her stockings.

On her it was the sexiest garment he'd ever seen. He didn't even realize he was staring until he heard her low, melodic laugh. "I thought you were in a hurry, love. Are you going to finish undressing me, or do you want me to do it?"

He swallowed and tried to find his voice. "I'll do it." He sounded raspy, as if his throat were parched. "How do I get it off?"

Even he could tell he wasn't making much sense, but she knew what he was talking about. "First you unfasten the garters, then there are hooks at the back."

He bent down and his shaking fingers grappled with the clips until he finally had all four of them lose. Then he straightened and put his arms around her waist. He could feel the fastenings and again his trembling hands made his task difficult, but he finally had the cursed thing off. As he tossed it at a chair Nancy removed her bra, then reached for the button at the top of his fly.

Her seeking fingers brought beads of sweat to his forehead as she released his zipper. She put both hands inside his briefs and slowly knelt as she pushed them and his trousers down his legs, then untied his shoes and helped him step out of them.

As she rose she paused long enough to kiss him intimately. The groan he'd been fighting to hold back escaped from his throat as he dug his fingers into her upper arms and pulled her up to crush her full length against him.

They fell together onto the bed, and it was then that he remembered what he had to do. It was almost more than he could manage to loosen his hold on her as he opened the drawer on the bedside table and groped for one of the small, square, foil packages.

He sensed Nancy's surprise, but didn't give her time to break the spell by asking questions. He quickly removed her panties, and the stockings she still wore, then lowered himself to her again.

His hands roamed freely over her smooth, bare flesh, seeking out well-remembered curves and crevices while his mouth ravaged hers and was ravaged in return.

His head spun as the pressure built to almost intolerable heights. When his seeking fingers finally penetrated the damp heat of her femininity she arched against his hand and moaned softly as her nails dug into his back. Her legs wrapped around him in a frenzied invitation impossible to resist.

Caleb's control snapped and with a guttural cry he plunged deeply, shuddering with need and intent on making her his, both physically and spiritually, for all time.

Nancy chanted his name as her undulating hips encouraged his long, hard strokes until they were both frantic for release.

When it came the whole world exploded.

Afterward it took a long time for Nancy's heart to stop racing, and her respiration to return to normal. She curled contentedly into Caleb's loving embrace, her head on his shoulder, one arm around his waist and one leg resting between his thighs.

She'd found heaven, and even though it might not last she intended to make the most of it while it did. For a little while she wanted just to love him and believe that he loved her. That in spite of their rocky start they could somehow make a life together and be happy.

His skin was damp with perspiration, and it tasted salty when she flicked her tongue along his shoulder blade. His heart was pounding as rapidly as hers, and his chest heaved as he struggled to control his breathing. If she had had any doubts about his fidelity during the months they'd been apart, or the depth of his need for her, they were gone—burned to a cinder in the searing fire of their melding.

They slept and woke hours later to sunlight and renewed passion. When sanity finally returned Nancy realized it was midmorning and she was hungry, but she'd waited so long to wake again in the shelter of Caleb's arms that she couldn't leave them now. Instead she rubbed her palm along his hip, loving his boney masculine structure.

He nibbled on her earlobe. "Unless you want to miss breakfast altogether you'd better not start that again."

She giggled like a teenager. "Surely you brag."

He took her hand and positioned it on his partially aroused manhood. "You think so?" he asked with an exaggerated leer.

"Caleb Winters, you're insatiable."

"Damn right, it's been a long time." He started out teasing, but ended on a serious note. "Don't you know that I'll never stop wanting you?"

She slid her hand up to his waist. "I hope not," she murmured, then hesitated before asking the question that had been nagging at her.

"Darling, why didn't you have the vasectomy repaired?"

Chapter Fourteen

Nancy had been surprised and puzzled when Caleb had taken measures to protect her. Obviously he hadn't had a second surgery to repair the failure of the first, but why? He'd been so adamant about not wanting their baby.

He cupped her breast and leaned down to plant little kisses on it before answering. "I thought you might want more children."

More children! Quick, uncontrolled rage exploded inside her, and she tore herself out of his arms and sat up. "You actually thought I would let you get me pregnant again after the way you treated me the first time?"

Her voice was low and taut and filled with anger. "Did you honestly believe that I would be masochistic enough to allow you to put me through that kind of hell a second time?"

She jumped off the bed and retrieved her dress from the floor to hold in front of her and cover her nakedness. She was trembling and only vaguely aware of what she was saying. "Well take my advice and do me, and any other women you may take to bed, a favor. Have the surgery again. You may be a great lover, but you're a rotten candidate for a father."

She whirled around and stomped into the bathroom.

The loud slam of the door vibrated in Caleb's head as he lay there staring at it in bewildered astonishment. For a moment he was too surprised to react, but then the full force of her words hit him like a powerfully wielded club. He rolled over and buried his face in the pillow as he pummeled the mattress with his fist.

Dammit to hell! Wasn't she ever going to forgive him for his supposed sins? He was all too aware that he owed her an explanation, and he had decided after their total oneness last night to trust her, no matter what the danger, and tell her the story of his past. In fact he was working up to it when he had inadvertently said something to start her railing at him all over again.

He heard the shower running in the bathroom and got wearily off the bed, then pulled on a pair of jeans and a T-shirt. No matter how much he loved her how could he trust her with his secret if he never knew whether something he said might trigger one of these rages of hers? Especially when he would be placing others in jeopardy.

He was putting on his loafers when the phone rang. It was Barry with good news. "The authorities finally caught up with Tony Durante, and he's back in prison. If you still think it's important you can tell Nancy about your background now."

That fact wasn't as exciting as it would have been an hour ago, but it still was a relief. "Thanks, Barry," Caleb said. "Are Danny and Luke all right?"

"They're fine. We've taken the surveillance off them."

"Alina?"

"She never had a clue that she and the boys were being watched. You can go back to Salt Lake City, now. In fact, I'd advise that you do. Your boss is getting pretty annoyed because you've been gone so long."

"I'll do that, and thanks again. I'll keep in touch."

"By all means. Good luck with Nancy. I wish I could come to the wedding."

If there ever is a wedding, Caleb thought wretchedly as he said goodbye and hung up.

Nancy finished drying her hair and stepped out of the bathroom wearing the white terry-cloth robe she had found hanging on a hook. It was big on her, and she'd had to roll back the sleeves. She felt as if she looked like the lost and frightened orphan she had been in childhood.

She knew her eyes were red and swollen from crying, and she could hardly keep the tears from welling again when she saw the pain in Caleb's eyes and knew she had inflicted it.

The weeping and the soothing shower had calmed her, and she was aware that once again she had overreacted. Why couldn't she control those outbursts instead of just letting fly and then regretting it later? She was hurting, but that was no reason to be so brutal.

Caleb was dressed and sitting on the side of the bed next to the telephone. She took a few steps toward him, but he didn't look either forgiving or welcoming so she stopped and looked down at the floor.

"Caleb, I . . . I owe you an apology. I'm sorry for some of the things I said."

"Are you?" His tone was cool.

She looked up and saw that his expression was as cool as his voice. "Yes, I am. You were right when you said the subject of the baby is still a raw spot with me. I don't seem to be able to discuss it with you at all without going off the deep end."

He stood and turned away from her to walk to the window. His limp was more pronounced than usual, and he moved with a dejected gait that added years to his age.

"I don't know what you want of me, Nancy." His tone was as full of anguish as his eyes. "I've admitted my mistakes, and tried to explain things that weren't my fault, but no matter what I do or say you'll neither forgive nor trust me."

He turned and faced her. His expression was bleak. "Do you blame me because you lost the baby? Did it happen because of the strain I put you under? Was the fact that I wasn't there to take care of you so you wouldn't have to work a factor?"

Nancy was stunned. It had never occurred to her that he might have been blaming himself for the miscarriage. "Oh, darling, no!" She started toward him but stopped again. "I would have lost her even if everything had been ideal. It was one of those accidents of nature that can't be anticipated or controlled. You mustn't ever blame yourself."

She saw relief wash over his face, but he didn't relax or beckon for her to come to him. "Thank you for telling me," he said formally. "Do you want to go downstairs for breakfast?" He looked at his watch. "Or we can have it sent up if you'd prefer that."

Why was he being so damned polite? Obviously she'd gone too far this time. He acted as if she were a stranger that he'd been ordered to treat well, but all the time his expressive brown eyes told her how badly she'd hurt him.

"I . . . I'll get dressed," she stammered.

He nodded. "Do you mind if I use the bathroom? I'd like to shower and shave."

"Oh, no, please, go ahead. I have my things right here."

She dressed hurriedly, then applied her makeup with the aid of the big mirror over the chest of drawers. He finished showering and emerged from the bathroom wearing slacks and a lightweight sport coat.

The meal was a total disaster. They sat across the table from each other and pushed their expensive food around on their plates. They talked about the weather, the decor of the dining room, and whether or not Ricardo Gutierrez was busy at the clinic on this morning—everything but what was tearing them up inside.

Caleb's manner was so forbiddingly polite that Nancy couldn't even knock on the barrier he'd erected between them, let alone destroy it.

Finally he put his fork down and looked at her. "I had a phone call while you were in the bathroom this morning. I'm needed back at work on Monday so I'll have to catch a flight to Salt Lake City either later today or early tomorrow."

Nancy felt the blood drain from her face and her stomach lurched. "You're leaving?"

He nodded. "Yes. I can see now that I've been unfair. I've been pressuring you to make a decision that you're not ready for. Maybe time and distance will help us both to gain some perspective."

She felt a wave of panic. Caleb was leaving her! "But..."

He reached over and patted her hand in a brotherly gesture. "Don't look so stricken. If you still feel guilty about your outburst this morning, don't. I deserved it. I've been selfish and thoughtless, thinking of my own needs and ignoring yours."

"No! Oh, please, Caleb. I just need a little time..."

He signed the bill that lay on a small tray and stood. "That's what I'm giving you, Nancy. Now, if you're ready

I'll take you home. I'll be tied up the rest of the day making travel arrangements and packing.''

Nancy winced. Originally they had planned to spend the weekend together. Now he couldn't wait to get rid of her.

Yes, this time she had definitely gone too far.

They were both silent on the drive to her apartment. Nancy was too stunned to think, and too afraid to talk. If she did she was sure she would say something stupid and drive Caleb even further away. Instead she twisted her hands in her lap and wondered if he was feeling any of the torment that was wracking her.

At her building they walked into the empty foyer and he pushed the button for the elevator, then turned to her. He made no attempt to hide either his pain or his dejection.

"I'll say goodbye here," he said courteously.

Her eyes widened. "You're not coming up?" Surely he would at least come to the apartment long enough for a private goodbye kiss.

He shook his head. "No, it's better this way. Stay in touch, Nancy. If you should decide to leave Dallas let me know where you are. Will you do that?"

Oh, my God, he wasn't only leaving, but he didn't intend to come back or send for her to come to him! He really was saying goodbye and meaning it.

A wave of nausea clutched at her, and for a moment all she could do was stare at him. Then, instinct telling her to salvage at least a remnant of her pride, she managed to pull herself together and nod. "Yes...yes, I will."

He reached out and she thought that at last he was going to take her in his arms, but instead he just patted her shoulder. "Good," he said and dropped his hand. "Take care, and let me know if you ever need anything."

Almost before she could blink he had turned and left.

The elevator door opened behind her, but she was too dazed to move. Instead she huddled against the wall in stunned wretchedness. Caleb hadn't even kissed her goodbye! He was leaving and he wasn't coming back, and he didn't want to kiss her one last time.

Upstairs Nancy's apartment was hot and stuffy. She turned on the antiquated air conditioner and looked around the small, drab room. Why was she living like this? She could afford a better place. She had rented it in the beginning because it was cheap and close to the clinic, but she had never intended to stay here once the baby was born.

The familiar feeling of grief and hopelessness gripped her at the thought of the baby. She'd lost it. That was a fact that couldn't be reversed, but she wasn't the only person in the world it had happened to. Hundreds, no, thousands, of women had miscarriages every day, and most of them came to terms with their disappointment.

Why couldn't she?

Was it possible that she *was* blaming Caleb? No, she couldn't be. She knew it wasn't his fault, or hers. It was just one of those unfortunate things that sometimes happened in the early stages of pregnancy.

She started pacing in the confined space. Could she be hanging on to the grief as a way of punishing Caleb for not wanting their child?

The thought was so abhorrent that she stopped short. She would never do a thing like that! She wasn't vindictive....

The hell she wasn't. She had actually taken a perverse pleasure in telling Caleb that he'd gotten his wish, and there was no baby.

Nancy shuddered as the memory of his agonized reaction ripped through her. If she could do that to him she was capable of punishing him further. What better way than to play the martyr? To let him see how she had suffered because of his shortcomings.

She sank down on the sofa and buried her face in her hands. That's exactly what she'd done. She'd let her grief feed her bitterness until her objectivity had changed into something twisted and destructive.

No wonder Caleb had finally lost patience with her. If she wanted him she would have to go after him, because she had a gut feeling that he wouldn't come to her again. As he'd told her, he had done all he could to apologize and convince her that he loved her. She knew he wouldn't try again.

She raised her head and looked at her watch. It had been nearly two hours since he'd left her in the foyer. Surely he couldn't have caught a flight out so quickly.

She reached for the telephone, then hesitated. If he was in his room and she told him she wanted to see him he would almost certainly refuse. She would do better to take a chance and just go to him. She had to talk to him. She had to at least try to make things right.

The bus ride to the hotel was a short one, but it seemed to take forever. They had missed each other by a few hours last year, and she couldn't bear it if she missed him by minutes this time.

The lobby of the Fairmont was crowded with people checking in, and the hall in front of the elevators was packed with guests trying to get to their rooms. She missed the first car, but elbowed her way into the second. Oh, God, don't let him be going down in one while I'm going up in another, she thought desperately.

She was nearly frantic by the time she finally reached Caleb's room. Her hand shook as she knocked on the door, then stood to the side so he couldn't see her through the viewer.

There was no answer and she knocked again, harder this time. Maybe he had checked out after all.

Still no answer, and she banged at the hard, thick wood with both fists. He couldn't be gone, he just couldn't!

Finally his voice sounded through the barrier, strident and demanding. "Stop that racket and stand in front of the door where I can see you or I'll call hotel security."

Relief flooded through her, and she quickly stepped into his line of vision. "It's Nancy, Caleb. Please let me in."

There was a moment's hesitation, then she heard the bolt slide back and the door opened. Their gazes met and clung, his questioning, hers pleading, then Caleb stepped back and motioned for her to enter.

"I—I'm sorry for ma-making such a commotion," she stammered, suddenly shy. "I was so—so afraid that you'd already left."

She was shaking with anxiety, terrified that he would send her away without even listening to her.

They were standing close together in the narrow entryway between the closet and the bathroom, and she wanted so badly to touch him. As if sensing her need he put his fingers under her chin and lifted her face. His glance took in her red eyes, her pinched expression and her trembling lips.

"What's the matter, Nancy?" he asked softly.

Without breaking eye contact she reached up, took his hand from under her chin and raised it to her mouth, then kissed the palm and held it against her cheek. "I love you, Caleb," she said huskily. "I love you so much."

He sighed and put his arms around her, drawing her close as he nuzzled her temple with his lips. "There's never been a serious doubt about our love for each other, sweetheart,'' he answered sadly. "It's other things that keep coming between us, and if we continue the way we've been going it will destroy us both. I'm sorry, but I don't think I can take anymore.''

She had put her arms around his waist and clasped her hands together in an effort to lock him into her embrace. She needed his arms around her, his body twined with hers, his hands and mouth caressing her.

"I know you can't, neither can I." Her voice was raspy, hurried as the words tumbled out. "I've been wrong, darling. I know that now. I've been vindictive and blind to everything but my own uncertainty and grief.''

Caleb attempted to interrupt her, but she continued on, "Losing the baby seemed to bring out deeply buried grievances that I wasn't even aware of. I've been punishing you, Caleb. Making you pay for what I saw as rejections during my childhood. I didn't know...I never realized..."

Her voice broke and she buried her face in his shoulder.

He grasped her arms and held her away from him. "Stop it, Nancy," he said firmly. "There's no need for you to assume all the blame. I started the whole mess by lying to you, and then avoiding the truth.''

She shook her head, but he paid no attention. "Actually, I'm the one at fault because I knew that I could never have a close relationship with a woman without courting disaster. I should have walked out of that clinic alone the day we met and never returned. I knew even then that you were dynamite. Once you took me home and warmed me with your tender, loving care it was too late. I had to see you again, and again, and again..."

He straightened and walked away from her into the larger area of the room, leaving her desolate and alone.

She followed him and noticed the open suitcase on the luggage holder. He was packing.

She sat on the edge of the bed where they'd made such passionate love just hours before. It seemed like weeks.

He had said he'd lied to her, but that no longer seemed important. He had also said he loved her, and that was the truth she clung to. She drew in a long breath. "Caleb, you asked me to marry you? Is the offer still open?"

She heard him gasp from behind her, but then the silence stretched on and on until she wanted to scream. "I— I'm no longer sure it's a good idea," he said finally.

She clutched her hands in her lap and forced herself to speak again. "Do you mean that you don't want me anymore?"

This time there was no hesitation. "I'll always want you, Nancy. That's both my joy and my curse."

He had told her everything she needed to know, and her raw nerves quieted as she got up and walked over to where he stood on the other side of the big bed. Conquering her fear of being repulsed, she put her arms around his neck and snuggled against him.

His stance was rigid, his muscles taut and his hands clenched at his sides. She massaged his tense shoulders with her strong fingers as her lips sought and found the leaping pulse just below his ear. "I'll always want you, too, my darling," she murmured, her voice little more than a whisper. "And if you'll marry me I promise to spend the rest of my life giving you that tender, loving care you found so addicting."

She raised her face to kiss one cheek, then the other, lingering at each to taste his skin with her tongue. She was aiming for his chin when, with an agonized groan of surrender, he clutched her to him and eagerly claimed her caressing mouth with his own.

It wasn't a kiss of lust, or even passion, but of all-encompassing love. They held each other and murmured endearments and promises while their hungry hands fondled and soothed.

"May I take it that you're accepting my proposal?" she asked softly as she stroked her fingers through his thick, dark hair.

He was suddenly still, and she felt his withdrawal even though he didn't move away from her. "Before we make any commitments I have something to tell you. You may want to take back the proposal after you've heard me out."

Chapter Fifteen

Nancy's fear returned, and she searched his face for a clue. Was he teasing?

She saw that he was deadly serious. "In that case I don't want to hear it." Her voice was tinged with panic.

He disengaged himself from her and walked away. "I'm afraid you'll have to, love. It's an explanation long overdue, but it reveals information I haven't been free to give. I'm still not since it involves other people, but, while I've always been willing to trust you with my own safety, I know you well enough now to trust you with the lives of my two young sons also."

Nancy blinked, and the panic escalated. "Sons?"

He nodded. "Yes, Damon, Jr.'s ten—we call him Danny. The younger, Luke, is eight."

"But you said . . ."

"I know. I said I didn't have children. I lied."

He jammed his hands in his pockets. "Technically I told you the truth. Caleb Winters doesn't have children, but Caleb Winters has only been in existence for two years."

Nancy's panic was full-blown now, and she wondered if she had lost her grip on sanity. Nothing she was hearing made sense.

"Until two years ago my name was Damon Photides," he continued, "and I had lots of family. An ex-wife, two sons, parents, two older brothers, one younger sister, an assortment of nieces and nephews, and more aunts, uncles and cousins than I could count."

Her head was spinning, and her confusion mounted. "Caleb, I don't understand."

A sad smile turned up the corners of his mouth. "No, I'm sure you don't, but it will clear up as I go along."

He reached out his hand to her. "It's a long story, and we might as well be comfortable. Come and sit here with me while I tell it."

His deep brown eyes were filled with apprehension, and she understood that he dreaded talking about this. She wanted to suggest that they curl up together on the bed while he talked, but he seemed cool and forbidding again, determined to keep her at a distance.

He seated her in one of the thickly padded chairs beside the round table and took the other one across from her. "Nancy, how much do you know about the government's protected witness program?"

She was getting used to surprises and managed to answer calmly. "Not much. Isn't that a way of protecting people who put themselves in danger by testifying against organized crime figures? They relocate them and give them a whole new identity."

"That's right, and that's what happened to me. Damon Photides died nearly two years ago when a bomb exploded in his car, and Caleb Winters was born a few days later."

Nancy was stunned with horror. She jerked herself upright and stared. "You mean the accident that nearly killed you was a bombing?"

"It was no accident," he said, "and it did kill Damon Photides, almost as effectively as if I had really died."

"But why? Why would anyone want to kill you . . . uh, Damon . . . oh, you know what I mean."

"Yes, I know," he said gravely. "Let me start at the beginning and tell you the truth about myself. My family owns a chain of prosperous Greek restaurants in Manhattan, and after I graduated from college and did my two-year stint with the army I was taken into the firm as a partner.

"At that time, I married the daughter of another Greek family who were long-time friends. I suppose you could call it an arranged marriage, although neither Alina nor I had any objections."

He paused, and Nancy felt a stab of jealousy. Was he remembering the happy times with his wife?

"After the children were born Alina was busy with them, and I was taking on more and more responsibility in the business. We'd never had a deep, passionate love to bind us together, and over the years the marriage lost its luster and deteriorated into a series of disagreements and picky quarrels."

He shifted uncomfortably in his chair, and rubbed at his stiff leg.

"About three and a half years ago a branch of organized crime moved in and demanded to be paid 'protection' for the restaurants," he continued. "I was outraged and refused. Accidents began happening at the cafés, and when I went to the police one of the restaurants was torched. No one was hurt, but the building was a total loss."

Nancy gasped, but he didn't seem to hear. "I was appalled. Instead of intimidating me as it was supposed to do, the incident only made me more determined to fight, and I began working with the Justice Department to gather evidence for prosecution.

"Meanwhile, when I still refused to pay the extortion I started receiving open threats. I tried to keep it from Alina, but they called the house and talked to her. Naturally she was terrified, and demanded that I give them what they wanted and stop playing the hero. I refused, explaining that it wouldn't stop there. That they would keep demanding more and more, and must be caught and put away before they took over completely."

Caleb's breathing had become shallow, and his facial features had a tight, strained look. Nancy wanted to reach across the table and touch him, but he hardly seemed aware of her as if he were absorbed by painful memories of the past.

"Alina wouldn't believe me. She accused me of grandstanding and putting us all in danger, and our already shaky marriage fell apart. A short time later, when the federal agents and I finally sprang a trap and got the evidence we needed the threats escalated.

"I was warned I would be killed if I attempted to testify." He jumped up and stood looking out the window with his back to her.

When he spoke his voice was raspy. "I was tempted. Hell, I was a businessman, not a cop. I was almost as terrified as Alina, but I couldn't back down at that late date.

"When I told her I was going through with it she moved out and filed for divorce. She got custody of the children, at the time aged five and seven, but I had visitation rights."

He walked over to the dresser where he picked up a bottle of whiskey, then turned to look at her. "Do you want a drink?"

She shook her head. "No, but Caleb, you don't have to put yourself through this. If you don't want to go on, I—"

He poured a generous amount of the liquor into a glass. "I'm almost finished," he said and took a long swallow. "I had the boys with me the weekend before I was to appear in court. We'd gone to a movie, and when we came out of the theater they ran ahead of me. There were moving cars all over the lot, and I called them back and held each of them by the hand.

His voice trailed off, and he gazed into space as though savoring the time with his sons. "That's the only thing that saved them. If they had opened the door before I did . . ." His voice broke, but he forced himself to go on.

"I don't remember the explosion, only the pain, but I learned later that the door had been wired to a bomb that misfired."

Nancy shuddered as pictures flashed in her mind of car bombings she'd seen on television and at the movies. Then she realized what he'd said. "Misfired?" Her tone was one of utter disbelief. "But your injuries . . ."

Caleb drained the glass and set it down. "If it had exploded full force, the boys and I wouldn't have had a chance of surviving. As it was I took the full brunt, thank

God. Both boys had second degree burns, and Luke, being the smallest, was thrown the farthest and broke his leg, but neither had any lasting damage.''

Caleb's face was without color, and his eyes had a dull, haunted expression. She'd noticed that the hand that held the glass shook. Nancy couldn't stand it any longer. She couldn't sit there and watch him relive the horror of his past without at least trying to help.

She leaped from the chair, and he held out his arms. Her face was wet with tears and she rubbed her cheek against his. "Oh, darling, I'm so sorry. What an awful experience.''

He held her as though he would never let her go, but after a few minutes he regained control and again put her away from him.

"No, Nancy, I'm not finished.'' His tone was heavy with regret. "You've got to hear it all before you make a decision.''

She started to protest, but then, realizing that he had to do it his way, she sat back down.

He began to pace. "I was unconscious for several days and heavily sedated for a couple of weeks after that, but finally I was able to give my testimony for the trial from my hospital bed. Meanwhile Alina and the children had been taken into protective custody.

"A few days later the criminals were convicted, and appeals were immediately filed.''

Nancy was confused. "But if your testimony was on record, why was it necessary for you to go into the protected witness program?''

"Several reasons,'' he said. "The gangsters didn't want me around to testify again on the off chance that they could get a new trial. Also, these people are vengeful and vicious. They would do anything to get back at me, and no one close to me was safe as long as I was alive.''

Nancy felt sick. What a dreadful price he'd paid just for wanting to be a good citizen and help to put those animals behind bars where they couldn't prey on others.

''I had taken all the chances I intended to with my family's safety. Especially the children's. After careful deliberation I agreed to be declared dead.

''No one but a few government agents and the attending physician knows that I survived and spent long months in a military hospital in another part of the country. I was given a new name, Caleb Winters, and a fictional but well-documented background. When I recovered enough to leave the hospital I was sent to Washington Island to convalesce, and there I met and fell hopelessly in love with you.''

Unable to stay away any longer Nancy went to him. He held her, and buried his face in her shoulder. She put her arms around him while tears streamed down her cheeks, and her voice was choked when she spoke. ''Why didn't you tell me all this when I told you I was pregnant? Believe me, I would have understood—''

''I know you would have, darling.'' He raised his head and brushed his cheek in her hair. ''If I had been the only one concerned I would have. I had no qualms about putting my own life in your hands. I loved you dearly, but even so we were little more than strangers.''

He brushed his lips against her temple. ''We'd only known each other a few weeks, and you didn't really know me at all. You knew Caleb Winters and his fictional background. Everything I'd told you about myself, except for my medical records, was a lie. You're very young, I couldn't anticipate how you would react to the truth, and I couldn't gamble with the lives of my children."

She ran her fingers through his hair. "No, of course you couldn't. Oh, Caleb, I'm so sorry I wasn't more patient. I should have realized—"

"Don't blame yourself," he said. "I was the one who botched the whole thing. I'd wrestled a long time with the decision to have a vasectomy. I love my sons, and it's possible that I'll never see them again. They think I'm dead. Alina might marry again, and they'll call another man daddy."

His voice broke and his arms tightened around her, but he took a deep breath and continued, "I couldn't go through that with another child. That's why I had the surgery, and that's why I was being such a bastard about your baby...our daughter."

A sob tore through him, and he released her and turned away.

Nancy understood that he needed privacy, and the only place she could go to give it to him was the bathroom again. She was beginning to hate that room. It seemed that one or the other of them was always taking refuge there.

When she came out Caleb was sitting in the middle of the bed propped up with the thick down pillows.

He held out his arms to her. "Come join me."

She slipped off her shoes and curled up next to him.

"There's not much more," he said. "I knew I had to talk to someone so I arranged to meet my contact with the protected witness bureau, Barry Young, in Chicago. That's when I wrote that ill-fated letter to you and left the island."

Caleb told her about his conversation with Barry and the advice he'd received. "That's why I didn't telephone you, but the whole two weeks was a waste of time. I never had any doubt about how much you meant to me."

He held her away from him and looked at her. "There's one thing you have to understand, though. If you marry me there's always going to be an element of danger, and if we have children they'll be endangered, too."

Nancy snuggled closer into his embrace. "As I understand it, we'll be safe as long as no one knows that you're still alive."

"That's right." Her skirt had pulled up, and his hand rested on her bare thigh.

"I'm not going to tell anybody, are you?" She unfastened the buttons on his shirt.

"Never," he murmured and trailed kisses down the line of her throat.

"Then it would be pretty silly to spend much time worrying about it, don't you think?" She ran her hands over his bare chest, then pulled his shirt out of his trousers.

"Definitely." His thumb caressed the inside of her leg.

She shivered with anticipation and caressed his back under his loosened shirt. "Caleb," she said, and the playfulness was gone from her tone, "I know that nothing can replace the sons you can't acknowledge now, but would you like to have more children?"

He looked at her, and his expression was solemn. "Yes, sweetheart, I want children with you. Even though I was shocked and fearful, I wanted the one we lost, and I'll be deeply grateful if you decide to give me more." He kissed her tenderly. "Ours will be special to me because they'll be part of you, and you are my heart."

Nancy could feel tears gathering again, but this time they were tears of happiness. She put her arms around his neck, and lifted her face to his. "Then don't you think we'd better get started on them?'' she whispered seductively. "It may not happen as quickly this time.''

A smile lit his face, and his hand moved upward, making her gasp as it found her heat. "I think it can be arranged,'' he said huskily, just before his mouth captured hers and put an end to the conversation.

*   *   *   *   *

Silhouette Special Edition

MORE SPECIAL THAN EVER,
SAY THESE TOP AUTHORS:

LINDA HOWARD

"Silhouette Special Editions are indeed 'special' to me. They reflect the complexity of the modern woman's life, professionally, emotionally and, of course, romantically. They are windows through which we can see different views of life, the means by which we can experience all the depths and altitudes of the great love we want and need in our lives. Silhouette Special Editions are special dreams; we need dreams—to take us out of our everyday lives, and to give us something to reach for."

EMILIE RICHARDS

"I write stories about love and lovers because I believe we can't be reminded too often that love changes lives. I write Silhouette Special Editions because longer, in-depth stories give me the chance to explore all love's aspects, from the mad whirl to the quiet moments of contemplation. There's nothing more special than love, and there's no line more special than Silhouette Special Edition. I am proud to tell my stories in its pages."

SSE-A1

ATTRACTIVE, SPACE SAVING BOOK RACK

Display your most prized novels on this handsome and sturdy book rack. The hand-rubbed walnut finish will blend into your library decor with quiet elegance, providing a practical organizer for your favorite hard-or soft-covered books.

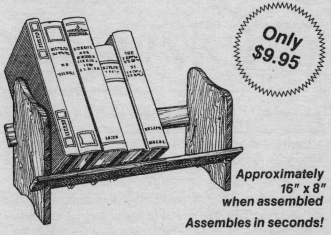

Only $9.95

Approximately 16" x 8" when assembled

Assembles in seconds!

To order, rush your name, address and zip code, along with a check or money order for $10.70* ($9.95 plus 75¢ postage and handling) payable to *Silhouette Books*.

Silhouette Books
Book Rack Offer
901 Fuhrmann Blvd.
P.O. Box 1396
Buffalo, NY 14269-1396

Offer not available in Canada.

BKR-2A

*New York and Iowa residents add appropriate sales tax.

1989
IS THE YEAR
OF THE MAN!

What makes a romance? A special man, of course, and Silhouette Desire celebrates that fact with *twelve* of them! From Mr. January to Mr. December, every month has a tribute to the Silhouette Desire hero—our **MAN OF THE MONTH!**

Sexy, macho, charming, irritating . . . irresistible! Nothing can stop these men from sweeping you away. Created by some of your favorite authors, each man is custom-made for pleasure—*reading* pleasure—so don't miss a single one.

Mr. January is Blake Donavan in RELUCTANT FATHER by Diana Palmer
Mr. February is Hank Branson in THE GENTLEMAN INSISTS by Joan Hohl
Mr. March is Carson Tanner in NIGHT OF THE HUNTER by Jennifer Greene
Mr. April is Slater McCall in A DANGEROUS KIND OF MAN by Naomi Horton
Mr. May is Luke Harmon in VENGEANCE IS MINE by Lucy Gordon
Mr. June is Quinn McNamara in IRRESISTIBLE by Annette Broadrick

And that's only the half of it—
so get out there and find your man!

Silhouette Desire's

MAN OF THE MONTH . . .

MOM-1

Silhouette Special Edition

COMING NEXT MONTH

#511 BEST LAID PLANS—Nora Roberts
Headstrong engineer Abra Wilson and cocky architect Cody Johnson
couldn't cooperate long enough to construct a hotel together—could
they possibly hope to build a lasting love?

#512 SKY HIGH—Tracy Sinclair
When client Jeremy Winchester insisted that pilot Meredith Collins
masquerade as his fiancée, she knew something was fishy—so why
did his pretense of passion feel so real?

#513 SMALL-TOWN SECRETS—Kate Meriwether
Their high-school reunion unveiled forbidden longings . . . but could
Reese finally beat the ultimate rival for Sadie's love without revealing
secrets that would tear the community—and Sadie's heart—apart?

#514 BUILD ME A DREAM—Pat Warren
Toy designer "Casey" Casswell created dreams for children . . .
and dreamed of having children. Pretty, practical Sabrina Ames
would be his ideal mate—if she weren't so terrified of marriage
and motherhood!

#515 DARK ANGEL—Pamela Toth
Julie Remington and Angel Maneros had crossed class boundaries to
fall in love, only to be thwarted by the bitterest misunderstanding.
Ten years later, they were facing temptation—and betrayal—
once again.

#516 A SUDDEN SUNLIGHT—Laurey Bright
When heiress Natalia awoke from a coma—pregnant—she didn't
remember the horrors she had survived. Nor did she remember Matt,
who claimed to be her lover, her fiancé. . . .

AVAILABLE THIS MONTH:

#505 SUMMER'S PROMISE
Bay Matthews

#506 GRADY'S LADY
Bevlyn Marshall

#507 THE RECKONING
Joleen Daniels

#508 CAST A TALL SHADOW
Diana Whitney

#509 NO RIGHT OR WRONG
Katherine Granger

#510 ASK NOT OF ME, LOVE
Phyllis Halldorson